P9-ELO-410

# THE PASSION DREAM BOOK

BY WHITNEY OTTO

*How to Make an American Quilt*

*Now You See Her*

WHITNEY OTTO

# THE PASSION DREAM BOOK

A NOVEL

HarperCollins*Publishers*

Grateful acknowledgment is made to the following for permission to quote from copyrighted material:

From *A Coney Island of the Mind,* by Lawrence Ferlinghetti. Copyright © 1972 by Lawrence Ferlinghetti. Reprinted by permission of New Directions Publishing Corp.

From *The Captain's Verses,* by Pablo Neruda. Copyright © 1972 by Pablo Neruda and Donald Walsh. Reprinted by permission of New Directions Publishing Corp.

From *The Collected Poems of Langston Hughes,* by Arnold Rampersad, editor; David Roessel, assoc. editor. Copyright © 1994 by the Estate of Langston Hughes. Reprinted by permission of Alfred A. Knopf, Inc.

THE PASSION DREAM BOOK. Copyright © 1997 by Whitney Otto. All rights reserved. Printed in the United States of America. No part of this book may be used or reproduced in any manner whatsoever without written permission except in the case of brief quotations embodied in critical articles and reviews. For information address HarperCollins Publishers, Inc., 10 East 53rd Street, New York, NY 10022.

HarperCollins books may be purchased for educational, business, or sales promotional use. For information please write: Special Markets Department, HarperCollins Publishers, Inc., 10 East 53rd Street, New York, NY 10022.

FIRST EDITION

*Designed by Ruth Lee*

---

Library of Congress Cataloging-in-Publication Data

Otto, Whitney.
The passion dream book : a novel / Whitney Otto. —1st ed.
p. cm.
ISBN 0-06-017824-8
I. Title.
PS3565.T795P37 1997
813.'.54,dc21 97-3563

---

97 98 99 00 01 ❖/RRD 10 9 8 7 6 5 4 3 2 1

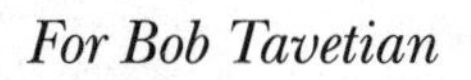

*For Bob Tavetian*

"We *think* differently at night"
she told me once

lying back languidly

And she would quote Cocteau

"I feel there is an angel in me" she'd say
"whom I am constantly shocking"

LAWRENCE FERLINGHETTI

In colonies are found:
ants, lepers, bacteria, and artists.

In migration are found:
geese, whales, and artists.

THIS IS A WORK OF FICTION. THOUGH I HAVE BORROWED ACTUAL characteristics, locations, anecdotes, and works of art, it would be a mistake to assume the people and places are anything but fictional creations. The story is a complete invention, as are most of the events.

With that in mind, I would like to thank a number of authors and recommend their books to anyone interested in the factual basis of some aspects of my novel. A list can be found at the back of the book.

I wish to thank Simone Seydoux, Jan Novotny, and Gigi Arino.

Thank you to Joy Harris and Diane Reverand, who make all aspects of my writer's life possible.

Love and thanks to John and Sam, the boys who mean everything to me.

# Contents

# Book One: Florence

1501–1504

## *1. The Gates of Paradise*

For much of the Renaissance, Florence was ruled by a rich and powerful family who loved the arts and fame and their good name in equal measure. They understood that to protect their land and other holdings meant the liberal use of physical force, but that there must be something worth protecting. Worth preserving. Art, they decided, art is the measure of a man. They viewed churches, paintings, and statues as monuments to their glory. In that regard, they understood further that all their accomplishments would come to naught if there was no remaining record. The only record that could possibly remain was art.

Art that bears their image, their stamps, their victories, their mistresses, their wives, their children, and their beliefs would insure their immortality.

Artists, on the other hand, saw the power and money and need of their patrons as a way of doing their work.

This arrangement, which resembled two brilliant mirrors placed face-to-face, each reflecting the other's image, produced the errant shards of split light that fell on the realm of the Renaissance.

The alliance of artist and patron was not limited to secular men with money. When the papacy returned to Rome and strove for unfettered power, the first thing for which the popes emptied their coffers was art.

Artists began showing up as dinner guests, seated beside cardinals and dukes. They discussed theories and ideas. The citizenry sought the extravagant beauty the artist could provide in designing something as grand as a cathedral or as mundane as the handle of a dagger. If a poor boy showed the slightest talent or inclination toward art, he was given instruction. An indication of the great numbers of artists and their need to organize was the establishment of their own guild, the Guild of Saint Luke.

All this courting and whispering and the promise of wondrous life seeded a competitive spirit among cities and individuals and the artists themselves. Everyone wanted "the best." But how could the best be determined when judging something as ephemeral, as smoky, as shape-shifting as art? A competition, it was decided, would provide a winner, one artist who would be declared the best.

In 1401 a design was needed for the east doors of the baptistery in Florence. Three artists—Ghiberti, Brunelleschi, and Jacopo della Quercia—submitted bronze panels depicting the assigned subject: The Sacrifice of Isaac.

## 2. *The Sacrifice of Isaac*

*Next to the water of winter/she and I raised/a red bonfire/wearing out our lips/from kissing each other's souls.* And that, son, writes Neruda, is how you came into the world.

From kissing each other's souls.

The story of God asking Abraham to sacrifice his son Isaac is not a tale of the soul-kissed love that can bring a child into the world; rather, it is a lesson in the stern-voiced devotional love that would take a child out of it.

Abraham and his wife, Sarah, lived one hundred years without children. Then they had Isaac, promised to be the first of as many descendants as there are stars in the sky. However, after Isaac was given to them, God asked for him back.

What did Abraham think as he climbed with his boy toward the sacrificial altar? Did he think:

It is far easier to live a century without a child than it is to exist for a single day once that child has been taken from you?

Is this the unraveling of God's promise of all those thousands of confetti-tossed stars?

What is the sum of divided love?

Or maybe he told himself that the first thing he must do once the deed is done is to begin to forget the memory of Isaac. Forget the look of trust on Isaac's face as he looks upon his father's face for the last time. This thought is the one that starts to break him down as he makes his climb.

*and I, to clasp/her tiny waist,/walked all the earth,/with the wars and mountains/with the sands and thorns/That's how you came into the world.*

Only a broken man could carry out such an act of

murder against his child. Something must have torn inside Abraham to allow himself to consider this killing.

Or was it a form of love? Was it love or duty that made Abraham lead Isaac to the altar? Was it a need to know something about love or duty that drew the demand from God? Was it love, finally, that stayed Abraham's hand when God's angel reached out, sparing Isaac? This father-and-son sacrifice, this dress rehearsal for another father-and-son sacrifice.

Neruda writes: *You come from so many places/toward the two of us/from the terrible love/that has enchained us.*

..............................

It is good to keep in mind that winning such a competition could garner for the artist admiration, fame, money, praise, and a desire for his company. As compelling as all that might be, much of the time the artist just wants to do his work.

How can "the best" be judged?

*Jacopo della Quercia's panel:* It did not survive to the present day.

*Ghiberti's panel:* The figures are fluid, graceful, elegant, as carefully choreographed as a dance. Spatially pleasing, not too daring, the disturbance of the source material muted. His Abraham is as threatening to Isaac as beautiful actors in an unpleasant play.

*Brunelleschi's panel:* His Abraham grips Isaac's small head, forcing it back to expose his smooth throat. He presses the blade of the knife into the soft flesh as an angel seizes Abraham's arm to prevent the murder. Abraham's posture with Isaac resembles that of an animal lunging toward prey.

Ghiberti's panel allows no contact between the figures; Brunelleschi's panel has Abraham grasping Isaac, with the angel restraining Abraham. Ghiberti's panel is a pantomime of murder and salvation, his Isaac a delicately wrought child balancing on his knees, facing his father without resistance. While Brunelleschi's Isaac is awkwardly placed, his head thrust back by his father's hand, his mouth open as if in midcry, he has one foot behind him, the other before him, poised to bolt.

How is it possible to judge the better interpretation? Which is preferable? The slightly unsettling loveliness of Ghiberti's bronze or the fierce heartbreak of Brunelleschi's rendition?

*What constitutes the best* is the question that will dog art lovers forever; it will be the source of heated discussion; it will result in the squaring-off of loyalties. It will refuse any sort of answer. It is not the problem.

When Ghiberti won the competition for the baptistery doors in 1401, he said, "To me was conceded the palm of victory by all the experts and by all . . . who competed with me. . . . To all it seemed that I had at the time surpassed the others without exception." This is the problem.

The problem with proclaiming someone "the best" is that everyone begins to believe it. Including the artist. And once the best is declared, then everyone else, by definition, is only *pretty good,* but not as good as the best. If a city is able to hold a competition such as the one in 1401, then it is probably due to having a number of worthy artists living in close proximity. None of them want to be labeled "not the best." Since money and fame are part of being "the best," the colony can become as inflamed as if in a state of siege.

Money changes everything. It brings the artist recognition, invitations, desires realized and desires unknown; it plucks a painter from obscurity and makes him a hero.

It means an artist can do his work.

Money breeds a strange sort of envy in that the artist may covet the attention paid and the commissions of another, more fortunate artist, without coveting his ability. It is a hard life that is subject to the whims of taste. It is a powerless life. Though it is well to remember that Florence was a place that generally respected its artists. As Albrecht Dürer said during a visit to Italy in 1505, "Here I am a gentleman, at home I am a parasite." Still, you have to accept the preferences of taste. You can't make anyone love you. This is true of love in general. You can't make them.

Lorenzo Ghiberti, the great artist who won the famous 1401 competition for the baptistery doors in Florence, left his heirs rare and delicate bronze work; marble and bronze antiques; a life-size bronze model of a human leg; several male and female heads; a variety of torsos. He also passed down the secret of his bronze technique, only to have finally a great-grandson who made bad sculpture and was robbed and murdered, ending the family line.

What succeeds Ghiberti is his fame and his work. This is why the smart men with money during the Renaissance funded the arts, requesting their likeness painted on canvas and wood, and why they collected, eventually, for the sake of collecting.

The reverse of this demand for immortality can backfire if patron and artist are not on civil terms. Leonardo da Vinci wanted to depict a prior as Judas. Not to mention all the kings and princes and noblewomen captured forever in the grip of their own folly. Whistler, centuries later, painted two peacocks, bitterly locked in battle, on the dining room wall of a patron who did not want to pay for Whistler's work; the patron was one of the pugnacious birds.

When Brunelleschi lost the competition for the baptistery doors, he was as ungracious a loser as Ghiberti was a winner. He turned his talents toward architecture, earning great praise and success. And when the builders of Florence could not figure out how to complete the enormous dome that now sits atop the cathedral, Brunelleschi approached them saying, after thinking it through for the past three years, he had the answer. They were so grateful, they invited him to work on the project.

Then they mentioned that his old rival, Ghiberti, would be overseeing the design and construction of the dome.

It is well to remember the terrible fearsomeness of Brunelleschi's competition panel for the east doors, and his bitter disappointment at being told Ghiberti was the "better" artist, when he knew it was simply a matter of taste. And then there was Ghiberti's tactless announcement. It shouldn't have surprised anyone when Brunelleschi suddenly became "unavailable" until Ghiberti voluntarily retired from the project.

Some like to think that because artists appear to listen to other voices and to live so much of their lives in the clouds, they are, perhaps, a more refined version of humanity. More sensitive, more intuitive, more compassionate. This is, of course, the dream artist because everyone knows that often artists are more shameless, more wicked, more jealous. A number of them have extremely long memories.

Though Jacopo della Quercia's bronze panel did not survive to the present day, enough of his work exists to understand his style. His figures are less graceful than those of Ghiberti, and more like the monumental and grand figures Michelangelo painted on the ceiling of the Sistine Chapel.

Michelangelo was one of the greatest gifts ever given to man from whoever bestows such things. He was a solitary man who believed his vision was solely his own. He disliked Leonardo da Vinci, was jealous of Raphael, did not finish his apprenticeship with an artist whose name does not easily come to mind. He said his genius came from God and his influence from the natural world. Then he contradicted himself, conceding one human, creative influence: Jacopo della Quercia.

For Michelangelo, figures sculpted by Jacopo della Quercia overrode envy and went straight to his heart. It was said of Jacopo's people that they looked as if they were trying to escape the confines of stone.

Michelangelo considered himself a sculptor above all, saying this particular act of creation is more "godlike."

And here is a sort of biblical law of art: One artist can beget another artist who begets another artist. Another angle in the refracting prism of the immortality question.

There are two artist myths. One says that an artist will have acclaim and riches at some point in his life but that his life will be longer than his fame and wealth. That he will fade into obscurity, all the more bitter for having once known such shining acceptance.

The other myth is the polar opposite of the first, and it says that a deserving artist will be ignored, impoverished, demoralized in his lifetime, only to be "discovered" by later generations who will laud him endlessly.

So, did the boastful Ghiberti fall into obscurity upon completion of the first set of doors for the Florence baptistery? What became of Brunelleschi and his unlocking of the mystery of the Florence cathedral dome? Poor Jacopo della Quercia, his panel is no longer with us.

Neither myth held true for any of the three competitors. Brunelleschi is remembered as the greatest architect of the Renaissance, as he was so noted in life. Jacopo della Quercia's echo resides in the people who populate Michelangelo's Sistine Chapel. And Ghiberti's east doors were eventually relocated to the north side of the baptistery to make way for a second set of doors, to be placed on the now vacant east side, also designed by Ghiberti. This second set of doors were finished the year Leonardo da Vinci was born. And when Michelangelo beheld them many years later, he said, They are the Gates of Paradise.

### *3. Michelangelo*

This is not the first time that Giulietta Marcel conceals herself in order to observe the young artist at work in his studio. It is not even the second time. The artist, M., has no awareness of her presence, for she goes to great trouble to insure her invisibility. He is deeply, profoundly involved in coaxing a breathtaking boy from a previously ruined piece of marble. The stone boy stands almost fourteen feet tall; the former sculptor's original intention was to fashion a giant. Now, in the hands of M., he will become David, killer of giants.

Giulietta, just thirteen, dresses like a boy (loose shirt, doublet, hose, a hat with a worn brooch of rubies and pearls that had been belonged to her mother, pinned at the brim) in order to sit more comfortably amid the dust and dirt of M.'s studio. Her boy's costume also makes it easier for her to climb in and out of the window that serves as her exit and entrance.

Once inside the studio, Giulietta hides behind a small grouping of enormous marble blocks—two of them have muscular, partially carved torsos that look as if they are straining to twist free of the stone—that serve as a sort of wall, or screen. The blocks are separated from one another and one of the walls by a couple of inches, and it is through these various "cracks" that Giulietta watches M. work. On one side of the marble blocks is M. and the statue he is willing into existence, and the scaffolding and the ladders; on the other side is Giulietta and the unlocked window.

All Giulietta's movements are practiced and precise; if she must move, she tries to coordinate her actions to the cadence of M.'s hammer and chisel. Her comings and goings are dependent upon M.'s arrivals and departures. If she grows thirsty or, worse, hungry, she has to find a way to quiet the growling in her stomach and resist the urge to moisten her lips repeatedly. The most difficult aspects of her covert life are controlling her bladder and managing the stiffness in her legs and lower back.

These are the necessities of her life, since she lives in dread of being discovered.

The worst days are when M. himself is restless, dissatisfied, working slowly, with a lack of concentration. She can hear him muttering, can sense how he might be easily distracted. On these days she is most afraid.

The good days are the ones where he works with a speed and a certainty that command her attention. It is as if he is incapable of making the false move. And it is on those days that she absolutely believes his claim about his line to God.

### *4. The Arrangement*

Giulietta considers the hours she spends in M.'s studio private spying, not to be confused with what she calls public spying, something that occurs daily as M. walks the streets of Florence. M. is a famous man, fortuitously connected with dukes and popes and people in power who supply him with work and materials. M. is an artist from a noble family. His *Pietà,* completed the previous year, is on display in Rome. The story that circulates about the *Pietà* is that M. was standing, unrecognized, with a number of people admiring his interpretation of sorrow, when a man was heard to credit another artist with the work. That night Michelangelo stole into Saint Peter's and carved his name across the sash of the Madonna's perfectly draped robes.

Certainly, Giulietta had noticed M. walking restlessly around the city, stopping to converse with the various men who lingered in the piazzas, or strolling by the river, seeming almost reluctant to return to work if it was a particularly fine day. She was mindful of the vagaries of expression on his face; she could see who pleased him during a chance meeting, who bored him, who irritated him, and who he pretended not to see at all as he picked up his pace, eyes focused in the distance.

This is public spying, Giulietta tells herself, this sort of close public observation. For M. was admired, feted, and courted by men of connection and means, and she believes that she, young, unknown and female, with artistic aspirations of her own, is meant to watch him as he walks the world. Everyone in Florence is supposed to pause, midconversation, replace their glasses on the table as gently as possible so as not to make any noise that would prevent them from eavesdropping on what he has to say. Everyone is meant to notice him. To notice him and, perhaps, whisper to each other something concerning his work, or temperament, or lovers, or enemies, once he has turned the corner and gone.

All this close listening to his private conversations, expounding on his private life, openly staring at him is not rude because M. is famous.

So when a friend of Giulietta's father, a man named Ferrante, sat with her one day on the piazza, pointed to M., and said, "That is who I want you to watch," it hardly felt like being asked to do something she wasn't doing every day. Why, she and Ferrante were doing it then, as they sat in the square discussing whether or not Giulietta would spy on him; they were spying on him already.

"I am too old, too conspicuous," said Ferrante, when Giulietta asked why he didn't spy on M. himself. "I am known. He knows me." Ferrante told Giulietta that he was writing a series of biographies of Italian artists, from a little more than a century past as well as the present. It would be a compilation of their work, their habits, their origins, their loves, their lives. Ferrante thought, who would notice a slight girl of thirteen, who lives alone with her semireclusive father, too poor to have a full-time servant, and too well educated to be a servant herself? From years of friendship with Giulietta's father, Ferrante knew that Alessandro Marcel did not closely supervise his daughter. In fact, with her unchained freedom she was more like a boy and less like the girls of her day and background.

Ferrante said, "You are not like other girls. Your life has not been sheltered."

Giulietta was not sure if that was a compliment or not, no matter that it was true. Her mother had died when she was a baby, and Giulietta behaved like a girl without a woman's influence; she finds it worrisome that she has so much difficulty embracing and following the expectations of her sex. Giulietta said nothing, her attention on M.

"From living with your father, you understand what I want," said Ferrante. "It is your life as well."

Ever since Giulietta had shown a talent and an inclination toward art, her father had been apprenticing her. Together they spent long hours upstairs in his studio, Giulietta understanding that, as a girl, she would never be allowed to study with another artist, or in an academy, nor could she join a guild. All of this was fine with Giulietta, for she loved her father's work.

"Will you do it?" asked Ferrante, naming a nice weekly sum for her efforts. She knew about the offer from the Monte delle Doti to supply the necessary dowry for Giulietta to become a nun, despite her lax religious instruction; she was aware that her father had had inquiries as to the possibility of his daughter being taught to spin cloth. Her marriage prospects were very slim, and while most girls her age were marrying either men or God, Giulietta was secretly relieved not to be in their number. Then her relief would fade and she would worry about her fate if she never married.

Giulietta looked over at M., who sat beside another

beautiful young man—younger and more beautiful than M. himself—to see him placing his hand on his companion's shoulder. She watched as he caressed it, then slowly, deliberately moved his hand down the young man's perfect, muscular arm, in one unbroken, fluid, pleasured motion, as if all perception lay in M.'s fingertips. When M.'s hand arrived at the young man's hand, M. held it palm to palm before he reluctantly, wistfully, it seemed to Giulietta, released it.

And it was in that moment, the observance of that single action, that Giulietta's previously unknown desires asserted themselves in a crazy jumble: She craved a life of art, she craved the artist (M.), and she craved to be the artist. Since this left her suddenly confused and unable to make any sort of distinctions, she simply answered Ferrante's proposal by saying yes.

### *5. Sandro of the Birds*

What brought Alessandro Marcel happiness was working out the problems of perspective, painting animals, his daughter, Giulietta, in general and her art instruction in particular, and the wonder of the birds. He so loved and understood birds, often choosing them as subjects for his pictures, that he was known around Florence as Sandro of the Birds. People did not usually call him Sandro of the Birds to his face, but he knew he was referred to by that name. He did not really mind; there are worse things to be called.

His fellow artists often said that Sandro was "more poor than famous." He supported himself and Giulietta with the money he made from assisting his better-known (though not always more talented) artist friends with their commissions. Occasionally a small project was passed on to Sandro, who gratefully accepted it. Finally, he was too shy, too melancholy, too quietly eccentric to pursue the altars, holy panels, frescoes, and vaulted ceilings that other artists campaigned to make. So he ended up living off the kindness of Florence's larger artistic community. It was not charity, for everyone admired Sandro's very fine work. It is his nature that stands in the way of greatness in his own lifetime.

Yet there is not a serious collector in Florence who does not count among his collection at least one painting by Alessandro Marcel. The late Beatrice d'Este, such a wildly prodigious collector of art and objects that it sometimes disturbed people to the point of disorientation when exposed to all the treasures she owned, possessed four works by Sandro. Most were tiny canvases or wooden panels that beheld a fragile, perfect bird.

Sandro once had a commission from a monastery just outside Florence, to paint its tiny refectory. He painted wall frescoes that wrapped around the diners with blue fields of grass, red cities, green skies, and purple wildlife. People wandered the blue fields touched with gold. He had offered to the brothers a fantastically hued world. Then, despite all his love of this project, he quit before it was finished. He stopped showing up and was neither heard from nor seen for two weeks.

Two friars went to find him, without luck, until the day they caught sight of him hurrying down a street in Florence. When they called out to him, Sandro nervously glanced in their direction, then quickly disappeared down an alley. They called again. He did not answer.

They went to his house. He did not answer.

They sent him messages. He did not answer.

Then they saw him, when he did not see them, in the piazza with Giulietta. "Why did you stop coming to work?" they wanted to know.

"Please don't ask me," he said as he tried to walk away, almost imperceptibly pushing Giulietta ahead of him.

"Well," they said, "the walls must be finished. We have an agreement."

"I can't," said Sandro miserably.

"Why?" they asked again.

And Sandro haltingly explained that it was because they fed him cheese every day: hunks of cheese, cheese soup, cheese pies, bread and cheese. "I was afraid if I ate any more cheese, I would turn to glue." His eyes would not meet theirs or Giulietta's.

The friars stood silently, then burst out laughing. "That's it, then?" and promised to vary his diet. Sandro agreed to honor his contract.

Giulietta thought of this incident as one more example of her retiring father's inability to cope with the world. She did not fully understand why his personality was constructed in this manner, only that it was, and why he was so entirely at ease in the solitude of his work.

As for the friars, they were not convinced by Sandro's story, thinking there must be another reason for his abrupt vanishing. But when they recounted the affair to three other artists who had also been employed at the monastery, the artists simply smiled and said, "That is Sandro."

And yet, Giulietta lives in a house with her father that holds a tribute, painted by Sandro, a tall, five-paneled portrait of the men he loves and why: There is Giotto (light and the origin of painting), Brunelleschi (architecture), Donatello (sculpture), and Manetti (mathematics). The fifth man in this polyptych history of art and thought is Sandro himself, representing perspective and animal portraits.

To Giulietta, this is the contradiction that sums up her father: the prospect of asking to be fed something other than cheese causes him to abandon his work and forces him into hiding, even as he places his own image confidently among the best of Italy's artists and intellects. His contributions next to theirs.

In the years before the colorful world that graced the refectory walls, Sandro picked up his first substantial commission by default. It turned out to be Giulietta's favorite work by her father.

The duke of a nearby village wanted someone to paint the vaulting of the town's cathedral. The citizens, along with the duke, wanted something spectacular to replace the plain night sky and stars that currently covered the ceiling. They did not have a lot of money, and because the town was small, unimportant, and largely unvisited it was difficult to attract some of the more popular Florentine artists. They finally settled on an older, moderately known painter, who asked young Sandro to assist him.

Sandro was newly widowed and wondering how to care for, not to mention support, his three-year-old daughter. He agreed to take the job on the condition that he could bring along Giulietta and her nurse.

Four days into the project, the older artist's heart failed and he died, leaving Sandro alone and in charge of the starry ceiling.

This was fine with the duke, whose sole words to Sandro were, "Remember, make it beautiful. Make it uplifting."

The result was a glorious illusionist ceiling unlike anything ever seen before, an impressive funnel of clouds and birds with stunning, shining luxurious feathers of rose, turquoise, washed yellow, lavender, and pearl gray, flying in a brilliant blue sky, with sunlight breaking and illuminating from the dome's small windows. There were insects: butterflies of cobalt, vermilion, ochre, and pitch; bees dressed in the startling black and yellow velvet stripes of a jungle tiger; peacock blue and watery green dragonflies whose bodies shimmered in *cangiante.* All of the creatures and the clouds and the light rising up, up, seeming to find no end except in a heaven too high and too distant for the human eye to discern. A great pale gold glimmering diffused at the apex.

Each day Giulietta watched with delight as her father brought this world of flight to life. (Sandro ended up adding some *putti* at the request of the duke, but these little angels are primarily found sitting on the ledges of the small windows, gazing up at the marvelous procession of birds and insects, lazy and amazed.)

As Giulietta grew older, she recalled less and less of the daily routine. Instead, it seemed to her that one day there was a vague outline and the next an extravagance of wings.

It is this ceiling that first comes to mind when Giulietta considers her father.

When Sandro thinks of Giulietta he cannot readily say what first comes to mind. He remembers her as a toddler without a mother; he considers her finely drawn features, her balance, her proportion, her deep brown eyes with their cast of evergreen, and the warm russet of her hair. He thinks of her stride, too loose-limbed to be feminine, a bit too restrained to be truly masculine; in general, she carries herself as if she believes the world is entirely unconcerned with her.

He ponders the hours they spend in his studio together, her face and hands taken up with the small practice fresco she makes as he instructs her regarding the difference between wet and dry fresco, the building up of the layers, the limitations of color and time, and the application of pigment.

He thinks of how her eyes meet another's unflinchingly, with curiosity, before looking away. He thinks about her almost involuntary reluctance to be the woman her time demands her to be and shakes his head sadly when he considers this may be one of the things he loves best about her.

### *6. Sfumato*

This is what Ferrante told Giulietta about Leonardo:

*Sfumato* is the smoky effect seen in paintings by Leonardo da Vinci. Leonardo was born on the day that Ghiberti finished the *Gates of Paradise* for the Florence baptistery. He was largely responsible for elevating the status of the artist to that of theorist and intellectual.

His pictures told many stories about the emotional lives of artist and subject alike.

He felt there was a connection between the body machine and the design of musical instruments: for example, the correlation between the tendons of the hand and the keyboard; the upper larynx and the woodwinds.

In the same way that Leonardo's flying machines prefigured airplanes, so did his notion of the body as musical instrument find its expression in a photograph taken in the twentieth century by an American photographer, who fashioned his Parisian mistress as a violin, complete with sound holes drawn on her shapely back.

Sandro and Giulietta are working on the technique of egg tempera.

"Once you add the egg yolk to the paint your time is limited," Sandro says as he mixes powdered pigment with water. "It sets quickly."

Giulietta reaches over with her brush.

"Wait," says Sandro, causing Giulietta to stop, brush poised in midair. "Is that the color you want?"

"Why?" she asks.

"Because you have to blend them before, not after," Sandro explains. "Once the egg is added, there is no mixing." Then he goes on to say that specific colors have certain meanings. Unmixed color reflects God's creation. Mixed color is a "corruption." Ultramarine is for Christ and the Madonna; vermilion and gold for saints. Yellow indicates cowardice; Judas's robes might be yellow. Red is blood.

"Earth colors are made from compounds of metal. Ultramarine, made from crushed lapis lazuli and imported from across the ocean—that is what the name means—is very dear. A patron will ask how much ultramarine is needed for your work, and the exact amount will be written into your contract." Sandro falls into embarrassed silence. He looks away. Giulietta is about to ask what is wrong when the reason occurs to her: She, in all likelihood, will never negotiate a contract with anyone. And Sandro, by apprenticing a girl instead of a boy, may as well be offering his gifts to a careless breeze.

Now she says nothing.

This is the way in which father and daughter stumble across the dilemmas of their separate lives, with mute understanding.

Time begins again.

Sandro stirs his brush in the paint. "Like this," he commands her, "not too thick. A thin coat can avoid shrinkage and cracking." Giulietta admires the way her father's hand moves quickly, assuredly across the surface. "You must learn to layer it," he continues, "particularly when painting flesh. For this you'll need lead white and vermilion."

As he speaks he spreads red across a panel. Sandro is working on a series of panels that represent the four elements. He is also getting paid for his efforts, though even if he were not, he would still be spending this late autumn afternoon with Giulietta. He is using animals to represent the four elements: Earth is a mole, Water a fish, Fire a violently red salamander, and Air a curiously constructed chameleon. Sandro has never actually seen a chameleon, but he believes it can change color because it lives on air. His interpretation looks less like a lizard and more like a camel with a distended belly.

When someone knocks at the door, Sandro wipes his oily, multicolored hands on a rag and walks downstairs to answer it. Inside the studio Giulietta can hear Sandro unlatching the door, hear his muffled voice. She imagines him illuminated all around from the bright autumn sunlight that spills into the house.

Then all is silence, and she knows that he has disappeared.

Giulietta, in imitation of Sandro, cleans her hands on the white shirt she wears over her dress, follows her father's path down the stairs, and sees that the door to their small house has been left ajar. As she goes to close it, she sees that the door between the street and the tiny courtyard garden they share with two other families is similarly open. Before closing this second door, Giulietta steps into the street, slightly squinting against the light, to see the errant Sandro walking beside Leonardo.

Leonardo is talking and gesturing calmly as Sandro nods. The two men draw second looks and remarks from passersby, and even Giulietta wonders what the great Leonardo wants with her father. She knew from Ferrante that Leonardo had recently returned from Milan, where he had lived and worked for the Sforza.

Ferrante had said that Leonardo wasted his gifts there. For nearly twenty years he designed costumes and scenery for masques, a heating system for bathwater, and painted the portraits of one or two girlish mistresses. He drew maps and drafted plans for irrigation systems and war machines and an automated lion that dropped lilies from its breast. He painted a refectory wall. "Most of the projects he proposed," said Ferrante, "were never realized due to lack of interest from his patron. There were mountains of notes, ideas, and sketches. He even made a massive clay statue of a horse, rearing up, bearing Francesco Sforza, Lodovico's father, on its back, but was not given the bronze to complete it." The bronze had gone into weapons of defense. Ferrante continued, "And, later, when the French took Milan anyway, they used Leonardo's horse for target practice."

As usual, Giulietta did not ask how Ferrante knew what he knew.

So what is this great man with his hundreds of pages of impossible inventions discussing with her retiring father? She smiles at the thought of her father with his feverish problems of perspective, and his passion for birds, and his faith that he can accurately portray animals he has never seen. This man who places his own image in company with the other eminent artists of his time on the five-panel screen that adorns their house. She tilts her face upward, inhales the smoky scent of the fall, loving the play of light and the lengthening shadows. And she decides that maybe it isn't so strange that Leonardo would seek out her father, even though they have not met before. It occurs to her that there is something tribal about artists; something beyond the guilds and patrons and renown, and that every so often this impulse, this bond, this strange blood tie, wills out.

She shuts the street door and wanders across the courtyard, closing the door to their house behind her, and returns to her work.

### *7. Angel Wings*

"He asked me if I would walk with him, and of course, I said yes." Sandro and Giulietta are sharing supper as her father recounts his afternoon with Leonardo. "He wanted to talk about birds."

"Birds?"

"Feathers. Wings. He fashions the wings of his angels after bird wings."

"Why would he come to you?" asks Giulietta, recalling Ferrante's description of a handful of flying machines that he had seen among Leonardo's sketches. Although Giulietta believes that everyone, at least once in his life, should want to spend time with her melancholy father and talk about the weightlessness of his flying sky of birds and insects and angels in the cathedral in the tiny, ignored town outside Florence. Or ask him about his camel that thrives on air. Maybe exchange ideas concerning the mathematics of perspective.

"Because," Sandro says with wonder in his voice, "someone had said to him, if you want to know about wings, you should go see Sandro of the Birds."

"What did he say during your walk?"

"He told me that when he was younger he used to free all the birds in the marketplace."

"What did you do?"

"We ate cakes as we sat beneath a tree. On the grass."

A result of that afternoon was Giulietta keeping track of Leonardo for the rest of his life. Though he was ignorant of her sense that he was her last link to Sandro. This sense intensified when her father died years later.

She even met Leonardo once or twice when she was older and he was quite old, without confiding what he meant to her in connection with her father; the way his name made her recall the day when the two men walked side by side down the street, and how her memory is filled with the light, shadows, and perfume of that afternoon.

Her father was a dreamer; Giulietta herself has always harbored big dreams, sometimes without fully surrendering herself to this truth. But Leonardo was an extraordinary dreamer. Since his visions had no precedence in this world, it seemed right to Giulietta that the handful of paintings he left behind should be imbued with the dreamy, vanishing quality of smoke.

It also made sense that some of his work would begin to show signs of damage even before his death. The mold that crept across and through his *Last Supper* did not surprise her. The connection of his ideas to this world was tenuous and slight, yet powerful, like an unforgettable dream that crowds your day with its memory.

When Giulietta had the unexpected opportunity to see Leonardo's notebooks (with their painfully small backward mirror writing) she could feel her own dreamer's heart begin to break as she read this sentence, written repeatedly, on one of the last pages:

*Tell me if anything at all was done . . .*

### *8. Terribilità*

*Terribilità* was the word often used to describe M., as "of the Birds" was to denote Sandro. Its rough translation is frightening genius, or awesome talent. Something like that.

This served to characterize M.'s temperament and ability. People were as drawn to him as they were afraid. Even the important men who patronized him were slightly cowed when exposed to his moods. The worst of him came out when he was working. When he was a boy even the great Medici kept their distance. In relation to other artists, Raphael said M. was "as lonely as the hangman."

Yet those M. loved, he loved.

It seemed to Giulietta that M. feared no one, which only served to make him more frightening. The changing weather of his personality also contained a seductive element because it is difficult for human beings to resist those among them who neither rule nor serve. M., like

Giulietta, seemed to live deep within himself. Even her father's unease with life was markedly dissimilar from M.'s, for Sandro lived in continuous retreat, his little, inner life formed from this particular pulling away from the world that surrounded him.

M. was not like that. It was as if he suffered the outer world without allowing it to force him to close into himself. As if its second-rate concerns neither touched nor moved him; as if nothing was more important than his fabulous solitary world. The universe over which he ruled.

Giulietta arrives at the studio well before M. It is freezing inside, and since she cannot light the fire, she walks around to keep her blood circulating.

The tall, unfinished statue is as intimidating as it is alluring, almost an exact embodiment of M.'s *terribilità*. Her reaction to it is much the same as her reaction to M.: She is afraid and attracted in equal measure.

To stand this close to the statue is to make her lightheaded and breathless, if only by its sheer size. The scaffolding that surrounds it reminds her of an enclosure necessary to keep the stone boy from wandering around the studio. He looks as if he can crush Giulietta with one enormous hand and little effort. At the same time, the way in which his hair curls around his face makes her want to caress his cheek.

Giulietta wants to climb the scaffolding, to pretend for just the briefest moment that this is her work, that this artist life belongs to her. She grips a supporting plank, then another as she begins her climb. Fear is causing her to perspire in this ice-cold room. Before she knows it, her feet are no longer on the floor but stepping up onto one of the horizontal planks. And she cannot tell which is making her more afraid: the possibility of M. rushing into the studio, discovering her, or this almost unbearable proximity to the statue itself.

And then, before she can ascend any further, she hears voices outside the door.

Half falling, half scrambling, she tumbles down the scaffolding, running to her hiding place behind the blocks of marble. She panics, thinking she will not be able to quiet her panting quickly enough and will surely be found out, gasping for air, as soon as M. comes inside. The more she tries to calm herself, to soothe her agitated breathing, the more impossible it seems.

Then she realizes no one has touched the door. This helps to relax her somewhat. What she hears next is very loud arguing. The loudest, angriest voice she knows to be M.'s. He is speaking quickly, just below a scream, and sounding, at times, as if he is snarling. That's what he reminds Giulietta of—a snarling, viciously protective animal. To whom the other voice belongs she does not know, but it, too, sounds upset. Then the other voice grows quiet, as if trying to reason with M., then it loses all patience and shoots up in volume.

The only thing Giulietta can make out, from standing very close to the window, which is slightly cracked open, is that the stranger is demanding to enter and see the progress M. is making with the statue, while M. is threatening to abandon the work altogether if anyone should set foot in his studio.

The man reminds M. that he is being paid four hundred crowns, that the city has graciously provided the studio, and that he is fortunate to have the chance to work with such a superior piece of marble.

M. replies that the stone was *ruined* by some inferior nobody and that he, M., is breathing a life into it that it never would have without him. He also says that a price cannot be placed on genius and that he is sick to death of being told to be *grateful* that he is allowed to practice his craft at all when those he works for are clearly receiving more than they are giving.

M.'s voice drops, and Giulietta can only piece together some of what he says, which is something like, you all think in gold, and there isn't enough gold in the world to pay for what I make. You decide the price, I don't, because we both know it has no price.

Giulietta is reminded of a story that Ferrante told her during one of their discussions regarding M. A man in Florence asked M. to make a figure, a sleeping Cupid, and it came out so perfect and classically constructed that someone commented that it looked "timeless." The man then got this idea that he would bury the Cupid, age it with dirt and carelessness, then take it to Rome and sell it as an antique. Which he did.

Those who knew about the sale told the man that he should share his windfall with M., but the man refused. Not long after that, the buyer of the sleeping Cupid discovered the deception and demanded that the man take back the Cupid and return his money.

As Ferrante told Giulietta, "It was an exquisite piece of work, well beyond the value of what the man paid for it, antique or not. But some people only value what they are told is valuable."

The studio door bangs open, and in stalks M. He is unaccompanied. For a second, Giulietta hears nothing. She imagines M. staring at his statue, scrutinizing it, suddenly understanding that someone has been near it.

That he is not alone. Her chest constricts with fear. She presses her thin body against one of the blocks that holds a partially carved torso. She pushes so hard that her spine begins to ache, all the while thinking that if she desires it enough, the unfinished figure in the stone will protect and enfold her little form. Giulietta closes her eyes, longing to pray not to be found out, but she will not do so, for it would be a sacrilege to ask God to help her continue a deception.

M. is moving slowly around the studio; his footsteps sound as if he is circling, then walking toward her, then doubling back again. He whispers something she cannot make out, and she can almost picture him cocking his head to one side, as if he has heard a foreign noise and is about to investigate the source. As much as she wants to, she does not dare to peek through the open spaces between the marbles, and so continues to imagine his movements, pictures him coming closer to her hiding place; she is overwhelmed by how exposed she is.

Then she hears him pick up his tools, curse, and fling them down again.

### *9. Her Ephemeral Legacy. Her Useless Dowry.*

For the first time Giulietta hates M. She despises the restriction and imprisonment of her life as M.'s spy. Why does she endure such discomfort and fear? So one man can write, with greater authority, another man's story.

As she grows older—almost fifteen—she understands that, as with her adoration of M., her love for her father is growing more entwined with her devotion to art. This awful dawning of this awful truth, which is that she wants nothing more in this world than to be an artist herself.

More and more she considers the question *who am I?*, and the answer, artist, is as inseparable from her identity as her love of art in general is wrapped up with her love for her father. This desire, this longing, has nowhere to go.

Did I choose this? she wonders, or was it proximity and inheritance? She has been around artists her entire life; they populate her days, they have infected her with their own unnameable quests, their wants are her wants, so how, she cries as she hides her face in her hands, how could she ever have been anything they are not?

She considers the passing of her father's knowledge and skill to her as her ephemeral legacy. Her useless dowry.

She observes the girls her own age who already have children, or, if they are still unwed, are almost never allowed out without a veil and a chaperone; or the courtesans with their immodest walks and momentary careers that inevitably end tragically.

"Why didn't you raise me more like a girl?" Giulietta demands to know. "Don't you care? You give me too much freedom. Don't you love me?"

"I love you more than you know," Sandro tells her.

"It's not decent that I should be so free. What if something happens to me as I go about without a chaperone? The world is perpetually unstable."

"If that is so," he says, "then I couldn't possibly protect you. I can't win against the world." He reaches for her paint-stained hand with his own. "I can't live forever, and with that in mind, that is how I brought you up."

"When you teach me how to paint, what are you thinking?" She is standing, her rough-woven green dress spattered with enough tiny flecks of paint so that the colors look as if they are part of the fabric. Sandro takes no notice; he is admiring the *cassoni,* bridal chest, she has been painting.

"I'm thinking how very good you are," he says finally.

When M. stormed out the day of the fight with the unnamed man, Giulietta stayed behind, her body relaxing, slumped against the marble that had so recently received her flattened spine.

She inhaled the scent of oil, dragged her foot across the layer of dust comprised of marble, powdered pigment, and the street. She sat amidst brushes, hammers, chisels, and panels of white poplar panels so paint-laden and wildly splattered that they are beautiful as they are. When Giulietta tried to nudge a panel with her foot, she is amazed at the weight and density of the accumulated paint. For one inexplicable moment, Giulietta has to stop herself from breaking off a chunk of color from one of the impasto pools in order to taste it.

She is so tired of simply watching.

### *10. What Does He Do?*

"What does he do?" asks Sandro. He and Giulietta are discussing M. at work. Sandro's voice is low and tentative with curiosity.

Giulietta thinks for a moment, hesitant because she did not know until now that to share her secret life with M. (her one-sided secret life) is to reveal herself. How can she talk about the pleasure of watching him work without a softening of her speech? Or the guilt she experiences from violating another's privacy? Or her resentment that she can only get paid watching someone else work, and not receive a penny for her own efforts?

How can she talk about the unexpected merging of her identity with his: her mind turning to a day when she sat on her side of the makeshift marble wall, dipping her fingers into the dust on the floor and sketching phantom pictures on the backside of the blocks. Giulietta worked quickly, confidently, her imagination filling in the colors and detail of expression as she made one picture after another. As soon as she completed a sketch, she wiped it away with the palm of the other hand, immediately beginning something new.

On her side of the marble barrier, Giulietta worked as breathlessly as M. did on his side. So accustomed was she to working alongside another artist, so great was her longing to record her own vision. She made one evanescent drawing after another and found herself in tears from the experience.

So, how can she say to her father when asked about M., I learned that as long as no one buys or cares for your work, you are an invisible artist?

How could she say, It's quite possible that I love and hate M. This mysterious *chiaroscuro* of her senses?

All she ends up saying is, "M. is mostly quiet."

"He says nothing?" asks Sandro.

"Curses, sometimes."

"Curses," repeats Sandro.

Giulietta could also say that M. recites poetry, some she recognizes, some wholly unfamiliar, and that his voice falls into rough whispers or rises dramatically. The enthralling music of his voice. And that the days of endless poetry are the days that make her worry about things like love.

### *11. Money and Intimacy and Obligation*

Ferrante insisted that Giulietta attend his party, and though she is uninterested in going, she has no choice. She is in his employ.

In her small room that sits atop the studio and is actually a closed area of the common belvedere of their shared home, she primps with the lack of expertise of someone unused to parties and celebrations. Tossed across her bed is the dress she will wear, a worn, dated gown that had belonged to her mother but still has a certain elegance. It is of malachite-green velvet, heavily embroidered with gold and red, and a slightly paler green. The tight sleeves reach down the back of her hands. The velvet is a bit heavy for the season, but it is the best that she has.

For now, she is still in her white chemise, arranging her russet-gold hair in a long braid held with two ruby-and-jade clips at the back and a ferronière that strings tiny semiprecious charms across her forehead. She stands before the ornate mirror that dominates much of her bedchamber. Though her hairstyle is current, her unplucked hairline is not.

On a table sits a box made by Giulietta. She has recently begun fabricating these rather small, beautiful boxes with tigers and panthers with lapis lazuli eyes, or, like the one in her room, a young boy and a young girl facing each other in a mirror. The boy looks to see himself as a girl, and the girl becomes a boy. From this box she extracts dangling pearl earrings that will adorn her ears. Rose-hued slippers for her feet. All her modest riches are a legacy of her mother, who was born to a financially comfortable family, only marrying into a less fortunate one.

Giulietta laces the dress, down the sleeves, across the bodice, along the side, understanding how her boy's disguise, with its ease and illusion of a life of possibility, has made these girl's clothes all the more unappealing. The restriction of the style reminds her that she will, most likely, always be at someone's mercy.

Walking out the door of her room, she stops to take in the view from the belvedere. Her rooftop, aviary room. The early summer evening is warm but not hot; she loves the long summer days, sometimes dragging her bed out onto the roof to sleep.

Downstairs her father waits to escort her to Ferrante's, though he himself will not go inside. He will meet her later to walk her home. When she enters the room she can see, for the first time, her own prettiness reflected in his look.

When Giulietta arrives at the party, Ferrante greets her warmly, happily, pressing a purse full of gold coins into her hand. Tells her that there is another artist present tonight whom he would like her to "keep her eye on."

Giulietta laughs, says after Ferrante has pointed him out, "Isn't there more than enough known about him already?" For this man's life has been so public, so unfailingly scandalous, though he is well liked for his easy conversation and good humor. She says, "I doubt there is much I can add."

His sole competition in the extremes of his bohemian life is a writer who devotes his talent to erotic tales that people seem to enjoy and deplore at various times. The writer is not circumspect about his opinions regarding politics, yet he seems to get away with his views. Recently, he wrote stories as companion pieces to a group of sixteen drawings deemed "unfit for general viewing" but that were exceedingly popular nonetheless.

Giulietta is trying to act indifferent, casual, but the truth is she is not ready to end her time with M. How curious, since she so often feels trapped and occasionally bored by the situation; resents the time that it takes away from her own work—her perfect, beautiful boxes, and her first *cassoni*—yet her peculiar relationship with him is the most intimate one she has ever known.

And she wants so much to speak with M. In the beginning, it had been enough to watch him, to listen to his poetry and temper and curses and the dull sound of the hammer tapping on the chisel, but now Giulietta wants to speak and be spoken to. She wants to show him her flawless boxes. She wants to tell him how afraid her impossible ambition makes her feel. She wants to talk to him because she senses kinship.

Everything circles back to love, to the male costume she chooses to wear, in the beginning for comfort but now for other reasons. She has never forgotten her longing, sitting in the piazza with Ferrante, as they glanced over at M. and his young man or the strength of her longing.

Nowadays the larger fear she faces when hiding from M. is not getting caught, but that she will give in to the impulse to call out to him, confessing everything.

"I'm partially through with his story," says Ferrante as he and Giulietta walk the loggia of the courtyard, the figures of the guests throwing shadows from the lamps, discussing the new artist she is to observe. "There are things you can find out that I cannot discover any other way."

By way of background, he tells her:

Michelangelo sings his praises (Ferrante cannot know the effect this information has on Giulietta).

At age seventeen he ended his life in the monastery, then claimed he was kidnapped, along with others, and bound in chains. Held by Moors, he said later. Then spirited away to Barbary, where he was a captive for eighteen months, until he came upon a piece of coal. With that piece of coal he drew, on the dirty white wall of his prison, a likeness so stunning, so true to his Moorish captor, that he was set free.

Ferrante says, "That is why he always says, 'I owe my life to art.'"

From that moment on, he lived on his work.

He also lived for women. He pursued, lusted after, courted, seduced, promised the moon, sulked, bullied, argued, cajoled, used sweetness, used violence, used anything to get a woman. His conquests were many, though he only had one wife, a nun whom he persuaded away from the convent, and they produced a son. No one knew if they were married or not, but she was always referred to as his wife. He captured her fragile beauty, made earthbound, in pictures.

Ferrante says, "They say if he cannot have a woman, he paints her. And often has her anyway. I need to learn about his work habits. Much the same as M."

Giulietta looks over at the man in question, Fra d'Este, who is laughing and spilling his wine on a woman who is not his wife, then clumsily wiping it from her dazzling dress, his hands freely roving across her body.

"I'm still watching M. How can I be in two places at once?" asks Giulietta, not wanting to show either her repulsion for d'Este or her attachment to M.

"Just sit for d'Este. I want you to be his model."

They are still strolling, circling the revelers.

"What makes you think he will want me?" asks Giulietta. Ferrante, stopping, touches her shoulder and faces her. The expression in his eyes as he gazes at Giulietta is similar to the one in her father's eyes earlier in the evening, only less innocent, more immodest.

"He'll want to," Ferrante says, then, "I can't write about his life until I know his life."

"I'm not sure I should give up the other," says Giulietta carefully. "No," she says.

"I will pay you twice as much to sit for Fra d'Este. He paints in the evenings anyway, by firelight."

As they stand on the periphery of the crowd, Fra d'Este bounds toward them wearing a smile so infectious Giulietta is tempted to return it. Instead, she recalls his disgusting fumblings with the dazzling woman moments earlier.

"Is this the girl you told me about?" he asks Ferrante, as if Giulietta were deaf and mute. As inexperienced as she is, it is clear from d'Este's appraisal that Ferrante has already promised her to him. That their negotiation was an act of politeness without meaning.

Her father seldom painted live models. ("I cannot bear their discomfort," he said.)

She considers how this second job will eliminate almost any time at all for her own work. Her few boxes, with the exception of the one in her room, lined up in the studio alongside her nearly finished bridal chest. Sandro excited and proud of her progress and her skill and taste.

Fra d'Este continues to scrutinize her face and figure. No one has ever examined her this closely, and for the first time she feels her beauty enhanced by the look in a man's eye. *From the look in a man's eye,* she thinks, *a man I don't even like.* Which makes it all the more inexplicable that her untried heart should shimmer in anticipation.

As Giulietta stands, motionless, in the unrelenting stare and laughing remarks of Fra d'Este, uncomfortable in her mother's elegant, tired clothes, seeing her own reflection in the shining, drunken look of d'Este, someone grabs him around the neck in a rough embrace. Giulietta's heart quickens, for the man holding on to d'Este was M.

In that second, Giulietta almost convinces herself that the strength of her longing has somehow willed M. in her direction, and now that he is here, she will not be able to stop the words that lately seemed so uncontrollable. Or maybe M. found her out and is going to publicly denounce her. He will shout, "This quiet girl has been deceiving me!" She will be vilified. She will be ostracized.

Instead, M. ignores her entirely. At first she doesn't notice because she is used to being in his presence without acknowledgment; then she has to remind herself that she is not a boy, hiding on the dirty floor of his studio. She is a guest at a party.

"I heard you escaped again," says M. to Fra d'Este.

"What's this?" asks Ferrante, his interest keen, and Giulietta can almost picture him mentally noting the exchange between M. and d'Este, eager for the party to end so he can stay up late into the night, writing it all down.

This causes a pang of guilt in Giulietta, as well as pity for the two unknowing artists. She thinks of the way she spends her days, and of Ferrante and his biographies, and she wants to blurt out to the two men, "Oh, you don't know the company you are keeping."

"Our friend," says M. to Ferrante, "was not getting his work done, so Silvestro, wanting his money's worth, locked him up in his house, not to be distracted." M. is smiling.

"What did you do?" asks Ferrante.

Fra d'Este shrugs his large shoulders, laughing. "I made a rather serviceable rope from the bedclothes, and ffffftttt," he says, slicing the air with his hand for emphasis, "I was gone. Women and wine," he says of the bender he embarked upon once freed. Ferrante and M. laughed along with him.

"Well, Silvestro didn't try it a second time," says d'Este. "Inhumane. To be locked up with one's work, as if that is all life is about."

Giulietta listens to the men, who have forgotten her. Imperceptibly, unthinkingly, their bodies begin to rearrange themselves into a tighter, closer circle, edging her out altogether. This is when she goes home, bidding good night to no one.

### *12. Two Men*

Sandro monitors Giulietta as she works. He has been teaching her about the difference between the opaque effect of oil paint and of glazing. He says, With oil, light is only reflected back. With glazing the light passes through, is trapped, then reflects the paint underneath before being released.

Giulietta mixes a glaze for a box she is making, of a blue and gold tiger with red eyes.

Since Giulietta left the party before their arranged meeting, Sandro was not able to walk her home in the deep violet of the summer night. Had he known she was traveling alone, he would have raced out the door to find her. Instead, he was upstairs reading in the studio when she came in the door. At the moment of her appearance in the doorway, Sandro, in his confusion at her unexpected appearance, as well as her being clothed in his wife's old dress, Sandro thought she was his wife, come back to him. For he had loved her so deeply, their romance always felt fated. Maybe they were given this enormous love because their time together would be so brief.

As Sandro looks over at Giulietta, he thinks of how his daughter calls up the image of his wife, in the chance, fleeting moment; a space of time so swift that in the second he seizes upon and tries to fix the resemblance, it is already gone.

Giulietta does not think about her mother as she paints the blue and gold tiger; she meditates on M. His blood is her blood. At night, she will recall the meter and rhythm of his voice as he recites poetry. His presence is powerful. It is as if he is a dream, or a trance from which she cannot awaken. For the first time she understands why the admission of love from one person to another is sometimes spoken in low, hesitant words because what is said, besides I love you, is Please don't use this against me. You are saying, I am susceptible to suggestion. You must hold a hope and a faith that you will not be struck down in your vulnerable dream state.

She finds herself repeating to herself I love you I love you I love you I love you I love you I love you I love you.

* * *

The next day Giulietta dons her boy's costume and follows the narrow, turning streets that take her to M.'s studio. Instead of filling out with age, her body is growing taller and thinner, which makes the cut of her male attire fit her that much better.

With her red-gold hair shoved under her cap, she draws a few looks from men and one or two unchaste glances from women, older women she knows to be respectable and married. One woman allows herself a slight smile at Giulietta. Giulietta tilts her head in the woman's direction to acknowledge her admiration and keeps moving.

Everything is changing now that Giulietta purely loves M.

When she comes upon the painted, cloudy window of M.'s studio—her window, her entrance and exit—she listens carefully for the sounds of M. within. It is later than her usual arrival time. She knows it would make more sense to forgo her spying under such a circumstance, but she cannot stay away from the man who is transforming a beautiful ruined giant into a beautiful boy. This miracle she witnesses daily.

The window is shut tight. She stands still, reminding herself that she mustn't be inattentive to what she is doing. Pressing her fingers to the glass, she is afraid to open it. Then she realizes it is quiet inside.

Had she heard any sounds inside? Or did she simply assume M.'s presence? She takes her fingers from the glass, trying to determine what to do.

The two men arrive as Giulietta is leaning against the outer wall, chastising herself for her senseless rush to enter the studio without regard to secrecy. What is she thinking, acting in such a manner?

She glances up to see M. with a companion, conversing quietly as they pause at the studio door. Giulietta pretends not to notice, even as she is surreptitiously eyeing them.

Suddenly, M. catches her eye, holds her gaze in his; and, though he has put the key into the lock of the door, he is not turning it; his movements as leisurely as hers were hurried minutes before. He continues to stare at Giulietta.

All the symptoms that accompany her usual fear of being caught commence: the wild, almost incapacitating jump of her heart; her struggle for breath; the pounding of her pulse; and the heat that feels like a very small fever traveling her body.

She knows that he knows. But before she can get sick, or faint, or bolt, M. smiles.

And it is a smile of such invitation and promise that Giulietta finds herself returning it in kind. Her buried affection expressing itself in her face.

Then M. opens the door and, with a certain anticipation and lust, or so it seems to Giulietta, gathers his companion in his arms and brings him into the studio.

Now she slides down the wall until she sits in the street. Is it her imagination, or can she hear the laughter of the two men inside? Is it possible to hear the sound of a kiss? This uninvited crush directs her without regard. From the pinnacle exchange of a smile, she has now fallen into the dust of jealousy with such effortless ease it leaves her with a sense of detached wonder.

She sits slouched against the wall until the sky turns from dusk to night, then she makes her way home in the dark.

### *13. Firelight Tangled in Her Hair*

For months Giulietta has been sitting for Fra d'Este, in the evenings in his studio, where he tells her that looking at her with the firelight tangled in her hair makes him feel that he will live forever. She suspects that Fra d'Este has fallen in love with her.

No one has ever studied her this closely, with so much attention to her fluctuations of appearance and mood. It unnerves her and wears her out. This must be the nature of the relationship of painter to subject.

It is the strange dichotomy of her life that she should spend her evenings scrutinized by d'Este and her days unseen and unknown by M. On these winter evenings, frozen by command more than by the temperature of the room, she turns over in her mind this existence of similarities and opposites: similar in that her time with each artist demands the same patterns of breathing, that is, inhalation and exhalation must be slight and almost imperceptible, leaving her in a constant state of borderline light-headedness. Opposite because she spends her days as the invisible boy in M.'s world and her nights as the womanly center of attention for d'Este, who allows no detail of her face and figure to go unnoticed.

She feels, by turns, furtive and shameless.

Fra d'Este has begun to move her image around in his pictures. She has made the journey from town girl to seraph to Madonna (*It is said he paints the women he cannot have*). He talks with admiration of her face, her hands, the silhouette of her figure, the fine arch of her small feet. He sometimes refers to her in colors: shell pink, alabaster, glass ocean green, copper, my honey girl, my golden one.

* * *

"Are you paying attention?" demands Sandro, taking Giulietta step by step through the gold-leaf process, but she is so exhausted, so worn from all the lives she is leading, that her mind wanders freely.

"Here," says Sandro, handing her a panel of silver fir, instructing her to apply the bole to the ground of white gesso. "Giulietta," he says again sharply, "watch." He begins the pounding and polishing required of gold leaf.

Her concentration breaks over and over because she doesn't know how long she can keep up this life and cannot ignore her future.

What if she, so adept at deception, takes her boy's self into someone's studio, or enrolls in the academy? What if she becomes so good at her work that once they discover she is an impostor, they will forgive her, wrench social convention, and let her stay?

"Don't you want your work to shine?" asks Sandro, demonstrating the art of applying sliver after sliver of gold to the panel.

M. is getting closer to finishing his statue, and in one sense Giulietta is relieved for she thinks it will ease some of the lassitude that dominates her sessions with d'Este, who lately complains of her "lifelessness."

"I thought it preferable that I am still and docile," she says to him.

"Still, yes," he says, "but not dead. If I want a dead model, I'll call Leonardo." They both laugh at his joke, Fra d'Este laughing harder and longer than she, and Giulietta imagines him repeating the joke over and over among his companions. Giulietta fights to look lively without breathing.

* * *

Adding the gold leaf is the final touch on the wedding chest Giulietta has been making. It has a background of night sky and stars, some gold, some silver, and a man and a woman, not religious figures, walking on what looks like air. Their hands reach out to each other but do not, cannot touch. Their faces are turned almost entirely away from the viewer, as if they are taking in the infinite carpet of stars that unrolls before them.

Sandro takes in the effect of Giulietta's scene, proclaims it "odd." The disturbance in his face tells Giulietta that the subject matter is unacceptable: It is not religious, it is not of the natural world, it's not even (and this would be for the serious, secret collector of such things) erotic, exactly.

"Perhaps some wings?" suggests Sandro, though it is clear that neither figure resembles an angel.

She sighs, watches the sun go down, its diffused light spilling into the room, setting it aglow, enhancing the gold of her night sky, the hint of gold in her hair, and she sadly announces she must be elsewhere, reluctantly placing her own work aside.

Fra d'Este paints Giulietta in *cangiante* robes with halos of light illuminating her red-gold hair. Her gaze is cast down as if she were modestly receiving a blessing. She is so many things under Fra d'Este's brush: a messenger angel announcing the birth of Christ; a girl drawing water from a well. A Magdalene. A Madonna. D'Este paints her in an idealized state, picture after picture, as if repeatedly reminding himself of what he cannot have.

Giulietta suspects that Fra d'Este has fallen in love with her. She tolerates his affection without encouraging it. She allows him to worship her from afar because there are days when it is the only way she feels real.

*14. Snow*

On a crisp, cold, blue day, when snow lay upon Florence, the boy Giulietta walks briskly to M.'s studio.

Then, there is M. He is walking as quickly as she and carrying a sack. Just when she decides that she will follow him (without appearing to be following him, keeping him in her peripheral vision), he notices her.

"You're that boy, aren't you?" he says.

Despite the fact that she had dressed little more than an hour ago, she pats herself, checking as to whether she is clad in doublet and jacket or gown, to see if she is "that boy" or not. M. crosses over to her and keeps her pace. "You must be an apprentice," he says. She nods. "Well," he says impatiently, "with whom?"

And Giulietta quietly names her father.

M. looks surprised. "Sandro Marcel has opened his studio." He shrugs.

"Why did you ask?" asks Giulietta.

M. takes her uncovered hand in his own gloved hand. "Your hands."

She glances down at her fingers: They are stained with paint. M. and Giulietta fall in step; she does not ask where they are headed, nor does he inquire in regard to her destination. In front of a good-sized palace, M. comes to a halt. Giulietta stops as well. "Come with me," he says, abruptly, "and learn something."

After exchanging pleasantries with the owner of the house and being attended to by a very old slave, M. and

Giulietta are led into a garden courtyard. It is here that M. opens the sack he has been holding, extracting his sculpting tools, including a trowel and a knife.

"What are you doing?" asks Giulietta.

"I am making statues of snow."

"Is this what you want to teach me?" she says.

M. looks up at her from where he is kneeling by the sack, his clothes darkening from the wet snow. "No," he says, with an edge in his voice, "I want you to receive a lesson in time and money. If you want to assist me, that would be fine as well."

Giulietta is grateful to have something to occupy her hands. Though she has often longed for a day such as this, when she would finally be able to talk to M., she reminds herself not to speak too much, or at length, to stay remote lest she give herself away.

"Are you cold?" asks M., not waiting for her answer, "so am I. But that man in there is rich and influential, and when he asked me to come today and make snow statues in his garden, I knew I was not being asked at all. That is something you will need to know when you leave Sandro. That is something you will need to understand as an artist.

"I never talk when I work," continues M., "but this is not work. Sometimes I recite poetry, but that isn't talking. I had a patron in Bologna who said he loved the sound of my Tuscan voice and had me read to him for hours on end: Dante, Petrarch, Boccaccio. I even read some of my own poems. He was a very pleasant man.

"Another man I did work for, a man of means here in Florence, asked me to paint him a picture for seventy ducats. I sent him the picture, and he sent me forty ducats. I sent back the money and demanded the return of my painting. But"—M. smiled—"he loved the picture. So he sent the seventy ducats." By now M. and Giulietta had made separate, tall mounds of raw snow. "I sent back the money and told him the price had gone up to one hundred and forty ducats."

"Did he send it?" asks Giulietta.

"Yes. I told you, he loved the painting. But it made him furious, to be asked to pay more than the original price. He did not think, I love this picture so much that it is now priceless to me, no, he could only think in ducats, and crowns, and florins. And"—M. begins rough-cutting the snow figure with the knife—"if you want to do your work, you'll begin to think in ducats and crowns and florins, too."

The front half of the figure is emerging, as if it were trying to escape the confines of the snow. Much like the torsos trapped in the marble that hides Giulietta in M.'s studio. The resemblance to the torsos and the nearness of M. tighten Giulietta's throat with emotion. Then it passes.

"It will not be simply money that concerns you," says M., "it will be time. I displeased a pope, and for my penance I was forced to spend a year on a statue of which I am ashamed. It is all time and money."

He is now behind a snow figure, which stands not much taller than Giulietta. M. works quickly, cutting, shaping, smoothing. Every so often, the wealthy man of the house wanders out to the edge of the garden, wrapped in a fur-lined coat that falls almost to the ground. He nods to M., who nods in return.

M. starts on the second figure. Giulietta occasionally passes one of the tools to him. Or wipes the excess snow off the tools and onto her shirt. If M. had not spoken a single word to her, she would still understand how much he hates what he is doing. This waste of his time.

She wants to laugh a bitter little laugh when she thinks of her perishable dust drawings on the reverse side of the marble blocks, or of the wedding chest that will never hold the treasures of a bride, or her small boxes bright with blue tigers and boy/girl mirror effects, or the fact that she would not have the dubious privilege of freezing beside M. in the snow had he known her true sex. For M. may have moments of resentment and powerlessness, but Giulietta was looking at a life of it.

She would not even be asked to make figures of frozen water that will be a memory tomorrow. She would not even be asked to do something as nonsensical, vain, and ephemeral as that.

M. says, "You can't offend anyone because you don't know who they'll be tomorrow. You have to stay out of politics and power because it cannot serve you to be a part of it. Oh, you can make claims to be apart from it, but not too apart from it or people will question your loyalties. So you choose the solitary life of an artist only to end up having to negotiate treacherous social situations because you want to continue to live the solitary life of an artist. One day I will make a mausoleum with figures representing night and day and dusk and dawn and eternity and resurrection, because it is all, all of it, time and money."

When he is done, he tosses his tools back into the sack. Giulietta examines the three figures in the fading light. It is then that she sees the snowman who matches her height, also has her face, its eyes lifted to heaven, its hands pressed against its heart.

### *15. Love*

Fra d'Este remarks daily on Giulietta's appearance: She has grown thinner, older, happy, sad, restless, worn, glowing, or her color is off.

He has taken to dressing her up in ever more elaborate costumes (angel, goddess, religious, noble, or foreign-born). His wife's jewels adorn her brow, fingers, ankles, and throat. She either wears turbans or scarves upon her head or he threads her hair with still more bright, glittering gems. Pearls drape her body like elegant bonds.

Gold hangs from her wrists and breast.

He feeds her peaches, tangerines, and grapes of purple, red, and pale pale green.

Giulietta genuinely enjoys Fra d'Este's company, for he is a fine conversationalist, funny, sacrilegious at times, nothing dour or dark about him. She is thrilled when he speaks his rough language so freely in her presence. In this respect, she is like a man to him. Yet she remains reserved in exhibiting any sort of warmth toward him, afraid he will seize upon it and construe it into a love she doesn't feel.

It actually repulses her when he talks of his love for her. The coarse language vanishes and is replaced by poetic, sweet, honeyed words that never reach her because she is too busy trying not to run from him. When he confesses that he adores the very essence of her, it is all she can do to keep from ripping the velvets and silks and emeralds and ropes of gold and pearls from her body, flinging the entire mess at him. Fra d'Este's romantic entreaties make Giulietta want to scream for silence.

Yet she does nothing. She does not end their sessions

together by the light of the fire in his studio; she does not refuse payment from Ferrante as she relates her observations. She allows d'Este to openly appreciate her body, while turning a deaf ear to his attempts to woo her. She lets herself like him without loving him.

When d'Este painted a picture of her not as an angel, or a Madonna, or a queen, but as herself, she understood the depth of his emotion toward her. She felt pity for him because she was lost to him in that way, and gratitude because by painting her he was giving her a tiny shred of immortality. She, Giulietta, matters.

Most of all, Giulietta sits for Fra d'Este as a reminder of how she must never behave with M., regardless of how tempted she might be to act on her affection or how confident she might be about her ability to win him. Regardless of his inviting smile. Regardless. For it is preferable to be ignored, she tells herself, than despised.

### *16. I Have Nothing Else to Give You*

Sandro responds to the approach of Giulietta's sixteenth birthday by avoiding the subject of her future entirely and concentrating on her art lessons. He is impatient and abrupt and apologetic. He pushes and pushes her, and she cannot help but wonder, to what end? Why is he forcing her into a life she cannot possibly have?

Then there is her current life with M. The closer he comes to finishing the statue, the closer she comes to calling out to him. To confess her love and ambition.

Fra d'Este has canceled their time together twice now (he claims he feels unwell), but she has heard that he is enamored of a new girl, barely twelve. How old she feels! How unwanted by the world!

On this day in the studio with her father, Giulietta takes her hands from her work and lays them flat on the table. She is staring at Sandro, who is singularly engaged in his painting. Then, as if newly awakened, her father glances up to see his daughter watching him.

"What are you doing?" he asks finally.

"I'm thinking," she answers. "I'm wondering which is preferable: the life of a spinster or the life of an ex-nun? If I enter a convent, I am certain I will one day run away."

"You might marry," Sandro says, to which Giulietta laughs mirthlessly, "I might not.

"And I'm thinking," she continues, "What were *you* thinking when you decided I should know how to mix and apply egg tempera but not know how to cook. Or to understand the properties of oil paint, or the economics of precious pigments, but not the economics of running a household. Why teach me the technique of gold leaf? The best wood for panel painting but not the most durable fabric for making clothes? Do I need to know about the hierarchy of color? The effect of the profile and the quarter-turned face? Would my husband's house require a fresco made by me?

"When my husband wants his dinner after a day of work, will he settle for a discussion on perspective? How interested will he be in your opinion, your life's work, and M.'s differing ideas? 'All proportion is in the eye,' I'll tell him."

"You don't know—" begins Sandro before his daughter breaks in.

"Why have you taught me all this?" she demands, her voice and figure rising simultaneously. She is sobbing and racing around the studio, throwing paint and wood and brushes and palette knives to the floor. Sandro never moves; does not interfere with Giulietta's volatile display. His stationary pose and his silence serve to expand her anger. Tools and paints are flung with increasing wildness; her crying gains volume.

She falls to her knees, her dress taking on the combinations of dust and paint. "No one will want my pictures," she cries softly, "or admire my boxes, or care if one of my *cassoni* ushers them into marriage." She looks up at Sandro, who cannot meet her eyes. "Who would marry someone who can make a triptych but cannot make a home?" She wipes her tears on her white work shirt, with its evidence of her many lessons in art. She shakes her head. "Your instruction has ruined me."

Sandro starts to wipe his hands clean on a cloth, then stops, then finishes what he began. He rubs his forehead with his hand; his expression is bewildered and sad, and his eyes slightly glisten. Giulietta thinks he might cry. Instead, he moves from his chair to sit beside her on the floor. With both hands open and turned upward he whispers, "I had nothing else to give you."

### *17. Rome*

Artists follow money.

Giulietta has heard that as soon as M. is finished with his statue he will be leaving for Rome. The future home of Leonardo da Vinci and Raphael, and for the same reasons.

She does not know what to do.

She throws on her male clothing and rushes to his studio, almost before it is light. In the early-morning shadows, she approaches the statue that by now she feels she knows as intimately as her own body. She runs her hands over the feet and legs of the giant boy. He still frightens and intimidates her, especially in this dim light. His dimensions threaten her. She is afraid of being crushed should he fall on her or, maybe, step down from his pedestal, although the scaffolding remains.

Instead of running, she rests her cheek against his disproportionately large hand. This makes her think of M.'s hands when he works, powdered white with marble dust, and then the flesh becoming darker, warmer, toward his upper arms. And when M.'s marble-dusted hands are placed against the marble of the statue, the blend is almost seamless.

All that is done now, because M. is done with this boy and, possibly, done with Florence.

Giulietta accidentally kicks something across the floor. She follows it and finds herself holding a piece of a marble curl in her palm. Her fingers gently close against the smooth, cold surface of the stone. Without looking up, she imagines the curls that frame his perfect face, and it almost makes her weep. She tucks the errant curl in her belt, brushes the marble dust that coats her hands on her shirt.

She exits the room through the window, closes it solidly behind her, then leaning against the outer wall, she begins her wait for M. So he will know, unequivocally, that she has been expecting him.

You, is all M. says when he sees her. I don't know your name, he says. She smiles but does not offer it. He smiles back and does not ask a second time.

But he does invite her into the studio, tripping the memory she has of that day, so long ago, when M. brought that young man inside, leaving her lovelorn and wild with jealousy in the street. Heartbroken at their intimacy. She recalls how the vision of their embrace served to drive her away and draw her back again. Now she is the boy being asked in from the street.

She thinks, if this is all the life I get, then this is the life I'll have.

When they enter the studio, it is evident to M. that she loves his statue, which moves him toward her.

M. is so physically close to Giulietta she wants to swoon. Her eyes close against the rush of her own senses; this inner battle to be him and to be with him.

Then, inexplicably, impulsively, Giulietta seeks the shelter of her hiding place behind the impromptu wall of marble. M. follows.

She suddenly cannot bear the discovery of her secret: that she is not the boy M. desires. She does not want him to reach out to her, then pull away as if struck; he will look upon her with the anger and mistrust of one who has been fooled; she can feel his dislike and his urgency to leave her.

It is all as clear to her as if it is happening already. His face, his shock, his fury, the terrible words.

And so she fights this conflict inside of racing headlong into the thing she is trying to avert.

Giulietta is again pressing her body deep into the arms of one of the unreceptive torsos. This captive. And the warring desires to delay M.'s embrace, even as she wants to rush and seize him.

As M. advances toward her, a whispered, unheard *No* falls from her lips, and her eyes watch him with undisguised passion, and her heart breaks with the knowledge that she is about to experience, simultaneously, his kiss and his immediate, inevitable absence.

# THE *PASQUINADES*

IF YOU WERE TO WANDER INTO ROME'S PIAZZA NAVONA during the years of the Renaissance, you would happen upon an old, weary-looking statue with messages affixed to it. These messages would carry opinions and criticisms, for example, regarding the pope, the government. And when you asked the name of this curious statue, you would be told *Pasquino,* after an unpleasant schoolmaster ("unpleasant" being the more charitable description of the schoolmaster's personality).

Then, if at some point you found yourself in the Campus Martius, you would be confronted with a second statue, similar to the first, festooned with small, written notes.

And, if you allowed yourself enough time in Rome, you would come to notice that these two statues—these *pasquinades*—carry on what can only be called a conversation, a sort of bizarre dialogue comprised of the notes they wear, speaking to each other from across the crowded city. The *pasquinades,* so beleaguered by the messages they carry and only talking to each other. Each understanding the other in a manner no one else can fathom; their bodies frozen in place but calling and responding just the same.

# Book Two: Los Angeles

1918–1919

## *1.*

THE EARLY SPRING HEAT PRESSES DOWN ON ROMY MARCH AS she half reclines on the wooden park bench, under the worthless shade of an oak tree, in La Luna Park. The vague seasonal changes of Pasadena allow little weather variation: a great deal of sun, not too much rain, occasionally morning gray, and more sun. The warmth of winter gives way to the immediate heat of spring. Nothing gradual.

Romy's boots are kicked off, tumbled across the grass, her stockings shoved into the crown of the upturned straw hat that sits beside her. Two silver brooches catch and toss the sunlight as they hold together her wrinkled cotton dress with its now misplaced belt that Romy is certain she left on the train she so recently disembarked.

Her bare feet rest upon an elegant, perfectly made suitcase of Italian leather, accented with a small solid gold lock and clasp. The suitcase's tidy appearance looks incongruous with the girl's naked feet, damp and disheveled dress, unkempt hair. A passing stranger might think the suitcase did not belong to the girl at all; that perhaps she is only just minding such a wonderful object until its owner returns.

The beautiful suitcase is practically empty, the result of the reckless packing that began her reckless journey. Most of Romy's clothes, shoes, books, and bottles of scent had been left behind; it contains a few undergarments, a skirt, two shirts (one paint-stained, the other pristine), a handful of photographs, a miniature watercolor kit, a silk pouch with a few pieces of jewelry inside, and, finally, a rather small and very old wooden box, depicting a girl's face looking at a boy's face in her mirror, and containing a smooth curl of marble.

Her parents are not yet aware that Romy is back in town, since she came directly to the park, needing to rest, reflect, and sit without her shoes in the shade.

At this point she cannot say which would upset her parents more: her casual public attire (her mother would scold), or that she has run away, midsemester, from the college she attends in Northern California (her father would deliver a very loud, very angry lecture).

Romy runs her hand across her moist forehead, sighs, and begins to collect her belongings. She stuffs the stockings into her pocket and carries the hat and boots that she does not want to put on until the last minute, enjoying the feel of the prickly Bermuda grass under her tender feet.

As she walks across the park, she notices a young man on his hands and knees tugging at some shrubbery, arranging it this way and that. Behind him is a camera on a tripod. She watches as he glances at the sky, checks his watch, then gazes upward again. His shirtsleeves are rolled up, and the top buttons of his shirt are undone. He sits back on his knees.

*I know him,* thinks Romy, but she cannot think from where. He looks a little older than she—maybe twenty-two or so—and although he is quite nice-looking, almost handsome, there is something that interrupts the near perfection of his face. Whatever it is, she decides, it is more compelling than simple handsomeness.

His discarded coat lies neatly folded upon the grass. The sun passes over the ceiling of the sky.

For the life of her she cannot move, yet he does not notice her at all. This sensation of familiarity makes her want to call out to him, but she stops herself because he is black and she is white, so where, exactly, did their paths cross?

Still, there is something about him that is so affecting she cannot leave, nor cease her observation. *Is this like being struck by lightning?* she wonders. *How very strange.*

Then, like a series of sparks racing down a wire, Romy remembers a handful of incidents.

In the first, she was about eleven, walking home from school, having cut down to an infrequently traveled area of the arroyo, alone and daydreaming. Suddenly, she was pulled from her reverie by the sound of boys. A clutch of voices. Her spine stiffened, her posture braced for their unwanted attention, which would probably include some sort of derision.

Their attentions were not personal; being female and solitary made her an irresistible target. When the boys do this to her or any other girl, she almost has the sense that they are practicing something, though she can't say what exactly. Though they had never physically hurt her, she didn't trust them. In a group, they seem to her wholly unpredictable.

As she walked slowly down the dirt path, she realized the boys' voices were not gaining in volume or intensity; they were not coming closer. She walked on until she arrived at where they were: standing a few feet from Augustine Marks, the boy who was the man now taking pictures in La Luna Park.

Romy froze when she saw the boys, unsure how to proceed and worried that they would harm this lone boy. She felt as apprehensive for the boy as she felt for herself only minutes earlier; she wanted to scream at the boys to stop, to pick on someone else, someone who can fight back, but she was too alone and too small and scared and angry to be of any help to anyone.

The white boys surrounded the solitary boy, who did not run or look afraid. They moved a little closer. Though it was difficult to make out the words of the group of boys, Romy distinctly heard Augustine say, with great care in his voice, "Why would you want to do that?"

With that, two women came upon the group. Romy could tell the women were taking in the situation; one of them caught Romy's eye and smiled. By virtue of their presence and without the exchange of a single word, the tension of the scene began to dissolve. The white boys wandered off toward their original destination; the women, who never stopped or slackened their pace, continued on their way; Romy's neck relaxed; and the boy leaned down to pick up a book that had been lying in the dust. He, like the others, said nothing and went along his way, seemingly unconcerned, as if he had never been detained at all.

* * *

The next time was the year Romy was in eighth grade and the school decided to hire a professional music director, a composer who ended up staying for a single year before moving back to New York and pursuing his "true vocation." This particular year, for Christmas, he organized the entire student body into one vast chorus of children's voices.

The students were loosely assembled in the auditorium, forming their own natural groups and couples, as the music director called out their names alphabetically.

"Romy March," said the music director. "Augustine Marks."

Romy looked around to see who would be standing beside her and saw the boy from the arroyo. She remembered her fear of the boys, and his bravery; the way he picked up his book and dusted it off. Her sense of recognition and shared experience was so strong that she almost expected an expression of gladness from him upon seeing her. Instead, he moved past her, without notice.

She slowly took her place next to him. Well, she thought, it's as if I met him in a dream. One of those strange, nocturnal one-sided relationships that fool the mind into thinking that the people we know in our sleep will suddenly know us in return when we awake.

Day after day, they stood side by side in the chorus. Augustine older and taller by two years.

Romy had an awful singing voice. During the first rehearsal, the music teacher stopped the carol midverse. "I'm sorry," he said impatiently, "something is wrong." Then began the song again. Again he made them stop. "Someone," he said, "is throwing everything off." When he had the chorus resume, he walked from one end to the other, listening, trying to isolate the offensive voice.

"Here," he said triumphantly, "the problem is here." He told the students in Romy's area to sing solo, one at a time. When Romy sang, it took the music teacher a split second before he said, "You, you will have to mouth the words. Your voice is a blight to the rest of the group."

She was mortified. There was nothing to be done; all students, traditionally, were included in the Christmas program, since it culminated in a performance for the parents. Romy silently moved her mouth.

It was at the end of the Christmas concert, when all the songs had been sung and the students were disassembling to join parents and friends, that Augustine turned to Romy, smiled, and mouthed the words "Merry Christmas."

"You too," she mouthed back.

The third time Augustine entered Romy's life was when she had been held back after class one day to complete an assignment that had gone unfinished in class due to her "socializing," as the teacher said. Sitting at her desk, across the room from the teacher, toward the back of the classroom, now empty and hushed, Romy struggled with the numbers in her textbook. She wanted to like arithmetic, and when she understood it she experienced a great sense of accomplishment, as if she were finally conversant in another language. But her understanding never lasted, and she found she would do almost anything to avoid working numbers.

Another teacher came quietly into the classroom, and the two teachers spoke softly. Every once in a while Romy would catch some of what was being said. Or maybe the teachers forgot that Romy was in the room and grew less guarded in their conversation, for it was close to summer and the lights had been turned off, leaving the classroom slightly darkened and cool. In the quiet and shallow shadows, Romy understood that the teachers were discussing Augustine Marks, valedictorian of the graduating class.

It seemed the school wanted another student to give the traditional valedictorian speech, instead of Augustine ("He is easily one of the best students I have ever had," said the one teacher). They agreed on his fine record and clear intelligence, but Romy's teacher said, No, I must go along with the principal in this matter, giving Augustine his due in private, while the other teacher ever more emphatically disagreed with this approach. Romy's teacher mentioned something about taking the majority into consideration.

The majority, of course, was white.

The other teacher was upset; she had come to enlist Romy's teacher as an ally and found her largely indifferent. At that point, Romy looked up from her numbers to see the other teacher looking away from Romy's teacher in silence. They accidentally caught each other's eye. Reflexively, the teacher smiled, and Romy was startled to recognize her as one of the two women who had come upon the scene in the arroyo that day. The teacher hurried from the room.

Augustine stands up and walks back to the camera, disappearing under the worn, velvet cloth. When he is obscured, Romy shyly moves closer.

"Damn," she hears him mutter. "You," he says, as Romy steps back slightly, "yes, you. Do you think you can move? You're in my light."

She looks down to see her own shadow darkening the plants he had so painstakingly arranged.

He tosses aside the cloth, asks again, his voice soft, tightly controlled.

Romy stumbles back a little, apologizes, trips over her own words. "I didn't mean to—I didn't know—"

"Well, now you do," he says.

She is annoyed. His abruptness seems uncalled-for. When he again throws the cloth over his head, she impulsively walks forward, filling the frame of his picture with naked feet flanked by her hat and boots in one hand and her beautiful suitcase in the other.

Very quietly, his voice tighter and edgier than before, he says, "I now have a picture of your feet."

Immediately she is sorry, but instead of saying so she mumbles, "You are just so rude."

To which he comments, "You are just so inconsiderate."

And she says, "I'm sorry."

He is visible again and beginning to pack up his belongings. "Never mind," he says without looking at her. She sees him check his watch, then the sky, then, "My light's almost gone," and she is not sure if he is talking to her. "The plants are crushed anyway." This is definitely to her.

"Why don't you use your own backyard," she asks, "if you don't want to be disturbed?"

"Maybe I don't have my own backyard. Maybe I want to be here." Clearly angry, he turns to walk away.

It is then that she whispers, "Augustine."

Augustine stops, and very slowly he looks over his shoulder at Romy.

In the course of this exchange Augustine has not

once made eye contact with Romy. He has looked past her, spoken to her intrusive shadow, talked as he packed his camera. He has allowed a certain amount of irritation to color his voice. He has noted her presence in the periphery. He took a ruined photograph of her feet, but he has avoided her face.

Now, with the mention of his name, he is turning to stare directly at her.

"Romy March," she says. "The Christmas pageant? Romy March," she tells him again.

Augustine looks at her for a minute without answering, then she sees a glimmer of recognition without any sense of how he feels toward her. He nods, turns forward again, and continues on his way, carelessly waving his hand above his retreating figure in the most casual of good-byes.

*2.*

The Marks family was a sort of badly kept secret: Everyone in town knew how smart they were, but no one talked about it. They lived in a house of wood and roses and rundown beauty. The light-filled attic was cleared for tables and chairs on which to read and study, while the cool basement contained Orlando Marks's workroom, inventions in various stages of completion, and a darkroom. A small shed in the back housed an impromptu photography studio.

Augustine's parents, Orlando and Suzanne, came out to Pasadena from Florida, where Orlando proclaimed that anyplace this routinely hot was in need of something sweet and cool. So, *Orlando's Gift*–brand ice cream came into being, as well as his ices in flavors of lemon, raspberry, peach, and melon. Every year he added and subtracted new flavors, all equally fine, though some were more popular than others.

Orlando's family and business were in states of expansion. He and Suzanne had five children: Françoise, Matthew, Meridian, Hazel, and Augustine.

His business interests included, besides the popular *Orlando's Gift,* cartography and surveying (noting how the area around his home kept widening and building and getting paved and straightened and crooked); the fabrication of eyeglass lenses (he and his boys needed spectacles, which eventually kept them out of the war). The eyeglass lenses led to an interest in photography, which eventually gave way to still another venture: spirit photography.

Spirit photography was an invention of the nineteenth century; Orlando became aware of it when he read about the case of a photographer named William Mumler, tried for fraud. A photographer took a picture of a single subject, only to have a second "person" or "extra" show up sometime during the developing process. The finished picture showed this ghostly presence hovering next to, or behind, or before the sitter, maybe placing a vanishing hand on the shoulder or gently laying its translucent head upon the sitter's lap. The spirit developing more quickly than the subject.

Orlando did a little experimenting, and when what was supposed to happen happened, he let it be known, discreetly, that he was for hire.

His secret was that his pictures were genuine. How he achieved the desired effect was utterly mysterious to him. And since he could not control the outcome, there was always the risk that nothing would come at all.

Shy subjects would come by Orlando's shed behind his house, having heard about him by word of mouth, and ask if he was "on the level." Orlando would reply, Do you ask a magician if his work is a lie? And that would be the end of it; Orlando treated his other gift as some sort of entertainment, allowing the sitter to do the same. His work was real, but it was safer to treat it as an entertainment.

This sort of thing was not for everyone. Those who sought out Orlando were people who had a hard time saying good-bye. Not all losses were recent: men in their sixties longed to see their fathers once more; women craved girlhood lovers and husbands; friends sought to assuage loneliness. Children never sat for him. As Orlando made clear, "You have to understand, this is not for them."

The astonishment on the subjects' face when Orlando handed them the photograph was always the same, as if they wanted to blurt out, But how did you know! They said nothing, because the collusion of trickery was understood before Orlando set to work. He had not forgotten William Mumler's trial.

The images in the pictures floated and faded; they caressed unaware faces with a tender ghost touch; they left kisses in the subject's hair. And for those whose pictures came out empty, there was no argument or threat to expose Orlando. His theory was that the sitter was not surprised, and too embarrassed to argue, when a ghost failed to appear. Or, to put it another way, Orlando told Augustine, only love brings us back again and again.

Money exchanged hands, recommendations were passed along, appointments made.

And in this way Orlando put all his children through college, Augustine the only one who almost didn't graduate for lack of interest.

*3.*

The small, exclusive Arroyo Hunt Club would never allow someone like Romy's father to join. The members are, in fact, grateful that Lorenzo March does not ask, and of course, they do not offer. Lorenzo is not from here, they reason, but that is not the genesis of their reserve. It is because Lorenzo is Italian and very, well, *Italian*. That is to say, his complexion is dark, his hair is dark (and thick), and he doesn't look much like those in the club.

The only one who looks like Lorenzo is Romy, with her smooth, olive skin and her wild, wiry dark hair. Helen March, Romy's mother, like Romy's brother, Edward, is fair and golden. As if she carries and gives off her own personal shine.

The Arroyo Hunt Club members know that in another respect, Lorenzo is as golden as his wife: He made them wealthy, or wealthier. Lorenzo invests and watches their cash and transforms it into more money. This serves Lorenzo well, leaving him very comfortable, as he likes to say. They also enjoy his company, befriending him without fully accepting him. Much of the time, Lorenzo is fine with the arrangement; he has no desire to join their silly little shooting parties in the arroyo below his splendid house. His life is the embodiment of the American Dream, with his Titianesque wife and his foreign looks that call up, for his clients, a vague violence and the heat of the Mediterranean.

Augustine's home is as lived in and loved as Romy's is grand and untouched. An elegant place that invites admiration more than habitation. The dark green bungalow was designed by the Greene brothers, with sleeping porches onto which the family can drag their mattresses on restless, hot nights. There is a perfect pond of river stone. From its perch above the arroyo, Romy can hear animal sounds and movements all night long.

The animal noises thrill and frighten her. Romy could never, no matter how hard she tried, understand the urge to hunt and thinks it is probably because when she imagines someone holding a rifle (one of her father's affluent, cold clients for example) all she can see is herself in the sights.

*4.*

Augustine, upon leaving La Luna Park and Romy, has his own pressing engagement with a young woman named Polly, who lives in the area between Pasadena and downtown Los Angeles. She is a year younger than he. People often notice Polly because of the languor in her step and the lack of clear racial definition in her face. As she says, "No one thinks I'm white, but I am white—and Indian, and black, and Japanese. I am, you might say, everything and nothing all at once."

Polly has an evanescence of spirit that, combined with her carriage and movements, tricks those who see her into believing her to be more beautiful than she is; not that much more, because her looks are considerable, but all these elements combined lend her face and figure a sort of perfection.

She often trades on her loveliness. Polly counts among her acquaintances men grateful to spend time alone with her; men who generously tip her when she collects and returns their coats in a club or restaurant; men willing to give her the part of The Beautiful Girl briefly seen in the occasional movie short; a little bit of this, a little bit of that. Polly resides alone in her own apartment, with no one telling her what to do. Since her spirit is so light as to be almost insubstantial, her life suits her very well.

Augustine is unhappily involved with her. He wants her all to himself, and since his nature is neither acquisitive nor possessive, this confuses him.

"I don't understand how we can get on so well together and how you can't want it to continue indefinitely," Augustine says to Polly.

"Who says I don't want it to continue?" Polly asks, laying her body on his, her arms upon his arms, her chest resting on his, belly to belly, her legs wrapped around his legs. Though she is thinner and slightly shorter, she twins him just the same.

He reaches behind her head, threads his fingers in and out of her loose curls. "I want an unconnected life," she tells him. "I want to love whom I want, when I want, leaving no debts behind me."

"You just don't want the responsibility," he says unhappily.

She laughs, holding him tightly. "You are right. I don't want it. Oh, as if anyone *wants* it."

And Augustine, so weary of trying to coax affection from her elusive heart, says nothing.

Polly says gently, "Honey, it doesn't mean we can't see each other. I want to see you. It just can't be life and death."

How he wishes they'd never met. This conversation is like so many they've had during the past year or so. Sometimes he doesn't even know if he loves her, or what it means to love her. And he finds himself thinking that maybe he doesn't know her at all, and that the first thing we are attracted to in each other is the first thing we demand to be changed. He laughs at himself, then stops, says, "It can't be any other way for me."

"Oh, honey, if you'd just relax, we could have some fun."

"I don't think I'm the only one you can have fun with."

"That's true," she says, "but it's the best with you."

Then his voice cracks. "I can't stay here." He disengages his body from her warm embrace and begins to dress.

Before he can stand, Polly reaches over, caresses his face, and says with a trace of regret, "You really are that sort of man, aren't you?"

"Unfortunately," he says, "you're right." He turns his face into her palm, leaving a kiss before he pulls away.

"I don't get much pleasure out of being right," Polly replies, letting him go.

Then he is again holding her close against him, kissing her, his mind racing with all the unhappy, incomplete conversations they have, all his words of love that tumble through his mind. There are moments when he lets them fall from his lips, but most of the time he remains silent, wordless, because he cannot keep risking his heart endlessly for her.

*5.*

"What does this mean, 'devote your life to art'?" demands Romy's father, who, Romy can see, is not even trying to understand. The edge in his voice disheartens her. "You can't devote your life to art, Romy. That's childish."

"How is it childish?" asks Romy.

"Because, sweetie," answers her mother in her conciliatory tone, "it is a permissive way of life. It is as if you are telling the world that you are too good to be like the rest of us."

A number of responses occur to Romy. She wants to say, I don't think the rest of the world ever gives me a thought. She wants to say, Then why did you expose me to paintings and dancing and music and books? To teach me to admire but not covet? To show me that it is noble to love the arts without loving the artist? And what about the gifts of paints, pencils, and paper? Was it all just to fill up my childhood time?

She wants to say, I've lived the life of the Good Girl. Obedient, thoughtful, empathetic, never a moment's trouble, and you've taken this behavior as evidence of fine parenting, as your due, almost. But I made a decision a long time ago that this path-of-least-resistance life was credit on my account for the day I ask something of you in return.

Romy has always been what might be called a private rebel, that is, her contrary manner is not apparent but hidden, dormant, closeted until the day arrives when it expresses itself and everyone says, shocked, "What's gotten into her?" when, of course, it was there all along.

"I mean to work hard," says Romy. "I don't see the life of ease that you see."

"We just love you, sweetie," says Helen, glancing over at Lorenzo, who looks like the personification of nasty weather. "We don't want you to be disappointed."

Disappointed?

She knew how fortunate she was to be able to attend the Northern California college (along with her brother

Edward) that she had so recently, abruptly abandoned. It was the same good fortune that provided her with the cool of a sleeping porch during the summer nights when the heat inside the house felt like a wool blanket stretched over her body. Yet this life she lived was not her life. The expectations that settled upon her were not the kind she could ever live up to, and she knew it. What she didn't know, however, was exactly what her life was meant to be, or the things she could realistically expect for herself.

Her grades had been good. In part, this was to distinguish herself from many of her female classmates who were sent to school, ultimately, to get a little education and marry well. And so many of the boys did not need to be there at all, with their fathers and grandfathers and uncles and friends of friends holding jobs for them.

Romy joined no sororities, honored no cliques. Instead she snuck out night after night to dance. Away she went into the tiny town, smaller than Pasadena, her college like a solid brick island afloat in the sea of pastures and fields, spending hours dancing until her legs ached. That was her first year.

The second year her grades began to slip because all the classrooms and ideas and lessons made her claustrophobic. The students were too passive, the teachers too dictatorial, and Romy felt she was suffocating, fighting for air that was altogether too thin.

By her third year it was decided that she would get a teaching certificate. Teach art, her parents suggested. This was before Romy ran away from school, informing Helen and Lorenzo that she did not want to teach art but to try to make art.

At Romy's college was a woman art teacher, twenty-nine years old, medium height, blue eyes, who never "fixed herself up," who actually had a rather handsome, androgynous look about her. She had a heavy, ungraceful way of walking, more like a man and less like a lady, which seemed altogether incongruous with her slender figure. That, and her very direct, unblinking way of looking at people when they talked to her, her smile slow, her expression ranging from serious to bemused, seldom stooping to charm, caused rumors to surround her like smoke.

The fact that she was not a local added to the foreign quality of her appearance, along with her obvious spinsterhood.

Then again, it was said that she had been married and left; that she preferred women to men; that she was heterosexually promiscuous; that she had a married male or female or underage lover; that she had a showing of work in New York; that her paintings were insensible abstractions an "eight-year-old could do"; that she was cruel to animals; that she was a drunk, a Christian, a heathen, an owner of numerous stray cats. In other words, the gossip was wildly contradictory because no one cared about the truth.

And since the teacher never spoke to anyone concerning her life, people took the liberty of saying whatever they wanted to unabated.

None of this was lost on Romy, whose previous example of womanhood was her mother: her life of love and privilege. Her good marriage, her pretty house and lovely children, her beauty. Romy was happy for Helen, but she did not crave such a life for herself and, instead, was fascinated by the mysterious, solitary life of this teacher. For

Romy, the teacher's life was like a sound from such a great distance that she couldn't discern whether it was real or a figment; this was the way in which Romy connected with this disconnected woman, and it worried her.

One night she saw the teacher walking the edge of town at sunset, and Romy had to say that the woman looked happy. This did not make things any clearer to Romy.

As far as teaching went, Romy panicked at the thought of a life devoted to the classroom, that world without oxygen. She saw herself growing older with each passing year, while her students remained young and ageless. The exact same age, year after year; their enthusiasm or studied ennui never spending itself. They would apply her teachings to the outside world, or disregard them immediately upon stepping out into the sunlight of the real world, and she would never see or know what became of them.

Worst of all was the pressure to set a good example for these impressionable minds. What, she wondered, could be less appealing than having to be somebody's good example?

So, during her third year of school, Romy is out of the school more than she is in it, for it can do nothing for her except render her breathless.

In the spring Edward asks if she would like to go to the spring dance with him and his date and a friend of his named Hugh. Hugh bores her; he tries too hard to make her laugh, and so she ends up with aching smile muscles from each encounter. They never talk about anything, and they don't flirt because Hugh is too busy performing for her; flirting requires interest, nuance, and genuine interaction, all of which seems beyond Hugh. Boys love Hugh because he is as in tune with what entertains them as he is out of touch with what entertains Romy.

She agrees to go to the dance because she wants to dance.

Hugh, it turns out, doesn't like to dance. Instead, he stands on the perimeter of the floor, watching Romy dance with a variety of partners, in the thrall of doing one of the things she loves best. Even the girls are generous with their partners, allowing them to dance with Romy, because her pleasure moves them.

She looks over between songs to see Hugh watching her, holding the drink that she occasionally walks over and sips. And suddenly she realizes that her parents are going to start talking marriage to her, since her final year of school is approaching, and it is not impossible that she could end up with someone like Hugh or Hugh himself. Stranger things have happened, and no one even knows *exactly* how they happen. In a rush, she considers Hugh, the art teacher, the various ways each man at the dance has of holding her, and making her excuses, flees the event.

She walks straight to her dormitory room, gathering her few belongings into her beautiful suitcase; tossing off her party dress for the crumpled cotton dress, without signing out, without looking back, and ready to face her parents out of a much greater fear than their displeasure, she heads for the train station. There she waits until the southbound train pulls in amid much steam and noise and the bright light of the moon.

During the night she hears the clacking of the wheels: the teaching life. Claustrophobia. The married life.

Claustrophobia. The Good Girl life. Claustrophobia. Until she falls asleep.

"I'm going to get a job," Romy tells Lorenzo and Helen. "I can't go back to school."

Lorenzo's eyes narrow. "What do you mean, 'can't'?" It is so much worse when his voice loses volume than when it escalates. "What are you talking about?"

"I can't," Romy repeats softly. "I can't bear it for another day." She looks into the face of the man who has her face. "You don't know."

He leans toward her with his quiet voice. "When I was your age, did I get to do whatever I wanted to do? Do you think I broke my back so you can be some bohemian? You think that's why I did it? I suggest—I *strongly* suggest—you think again."

Romy holds his gaze for a moment, then the Good Girl takes over and she averts her eyes.

"While we're on the subject here"—Helen lays her hand firmly on Lorenzo's arm as he speaks, but he ignores her warning—"what sort of *art* did you have in mind? This thing that you would devote your life to."

"I don't know yet," she whispers.

"I can't hear you," says Lorenzo.

Romy doesn't answer because she can't answer. How can she explain desire without meaning? This past year (the airlessness of the classroom, the solitary art teacher, the promise of Hugh or someone like Hugh) she has pushed aside the lives she doesn't want and is just starting to make sense of who she might be. Though she has not yet begun the pursuit of her "art" or her "life as an artist" (the two inextricably bound), she already feels there is no return from this fated, determined love affair.

"I thought you said, *I don't know,*" says Lorenzo, "but that can't be right or we wouldn't be having this conversation."

All this does is infuriate Romy, the Good Girl who has always asked so little for herself. Who was counting on bartering all those years of good behavior. Now she that she is being bullied and denied, she is thinking that she might as well have been bad for all her goodness has gotten her.

"No nice girl—" says Helen, but Romy turns a deaf ear to her parents' words, thinking about her quiet Good Girl life; it is like being a guest that everyone welcomes and nobody knows.

***6.***

A craze, practiced almost solely by Augustine, has renewed itself in Los Angeles, and it is from this particular fad that he draws his income.

Those with daring and money seek out Augustine to print tiny photographic portraits on their skin. It is a simple process, discovered at the end of the previous century, using chemical solutions, a negative pressed upon flesh, and darkness and light. The pictures would not last forever, but usually they last long enough.

Women liked multiple pictures circling the upper arm or ankle; or a single, minuscule photograph nestled in the hollow of the throat or wrapped around a finger. Augustine carries considerable skill into his work. His images are detailed and exceptionally sharp.

And, if a woman is so inclined, he can impress a sweetheart's face on or near the heart without embarrassment on the part of either the photographer or subject.

It is risky for him, being a man working so intimately with a woman, particularly if that woman is white. The appeal is usually from someone with a husband, son, or lover overseas in the Great War in Europe. Augustine is compassionate with these women, and he understands what they are after when they request an image hovering over the heart.

As he told Orlando, "They are too sad to care about the world, of which I am a part."

Augustine decorates fingernails. And he perfected a technique of adding color to the pictures, making them appear like small jewels.

Like his father, he relies heavily on word of mouth. Both men deal closely with closeted emotions: Orlando's spirit work touching on hidden hopes within, Augustine's expressing love and memory from without.

For all the myriad pictures Augustine has taken of Polly, never once has his body borne her face.

Sometimes men and women come to him for the sheer fashion of his skin photographs. They want body bracelets or brooches and say, "I don't care who's in the picture, I just like the way it looks."

Augustine will pull out pictures of Polly without mentioning that he knows her well, and ask if her image will suit. Polly's arresting look, of a beautiful stranger who exudes mystery without personality, invites the fantasies of those who look at her. She gives the impression of existing in some other human world, not this mundane place, and so is an ideal model. In this respect, her face is an easy sell.

Every time someone leaves wearing the image of Polly, Augustine has to fight the small ache within his heart, for it always feels as if Polly were walking out his door to lose herself, once again, in the crowd.

7.

In a train heading north Romy sits, in defeat. When Lorenzo demanded that she return to school to finish the semester, she had no choice but to yield. Maybe she can get a job come summer. Her hand plays with the handle of her beautiful suitcase as she contemplates flight.

Same train, different car, sits Augustine, his chin resting in his hand as he watches, without attention, the scenery sliding by his window. He sees what is inside his own head. His thoughts are full of Polly.

Thinking he would train himself away from her, he decided to take a trip up north. His parents expressed worry when he said he wasn't sure where he was going or when he'd be back but that he had to go and he'd be all right. Reluctantly, they agreed.

Romy's stop is before Augustine's. He looks out the window to see her refusing help on the portable steps placed against the door of the car. A young man walks confidently toward her; she gives him a shy smile and slight shrug of her shoulders. Augustine assumes the young man is her suitor, and it is only when the train has pulled away, moving rhythmically down the tracks, that he recognizes the young woman in the station as the one belonging to the bare feet in the ruined picture he took that day in the park.

* * *

Augustine walks the grasslands and rolling hills studded with oaks well north of San Francisco. He sleeps outside, beneath a star-scattered sky that looks so close and vast he would not be surprised to awaken in the morning amid a field littered with tired, fallen sparkles. He lies on his back, with no real knowledge of the constellations, spinning his own bedtime stories.

There is a tiger in the sky bound by a diamond chain; a horse whose tail streaks like a comet across the night; a beautiful maiden drops golden pears from a basket too full of the fruit; two mythical beasts engage in rough play, the one tearing at the wing of the other with its starry teeth.

And there is Polly's face and luminous figure moving carefully, casually through it all: Polly being the queen of the sky. Hers is the image that sets him to sleep each night, mercifully disappearing by morning. Every day erases her presence from the stellar landscape.

He tells himself that he will recover from this sensation of love, that each day it will lessen, and each night the stars that comprise the arrangement of her face will soon grow unrecognizable, the patterns becoming young bears, or enormous, scaly fish swimming through the darkness.

During the day Augustine writes her letters. He tells her how she rules the night sky, and how she echoes the colors of the sky, trees, fields, wildflowers, and roads of the day. He mails them to his house, not hers.

Augustine arrives home about the time Romy is coming back from college; they miss traveling on the same train by a matter of hours. His family makes a lavish dinner. The next day he collects all the letters addressed to Polly and tears them into confetti. As he stands in the center of the Colorado Street bridge, he releases the scribbled bits of paper. Like a million errant butterflies, that catch the wind and reject its advances.

*8.*

"Try this and this," Romy says as she rifles through Helen's closet, pulling out a few soft, slippery evening gowns, deciding on one that is a deep blue silk and heavily beaded, which Helen initially rejects because it is so warm outside. Romy ignores her, plucking dangling diamond-and-ruby earrings from her jewelry box, along with a plain sterling silver clip to hold Helen's blond hair.

Now Romy rummages through her mother's powders, scents, lipsticks, rouge, and eye makeup. Helen patiently allows Romy to make up her face; the final result is elaborate, dramatic, and wonderful. Helen would never leave the house like this, but she rather enjoys this overdone version of herself. "I feel silly," is all she says to Romy.

"Nonsense," Romy replies, "you look stunning. Besides, the camera will wash some of this out, so you need the contrast."

When Romy arrived home for the summer, Lorenzo left a gift in her room. It was a camera. How like my father, she thinks, to order me to do something I hate, then follow up with something I love. Not that he could've known, though she has had some experience with cameras and darkrooms. Today she has coaxed Helen into posing for her.

As Romy has been dressing her mother, she has been decorating herself. She wears a silk scarf of deep green, purple, and ochre around her neck; emeralds fall from her ears; two brooches are stuck though the lapels of her shirt; her lips are painted a reddish berry color.

Helen smiles at Romy's costume, thinking, Who gave me such a girl, who is still more girl than woman, despite her age, and how can I thank them? Further, she didn't realize until this afternoon of play with her daughter how sharply a parent can miss the child in her child.

In the kitchen, Romy directs and commands Helen, who is made miserable by the stillness of the process. In the middle of a pose Helen asks, "Why would I be cooking dressed like this?"

"Well, it's not meant to be realistic," she says without conviction. She is not sure why she pictures her mother dressed for a dance but puttering around a stove.

"I look as though I am without morals," says Helen, and Romy has to agree that there is something of the well-heeled prostitute in Helen's look, but also something mesmerizing.

"Let me think about this for a minute," says Romy, then, catching sight of her mother, all sparkle and beauty, asks, "What do you usually do at this time of day?" The afternoon is fading, though the June light is long. "I mean, what would you be doing right now?"

Helen laughs. "Right now I'm all dressed up with nowhere to go."

"But what would you be doing, if you were alone?"

Helen hesitates, but her closeness to Romy has made her brave. "Probably thinking about supper and if I have time to sneak out back for a smoke." She looks at Romy.

Her daughter smiles back. "Well, then, pretend I'm not here."

Helen's gown whispers with her movements as she

rises from the table, crosses to a low cupboard, and reaches in the back for a tin canister. Romy sits silently, trying to allow her mother the illusion of aloneness. She is fascinated by Helen's willingness to be dressed as if she were an enormous doll, and now by her charade of solitude.

Helen takes cigarette papers from the container and sprinkles loose tobacco into the crease of the fragile bit of tissue.

"I want one, too," says Romy.

"Don't you think you're a little young for this habit?" asks Helen.

"Please," says Romy, "this once."

"Your father—" says Helen, which Romy interrupts, saying, "He's not here."

Helen rolls two cigarettes and goes out to the garden, where she motions Romy to join her at the edge of the pond. Romy brings her camera. They listen to the animals in the arroyo below.

Romy reaches over to remove the silver clip from Helen's hair. Then she says, "Take off your gloves and jewelry."

"Do you want me to go inside and change?"

"No, no, but"—she hands her mother a handkerchief—"can you wipe some of the makeup off?" Romy tosses the cigarette to the grass. "These are awful."

Her mother picks it up and lays it on a stone. "Your father," she reminds Romy.

Romy begins taking pictures of Helen smoking by the pond, still gorgeous in her blue dress but with less ornamentation, looking as if she has recently left a social gathering that was not much to her liking to seek out the pleasure of her own company.

*9.*

There are some handwritten flyers fluttering down the boulevard, finding their way to Augustine's street, advertising a new moving picture by someone named Oscar Micheaux. Augustine notices that it will not be shown in the local theater but at a school in a Negro neighborhood.

That night Augustine, sitting alone in a too hot and too crowded auditorium, sees something he has never seen before: a full-length film starring nothing but black people. And the story is glamorous, a love triangle. There are disapproving families, and friends who are honorable, and friends who betray. There are smoldering looks and impassioned kisses. There is a kind of smart humor.

He glances at the rapt faces that surround him and knows, no matter what, that his life's work will be about Negro people. This is the first time he has ever sat in a room of Negro people, watching a story about Negro people, made by Negro people. It feels strange and familiar all at once. It feels like real life for the first time, ever.

*10.*

Romy sits at a table strewn with paints and brushes and a cup of water. Before her are the pictures of Helen, elegantly captured in the kitchen, looking worn and fine in the garden smoking a cigarette. She is attempting to hand-color the pictures. The sparkling necklace, golden hair, and blue dress don't pose much of a problem, but she cannot work the flesh. So Helen's skin remains a whitish gray, with contrasts of dark and light.

There is something about these pictures, theatrical and ordinary, that appeals to Romy. They have a dream-like, fantastic quality. But they are not quite right.

The paint ends up on Romy's fingers, then from her fingers to her face, into her hair. She is filling in the colors of herself as much as her mother. And later, when she goes to wash up, Romy discovers that she likes the effect of being painted.

She begins to polish her toenails red, lines her eyes in pale gray, rubs her cheeks lightly with rouge, and wears a lip color so slight that it looks as if she has been eating some sort of wild berries. Her hair is rinsed with henna, leaving a trace of red behind to glint among the strands.

Her clothing is generally black or white, but now she adds bits of color: red gloves, a lavender underslip, a silk hat of spring green.

## *11.*

Two actresses, sisters it is said, one a vamp of some renown and the other lesser known, are coming to dinner at the March house. Their imminent arrival has a frantic effect on Helen, who worries about her clothes, hair, the help in the kitchen, and snapping after Romy like a particularly dedicated and not very likable work dog. No matter how hard Romy tries, no amount of begging and humoring deters Helen from her cycle of distraction and activity. Edward, too, is spending much of the day downtown: haircut, shave, manicure, new suit.

Only Lorenzo is unruffled and unchanged by the impending dinner. These women are his clients, and since he is not much interested in the movies, they do not affect him as strongly as the rest of the family.

Romy is excited for reasons beyond the actresses themselves. She sees in them a possibility for change.

"This is the first picture that we are doing together," says Gill, one of the actresses. "It's a comedy about a mistress and a wife." She laughs. "Of course, I play the wife." Everyone laughs because Gill is the sexy sister, while Rosalind is the perpetual sweetheart. "I've already done three this year, and Rosalind just finished her fourth."

"Oh, my," says Helen, "that seems like a great deal of work." Helen's words and movements are influenced by her shyness and admiration. Romy thinks her mother is prettier and, when not in this strange social state, more charming than these young women with their elusive charisma. Gill and Rosalind's personalities are causing the March family to behave in ways unlike themselves, with a mixture of curiosity and awe, though the actresses themselves are largely without affectation. They even defer a bit to Lorenzo because, as Rosalind points out, "You've made us quite a bundle."

When Romy had been arguing with Lorenzo about returning to school, she remembers thinking, as he questioned the work ethic of the artistic life, that all he did was make money from other people's money. Now, as she sits at dinner with Gill and Rosalind, she realizes that the respect they pay Lorenzo is not purely personal, they are also showing a respect for money. They are bound by it; they can do nothing but starve without it. That is, they would starve physically and spiritually, for one cannot act to an empty room.

Gill and Rosalind's personalities veer between a sort of tabula rasa marked by bright, blinding flashes of the aforementioned charisma; it is as if they are both projecting and inviting interpretation, thinks Romy. As she observes them she considers how close in age they are, yet they hardly seem blood related. Their clothing further underscores this point: Rosalind's dress of pale pink bleached almost white is of a cotton so fine she looks as if she were wearing silk trimmed with lace. Gill's attire is a lesson in contrast. She is barely wearing a gray dress, a sort of a slip over a slip, that reveals various little glimpses of her breasts when she moves. The undergarment is a slight, spaghetti-strapped sheath. The dress itself is gossamer, a spider's fragile web, without sleeves and plunging in front and back. Between the color and cut, Gill appears as ethereal as smoke.

Her eyes are smudged with kohl. Rosalind's face is clean of makeup, save for a bit of lipstick.

Additionally, they are awfully affectionate sisters. They finish each other's thoughts and sentences, frequently touching or holding each other's glance. They behave, Romy thinks, like two people besotted.

As Romy listens to Gill and Rosalind handing off bits of conversation to each other ("I said we need to do something together—" "—where we are seen equally—" "—that suits our image—" "—but that will not cast us as sisters—" and so on) she notices a dark mark on Gill's middle finger, initially taking it to be a bruise but now believing it to be a tattoo.

"It's interesting, isn't it?" says Gill, noting Romy's interest, breaking out of the round of movie talk in which she and Rosalind were engaged. "It's a photograph," says Gill, extending her hand with a practiced gesture toward Romy.

"You mean it's a tattoo of a photograph?" asks Romy, peering closer. The rest of the family is relieved that the actresses have turned their attention from them to Romy; it is exhausting to converse with people you are accustomed to watching. Because of the nature of the actresses' lives as portrayed on the screen, covered in various publications, not to mention gossip, any normal personal questions or discussions feel forced and tainted. The effort makes the Marches tired. Besides, who really wants to interact with someone so remote that she can only enter your consciousness in a dream in the dark of a theater? The actor offers and you accept.

When they watch Gill talking to Romy, the Marches can relax into their usual position of audience.

"Oh, no, no, it's not a tattoo at all," says Rosalind, taking Gill's hand lovingly in her own; their two hands now resting palm to palm, their fingers shallowly laced. "It's a real picture.'

"I'm not sure I understand," says Romy, noticing subtle tints of color within the small mark.

"There is this person, this man, who does this for a living, I think." Gill looks to Rosalind, who responds with a shrug. "He can place these pictures anywhere you like—"

"I have a bracelet wrapped around my upper arm," says Rosalind, and sure enough, beneath the lace of her sleeve, Romy can make out a shadow on her skin.

"They don't last," says Gill, "which makes the entire endeavor sort of perfect." Romy can finally discern the likeness on Gill's finger: It is Rosalind.

"Where do you do this?" asks Romy.

"Actually," says Gill, "right here in Pasadena." She glances at her own finger. "Strange, isn't it?" She smiles.

"What's the man's name?" asks Romy, but Gill just continues to smile, then turns her attention to Edward, inquires about school, which, Romy can see, bothers him, since he is roughly the same age as the actresses, but the school question transforms him into a child.

Dinner has ended and the dinner plates are being cleared from the table when Romy blurts out, "Do you think you could find a job for me?" to Gill and Rosalind. The table falls silent. "I would be willing to do anything. Really."

Gill and Rosalind look at each other, then Gill says, "Why not? We can see about it." She smiles at Lorenzo. "It is the least we can do for your father."

Lorenzo, Romy can tell, does not warm to the idea of his daughter in "that sort of environment," but Helen lightly touches his arm and he says nothing. Romy counted on the company at dinner to protect her. Besides, Lorenzo is flattered by the idea of someone giving him such a gift.

This was the possibility that Romy saw in the actresses: to forget about her last year of college. When she heard about Gill and Rosalind coming to dinner it occurred to her that even the lowest job at the studio would be preferable to being in an office.

"Just for the summer," adds Romy, and Lorenzo reluctantly agrees.

## *12.*

At the studio everyone calls Romy *baby* even though she is older than some of the actors. "It's a term of innocence, in your case," the wardrobe mistress told her.

Normally, her lack of worldliness doesn't bother her, but in this place it makes her self-conscious because it is preferable not to be so naive. The laughter that rises at her expense has a knowing, jaded ring. There is the studied boredom; the uncensored language (the filmed world is silent, encouraging this freedom of words); the flirting; the inconstant pairings; the vague sexual orientations; the elaborate clothing; the insubstantial sets that, on film, are often opulent; the illusory heroism of the actors; the weird reality of a life of mirrors, all trickery and reflected truth.

Aside from being called *baby*, Romy feels more at home at the studio than anywhere she has ever been before. Even with a hundred people, day in, day out, telling her what to do. Sometimes she hangs around watching the cameramen filming the action. They explain that they keep the timing of their cranking consistent by singing to themselves. They talk to her about lighting, and day for night, hanging miniatures, and depth of field with regard to the painted scenery. She likes hearing about the various techniques of illusion.

Her parents ask question after question as if taking her moral temperature and only stop when satisfied that she is still the same girl they've always known.

During her second week at work, as she sits on a discarded table from a movie about a murdered king, a young man, dressed as a groundskeeper, walks by.

"Augustine Marks," says Romy happily, forgetting herself for a moment.

Augustine stops, returns her smile, though it is not as unguarded as hers. "Romy March," he says. "How are you?"

"I'm fine."

"Good," he says.

"What are you doing here?" she asks.

Holding his rake to one side he says, "I'm playing the part of the gardener."

"Really?" says Romy, impressed.

He shakes his head. "I *am* the gardener. And why are you here?"

"I have a job," she says.

"Is that right," he replies with a look full of curiosity and envy because it is apparent Romy doesn't need to work.

"I mostly run around getting things for people, or taking things to people, and trying to be available and out of everyone's way." She hesitates. "They call me baby."

"Why?"

"Because," she says with a sigh, "I am such an innocent." She rolls her eyes and smiles.

Augustine laughs.

"I'm very happy," says Romy.

"Good for you, baby," he says.

After that, Romy and Augustine see each other almost every day. Their eyes meet in passing; they begin to say hello, how are you. Eventually, when their paths cross they exchange a few words.

Then, one morning, in the car on the way to work, Romy realizes that she looks forward to seeing Augustine, that his presence thrills her. She doesn't want to eat, requires little sleep, telling herself it is the heat and long days of summer, and is careful with her appearance. In short, knowing she will see him makes her happy.

Augustine is sitting, his back resting on a stack of scenery flats propped up against a wall. Since the painting behind him is of sky and clouds, Augustine looks as though he is reading his magazine and eating a sandwich in midair.

"What are you reading?" she asks.

He holds it up as she reads aloud, "*The Crisis?* "

"Yes," he replies, bringing the magazine back down and saying nothing more.

"Can I eat with you?" asks Romy.

Augustine reflexively looks around. The usual people are strolling or hurrying by, in singles or in pairs. Some are moving props, or scenery, or those enormous lights that have, on occasion, temporarily damaged the eyes of the actors, causing tearing and blurred vision. Though that happens less and less these days.

He thinks a minute, then nods.

Even though they spend every lunch break together, they still treat these meetings as if they were accidental. As if they cannot risk arranging them. They are not overly worried about what people will think; their concerns are more of a personal nature.

Life at the studio is so routinely unconventional that it sometimes feels to Romy like an alternate society. Gill and Rosalind are brazen in their affection; married men and women take up with each other; directors speak in hushed, close tones to very young girls, who gaze back with eyes lit by a thousand wishes; boys follow boys; those in front of the camera find their way to those behind the camera; composers of music give their songs informal names of those with whom they are involved. Who in this world, with its own laws and codes, would take notice of an errand girl and a groundskeeper, even if they are of different colors? Who in this place would care?

Romy and Augustine discover early on that a crowd of

artists are too outside, too removed from the rules of the general public, and too egocentric to care.

"I saw you once on a train heading north. A few months ago," Augustine tells her.

"Oh, I was probably returning to school," Romy says.

"Was that your boyfriend?" he asks.

Her mind settles on Hugh, then says, "Where?"

"At the station. He met you there."

"No. No. That was Edward, my brother." She resists mentioning that she doesn't have anyone special, notices that he doesn't ask.

"I'm not going back," she says. "Can I tell you something?"

"Of course."

"I talked my father into letting me live at home and attend a local school for my last year. But," she says, taking a deep breath, "I lied. I'm going to leave each day as if I am going to school, but I'm going to continue working here."

"What did you say to him to get him to keep you home?"

"I said he could keep an eye on me."

Augustine laughs out loud. "Never believe your child when she says she's making it easy for you to watch her."

Romy laughs with him. Then becomes serious. "I didn't know what to do. I couldn't go back because—well, I couldn't. I have some ideas and I want—" but she stops herself, looks down, and says, "I'm not sure what it is, but I want something *else.*"

"'Whether I shall turn out to be the hero of my own life or whether that station shall be held by anyone else these pages must show,'" quotes Augustine.

"Yes," she says, her sigh a sigh of relief and recognition. "You know."

"What is that magazine I see you reading sometimes?" she asks, sitting with Augustine in the balcony of an abandoned set of an opera house, sharing a huge piece of chocolate cake that she brought in her lunch. Indian summer is beginning to fade, and what passes for winter is coming in. When the first day of school came, Romy was apprehensive, scared to be found out. But as the days went by, she didn't think about it at all.

"My father reads it. It's about race building."

"Oh," says Romy.

"My father loves W.E.B. Du Bois, who has a lot to say regarding people like me, that is, the American Negro." He emphasizes the last two words, then falls quiet. He and Romy never discuss race. They don't even want to think about it when they are together. They understand that it matters. Every time they consider doing anything together off the studio lot, something any friends would do, they know it is not possible. So they avoid talking about race by never extending their friendship out of the boundaries of their workplace. "He writes, for example, about owning our own businesses, and progressive politics."

"Do you agree with what he says?" asks Romy.

"Yes, except when he talks about art, which he believes should be political, you know, serve a purpose beyond its own sake, and I'm not so sure about that."

Romy looks out over the low balcony of the imitation opera house and briefly closes her eyes, wishing everyone, except for Augustine, would simply vanish.

* * *

"I brought something." Augustine hands Romy a large photograph.

In it are Romy's feet, hat, shoes, stockings, and, of course, her beautiful suitcase. "I can't believe you kept it," she says, shaking her head.

"I guess I just never threw it out."

"That day," smiles Romy. "You had no idea who I was, did you? Even after I told you my name, you couldn't place me."

"That's true," he says.

"What did you think when I introduced myself?"

"Truthfully?"

"Yes."

"I thought, of course she remembers me. Who wouldn't remember one of four black students in an almost all-white school? I thought, this is the exact same reason that I don't recall her face." He says, "There were just so many of you."

"Augustine," Romy says hesitantly, "I know you spend a lot of time—well, here, for instance—is it hard for you to be around—" She shakes her head. "I shouldn't ask. It's none of my business."

"Ask me," says Augustine.

"Is it hard to be around white people all the time?"

He looks at her, thinking, if you have to ask, then I'm not sure I can answer. Then it occurs to him that within that question is another question, so he simply says, "Sometimes. I manage," to which she replies, I didn't mean anything, and he cuts her off and says, it's all right.

"I brought something to show you." Romy pulls the Renaissance box from a cloth satchel she is carrying.

"It's beautiful," says Augustine.

"Here." She hands it to him. "You can hold it."

"How old is this?" he asks, turning it over in his hand, admiring the painted boy and girl on the lid as they stand face-to-face, reflecting each other in a mirror.

"It's from the Renaissance. Early sixteenth century. And look." Romy opens the box to show him the curl of marble within.

"How did you get it?" asks Augustine.

"My great-great-great-great-et cetera-infinity-ad infinitum grandmother made it. I don't know anything about the piece of marble. I don't really know anything about her, except that she made this box. If you turn it over, her name is on the bottom."

Augustine sees the name *Giulietta Marcel* written on the underside. He hands it back to Romy.

"It is my most prized possession," she tells him.

He brings his camera one day to take pictures of Romy. They don't have much time, only an hour and a half, so Augustine ends up with two photographs of her.

"What will you do when you leave here?" she asks as he sets up one of the shots.

"I want to live in Harlem. I want to take pictures of the people who live and work in Harlem." He adjusts the focus. "I want to record their lives so they will know that they mattered." He trips the shutter.

At home, Orlando and Suzanne are pressuring Augustine to quit the studio. "I didn't send you to four years of college for this!" Orlando tells him.

How can he explain that he, too, hates his job. If artists are more open-minded, more enlightened, why is he trimming the grass instead of directing a movie picture, or even operating a camera? How can he tell them about Romy and how what he feels for her is nothing like the terrible attraction he had for Polly, but something more tender, more fundamental? That she is the bell that tolls in his heart? That one day, when Romy was nowhere near his thoughts, he suddenly found himself thinking, loving you just isn't what I had in mind.

"I made these. I took them and then I painted them," says Romy, showing the photographs of her mother, in the kitchen and garden, dressed for a party.

"You painted them?"

"Yes, I wanted the effect to be realistic, moving toward dreamlike." She looks at the pictures with him. They are somewhat crude in execution, not really very good. "I need to work on this idea more," she says.

"It's a good idea." He smiles.

"Do you think so?" She smiles back.

He nods, does not mention that lately his own photographs are of subjects posed among props so incongruous that they resemble dreams. Augustine catches himself staring at the girl beside him, wondering, where did you come from and how is it you understand the language I speak?

He does not mention to Romy how she is talking to him, in a whole other, private, mysterious, surprising way.

Rounding a corner on a studio street, Romy sees Augustine turning Gill's hand over in his own as they converse. They are friendly and easy with each other. They do not notice her, and Romy keeps her distance; in fact, she is torn between quietly leaving and briskly intruding upon them.

She cannot move.

Gill catches sight of Romy, waves in greeting. Augustine also looks up, and a certain softness comes into his eyes, but Romy cannot read what it means. She is distracted by the pounding of her own heart. As she nears the couple, she hears Gill making a date with Augustine, and the euphoria of knowing Augustine quickly shifts into a crash, a shattering, a break, a slap, a dive into ice.

Gill is going to meet with Augustine outside the studio.

Of course, Gill, almost the same age as Romy, can do whatever she wants with a modicum of discretion. She can passionately kiss Rosalind as she leans against a doorjamb and not be overly concerned with who passes by. She has a freedom of language unfathomable to Romy, who cannot imagine saying whatever she wants to say. Romy has never used some of the words she hears casually thrown around here daily.

Perhaps some aspects of Gill's life require a bit of decorum, an edge of secrecy; so what if she has to be a little bit furtive in her actions? Romy's entire life is a lie.

It is a lie when her parents think she attends class each day; it is a lie when she joins in discussions of marriage and children; it is a lie when she plays the part of the Good Girl willingly. She doesn't want to choose her china, but she also doesn't want to be one of those girls who rebel for the sake of rebelling. It strikes her as empty and purposeless to shock for the sheer pleasure of shocking. Who would want to command unwanted attention when you could just as easily be left alone?

Is she upset because Gill can make a date with Augustine or because it is a date with Augustine?

Is she in love?

Romy has seldom experienced jealousy; can jealousy indicate attraction? If jealousy defines love, then it is not possible to tell Augustine she is jealous without also admitting to love. Once she thought sex would lead to affection and was mildly astonished when she felt nothing. Does she love Augustine? She cannot remember now how often she daydreams about walking down the street with him, her arm through his, as the most unremarkable of lovers.

Romy cools toward Augustine, and when she again begins to warm to him, he finds it difficult to let her close again. The truths of their time press against him: *The problem of the twentieth century is the problem of the color-line . . .*

He thought about the debate among Negroes concerning the war in Europe; one side said Negroes could "earn" equality for themselves through patriotism; the other side said why fight for a country that wants to forget about you? He thought about Paul Dunbar's caged bird, and how everyone knew the poem and no one knew the poet.

He read about a songwriter named Marion Cook who had been trained as a composer and classical musician in the United States and Berlin, who ended up immersing himself in other musical forms because, as James Weldon Johnson said, there was no place for his genius. A white critic in New York wrote, after an evening of Cook's songs, "I am told that Mr. Cook declares that the next score he writes shall begin with ten minutes of serious music. If the audience doesn't like it, they can come in late, but for ten minutes he will do something worthy of his genius."

Augustine thinks about his college education and this job he keeps because it is the only way he can have a friendship with Romy. He didn't realize it immediately, but he does this for her. And now this. His life is always two lives.

He still makes his skin photographs on the side, recently doing a slim anklet for Gill, as well as freshening up the one on her finger. He experiments with other techniques, like the nineteenth-century style of gently blurring the model for an effect of remoteness.

Mostly he feels he is waiting for his real life to begin; everything seems a preamble to what he will become. How funny, he thinks, to say what I will be, not what I will do, as if he will one day be transformed.

Time passes, and after not talking, except in greeting, Romy bashfully asks Augustine if he wants to join her for lunch.

"Well, I don't know, baby," he says.

"I'm not a baby."

"Then what have you been doing with me lately?"

"Me? It's not what I'm doing with you—it's what you do with—" She stops, then says, "It's none of my business," and starts to walk away.

Instinctively, Augustine reaches out for her arm, to retrieve her, yet as soon as his fingertips brush her dress, he drops his hand, without taking hold.

It is enough of a gesture to turn Romy around. She is trying hard not to cry. *I mustn't let him see me cry.* Even so, tears begin to fall without a sound from her.

"Oh, dear." Augustine is at a loss. He called her baby to anger her, and now he is left with the useless satisfaction of having hit his mark. "I'm sorry," he says, "I'm so sorry, Romy."

"I have no right," she says, her voice catching. "You are not mine."

"Oh, Romy," whispers Augustine, "is that what this is all about?"

She shakes her head, the tears cease, and she turns mute. Her jealousy is an embarrassment to her; it flies in the face of all her good intentions and tender theories regarding love. "Forgive me," she says.

"Romy," he says again, and in his mind runs a line from a poem, *I love you for the breaking sadness in your voice.* He then does what he has long wanted to do, which is hold her face in his hand. Romy responds by closing her wet eyes and moving the curve of her cheek against his palm.

When Romy opens her eyes, with Augustine still touching her, she sees Lorenzo advancing on them, the fury evident in his rushing, brutish body language. She jumps away from Augustine, placing herself in front of him, so that when Lorenzo catches up to them she will be in the middle. Her father has never hit either of his children, but Romy thinks he might hit her now, and she will not allow Augustine to be struck. She could not bear to be the cause of someone else's beating.

Lorenzo stops inches from her body, then reaches out and yanks her arm with such bruising roughness it momentarily goes numb. As her father half-drags her to the car, it is strange to recall the gentle brush of Augustine's fingers, only moments before, in the exact same spot where her father now violently grips her arm.

* * *

Augustine's anger is as strong as Lorenzo's, his every impulse clamoring to rescue Romy, but the reality of his life is that he cannot. He can feel his blood race, his breath shorten from rage, but he cannot act.

And this, he knows, in the blindness of anger and frustration, is the cornerstone of all that is wrong with the world: A black man cannot challenge a white man. Augustine can love someone, honor her as a friend, but because of their color difference he is prevented from doing what he knows to be right and just. A country that will not allow its citizens to act honorably is an evil place. To stop you from goodness. To force you to ignore your own moral compass. There is no humanity there.

He quits his job. He worries about Romy.

Lorenzo calls his daughter an unrepeatable name, and after an evening of Lorenzo's wrath, the proportions of which Helen cannot reduce, Romy is made to sleep outside.

Helen cries, "She is your child!" Lorenzo responds by not allowing Romy back into the house. It was the discovery of Romy's lie that brought Lorenzo to the studio, but it was Augustine that pushed him beyond reason.

Romy settles herself on a lawn chaise, wraps her coat around her. February nights are cold, even in California. She shivers and weeps but in the one or two calm moments experiences an odd sort of exhilaration, as if she is finally free, her life unpredictable.

She dozes off, and when she awakens, the moon has risen and she is covered in a comforter, warm enough so that the cold no longer interrupts her sleep. With the first light of morning illuminating the garden, she looks toward the house and swears she sees Lorenzo watching her from the window. But when she looks again, he has vanished.

In the morning she asks to use the bathroom. She is told no. There is no choice but to relieve herself in relative privacy behind the garage; she is too weary for modesty.

Helen brings Romy's beautiful suitcase to her; Helen's eyes ruined from a night of tears. She embraces her daughter tightly.

Opening her suitcase, rummaging around inside, Romy looks up from where she kneels on the grass. "My box," she says to Helen, "I need my box."

Helen begins to explain that it is a family treasure, then says, "Wait," returning minutes later with it wrapped in a heavily embroidered scarf. "Your father will get over this," says Helen. "It will work out." But Romy doesn't want to tell her that, in a rather painful way, it *is* working out for her. Expectations fall away. She is scared and unsure, but within this terrible event there is something she has been longing for.

She kisses her mother good-bye. Helen is crying again.

As she walks, the sun is warm but not too hot. At one point Romy leans against a building and opens the box to see a wad of bills. She is not sure if they are from her mother or her father. Even if it is her father, she thinks, remembering the horrible name he called her, *We'll see who forgives who first.*

She walks and walks and walks until she comes to the train station. Romy is not sure where to go but settles on New York, someplace too busy to notice her. She considers Augustine's dream—art and Harlem—and wonders at what point their dreams entwined.

*  *  *

As she waits on the bench, her feet resting on her beautiful suitcase, the box still wound up in the scarf that carries the scent of Helen's cologne beside her, she reads a book.

When she glances up, she sees, outside at the window above the platform, Augustine. A mere glimpse of his face and pure joy overtakes her; she has to resist the impulse to rush to him.

And the light in his eyes illuminates his own happiness and surprise at finding her there; he doesn't attempt to go to her, instead presses his ticket to the glass: New York.

# Book Three: New York

## 1919–1927

the spring is not so beautiful there—
but the lads put out to sea
who carry beauties in their hearts
and dreams, like me.

THEY NEVER SAW EACH OTHER DURING THE TRIP FROM Pasadena to New York, for they were relegated to separate quarters and dining arrangements. Each was a little like Orpheus, who had been promised his beloved Eurydice on the condition that he never looked for her during the passage from the underworld to earth, in that Romy and Augustine had to take it on faith that the other would not lose his or her nerve and remain on the train.

When they arrive in New York, Romy stands on the platform gripping her beautiful suitcase and Giulietta's box wrapped in Helen's sweet-smelling scarf, until she locates Augustine. Her body relaxes for the first time in days, and her heart expands with a shockingly large measure of love. For the first time she understands intoxication in the presence of another.

They stand close, face-to-face, not saying a word. Though he has bags of his own to carry, Augustine still reaches for Romy's suitcase. She shakes her head no, and Augustine turns and begins to walk uptown. She wordlessly follows, never once taking her eyes from him, and he, unlike Orpheus, resists looking back. Neither is accustomed to the chill of a late February day in the city, but walking keeps them warm.

The other time she was in New York was exactly six years earlier, when her family took a vacation, during which they visited the Armory Show. All Romy remembers was the strangeness of the art and the crush of the crowds. Romy was quite young at the time, and deeply influenced by her parents' resistance to what they saw. Today makes her wish she could see it all again as an adult.

Romy follows Augustine to the heart of Harlem. ("I've spent so much of my life on the outskirts that now I want to be in the middle of everything," he tells her.) They take a room in a clean, modest hotel, where they honeymoon for days without the formality of marriage.

This is a new life, they agree, working out their relationship manifesto:

1: Neither one wants to be married. They are more comfortable on the outer edge of society, as well as not wanting their union sanctified by a country they love but do not trust. Yet, they see themselves as belonging to each other.
2: They want two cats. For balance, says Augustine, and Romy agrees that a single cat would feel "left out" of the lives of these two, who are clearly taken with a coupled world.
3: They will open a photography studio, calling it Perfect Fish Photography.

4: Should anyone ask, they will say that Romy is a Negro. With her curly black hair, olive complexion, and green eyes, she could pass. Augustine tells her that that first day in La Luna Park, when she stepped into the frame of his picture, he wasn't sure if she was white or not, he glanced up and away so quickly. It will simplify things, they agree. They don't expect anyone to ask.

This is Romy's first meaningful contact with a city. The first time she was in New York, she was happy to go home. The city overwhelmed her with all its traffic, odors, and noises, and the plethora of buildings. Mainly, it was the rush of people to which she could not get accustomed; in the West, people did not carry on their lives in the streets. At the same time, she noticed an innate politeness with regard to all this public living; people tended to allow privacy. In the West, people simply went indoors.

A few months shy of twenty, Romy thrills to the city. She loves Harlem at first sight: the wide boulevards, the brownstones, the striped window awnings, even the thick glass disks embedded in parts of the sidewalks to allow light in below are wonderful. The streetcars and the clubs and churches and theaters. Massive apartment buildings like small provinces. She's crazy for the countless windows that look out on the streets and backstreets and fascinated by the busy lives of the people behind them. Her attraction to the windows and the lives, she is sure, are one and the same. She is constantly curious. It's odd that the very thing that intimidated her as a child (too much humanity in too little space) captivates her as an adult. People talk, laugh, argue, kiss, embrace, scold, greet, ignore, and sometimes converse with themselves. She loves it all.

They rent an empty street-level studio with living quarters upstairs on 135th Street. Once they move in, the interior of the studio is almost a miniature of the movie studio with its extravagant and whimsical props. Clients entering the room are momentarily speechless at the variety of furniture and objects; there is such a wealth of stuff competing for attention that it is not unusual for each visitor to recall something different. They might mention the blue chaise longue of worn velvet; the stuffed crocodile suspended from the ceiling; the suit of armor; the ship of spun silver; the intricate, faded tapestries draped across the windows; the goddesses of stone; the Egyptian mummy; the replica of a chariot; the exotic foliage that barely survived the city extremes of hot and cold; the Japanese silk costumes and an obi tied to the neck of a polar bear; the crystal chandelier. Or someone might just say, How could you miss the sectioned mirrors and colored glass that refracted and multiplied the room over and over?

They paint scenery flats to resemble a lit fireplace flanked by columns of pink marble; a flight of stairs leading nowhere; a romantic, moon-splashed garden in Seville; Pisa's Field of Miracles; the view from atop Echo Mountain above Pasadena. A winter wonderland. Sitting rooms, music conservatories, plush bedrooms, and lush little sunrooms alive with greenery; an apple orchard; a gondola negotiating the canals of Venice.

Yet most people prefer the tableaux that resemble their own comfortable apartments. How funny, thought Romy, that the illusion that most appeals is the illusion of home.

* * *

Augustine informs his parents about Romy by simply dropping a brief note and a picture of the two of them into an envelope. Mostly he writes about Perfect Fish Photography, hoping to divert their attention, knowing that it will never work. But he tries just the same, and for the time being, Orlando and Suzanne make no comments regarding the girl in the picture.

Romy writes to Helen, who often sends her money. She does not reveal much about her life except that she has a job in a photography studio. Helen asks few questions; Edward sends his love; Lorenzo remains silent.

It is 1919, a terrible, shameful year as the country tries to pull itself apart with fits of violence toward its black citizens. Many of these men are newly returned heroes of the Great War; there are riots and beatings and shootings and lynchings. With so much blood spilled, the summer earns the name Red Summer.

Augustine and Romy dance at a place called the Garden of Joy, where they scratch the gravel, shiver, and ball the jack. So great is their happiness with each other that their original attraction to the club was its name.

The Garden of Joy is gay and straight. The folks dressed like the opposite of their own sex make Romy, who passes each day, feel right at home. Of course, there are the other, fancier Harlem clubs that draw the white crowds from downtown, but Romy, due to her new race, is not allowed inside.

One day, a very tall woman enters the studio as Romy and Augustine sit playing cards.

Business, for them, moves apace, so that they make enough money to live with nothing left over. They shoot church socials, weddings, business openings, anniversaries, graduations. Family photos, debutante portraits, and baby pictures. There is even the occasional funeral portrait. These Augustine does without Romy.

But there are vacant hours in between, which they often fill with play. They make bets concerning everything: cards, dice, how many pictures they will take in a given day, how many people will walk by the door without coming in. They idly make up possible lives for celebrities, then wager who will come closest to the eventual truth. They try to predict a client's reaction to a picture. They gamble over facts, trivia, dates. The payoffs might be cash, or objects, or "services rendered."

Sometimes their play is physical. One ambushes the other with a pillow, or an article of clothing, or a piece of food. Then they are off—chasing, laughing, out of breath, until one tackles the other. In times like these it seems to Romy that Augustine has six hands, four legs, and countless fingers that grab and tickle. When they are in the apartment, with the studio below, there is no one to bang a broomstick under the floor or complain of the noise.

Exhausted and disheveled and Romy has lost for the hundredth time, she says, "Don't ever change, Augustine."

Everyone speaks of sex as unthinkable in regard to one's parents, but what Romy cannot picture with Lorenzo and Helen is playfulness. Even though, to Romy, their marriage of Italian to American, working-class to upper-class, is essentially a "romantic" marriage, it lacks the active silliness of her affair with Augustine.

She says to Augustine, "One day I will be old and brittle and you will have to be careful not to break my hip or arm."

"Oh," Augustine says, "I'll still be taking you down, and I'll still be winning. I'm not cutting you any slack, baby."

"No," Romy says, smiling. "You'll be the one to receive no mercy."

And so on, in their world within the world.

The very tall woman asks, "Are you Augustine Marks?" She is easily six feet, and dressed in a man's silk brocade smoking jacket of blues and black. The jacket is held closed by a fringed sash of black silk and adorned with a cluster of amethyst and ruby grapes and green jade leaves fashioned as an enormous brooch. Earrings like exquisite miniature chandeliers play against her face. Her skirt looks as if it is made of many scarves. Her imported shoes have three-inch heels, adding to her already considerable height.

Augustine stands up when she enters, and since she remains standing, so does he, smoothing his suit, buttoning his jacket. "Yes," he answers.

She extracts an elegantly engraved card from her embroidered silk bag and hands it to Augustine.

He takes it from her without reading it, says, "I know who you are." Romy, who has been ignored by the woman, knows who she is as well. You could not mistake the woman for anyone else, with her lofty, strong frame and eccentric clothing that ranges from Russian princess to Japanese bride to artist queen. Everyone in Harlem knows this woman and her recently deceased mother, Madame Bisset, who invented a hair product and created a school that made her millions. When asked, Madame

Bisset said that the inspiration came to her "in a dream."

"I like the pictures you did for the beauty shops," says the woman. "Can you come to the villa weekend after next? I'm having a few people up."

"My wife and I would be honored," says Augustine.

The woman's eyes slide toward Romy, taking her in without comment. "Of course," she says after a moment. Then she is gone, leaving a scent as wonderful and as unusual as her clothing, in her wake.

The woman, Tea Bisset, weekends in the opulent home her mother built on the Hudson, and in which Madame Bisset lived and died. Tea also has a home in town, where she stays most of the time, for it is said that since her mother passed away in the villa, she can't bear to be there alone.

Tea is in the midst of a marriage, her third, which is unraveling. It is rumored that her husband is perpetually unfaithful, which has turned Tea predatory. When Augustine and Romy casually mention their invitation to the Bisset villa, Romy is told, "Keep an eye out, that's all I'm saying." Augustine and Romy laugh. As if anyone could come between us.

When Romy and Augustine arrive for the weekend, a party is already in progress. Some people are left over from the previous weekend's gathering, and new guests began trickling in as early as Thursday afternoon. Romy and Augustine are quite taken by their new surroundings: the Aubusson rugs, marble of rose and white, and velvets and silks, and the crystalline hall of mirrors that runs the length of the rear of the house.

Augustine and Romy set up their equipment in the hall of mirrors. The first person to be photographed is

Tea Bisset herself. As Romy moves behind the camera, Tea begins waving her long arms, saying, "What are you doing?"

"Setting up the shot," says Romy, her answer almost sounding like a question in its uncertainty.

Tea shakes her head and gestures to Augustine. "I hired Mr. Marks to record my likeness," she says, smiling.

"You hired Perfect Fish Photography, Miss Bisset," says Romy, without moving. Granted, Augustine can be found behind the camera more frequently than Romy, and Romy more often behind the desk, but they have an agreement that specific assignments are hers. Sumptuous women, of which Tea Bisset is an ideal example.

People begin congregating about the hall, waiting, listening. "Don't mistake me for a patient woman," says Tea.

"You know," says Augustine, moving slowly, like a graceful change of partners, displacing Romy from behind the camera, "I think we can get started now."

Romy is not unrealistic; she can look around this house and see who is in attendance. There are socialites, writers, painters, intellectuals, politicians, and self-made businessmen, black and white. They are, in short, future work for Perfect Fish; this particular weekend is of some importance. It could mean more money, which in turn will allow Augustine and Romy more time to devote to private photography.

But she is humiliated and doesn't know if she should direct her anger at Tea Bisset, Augustine, or the prying, indifferent crowd.

"You know, Tea is rich, and that isn't the same thing as being liked. I mean, folks don't necessarily come for her company." Romy glances over to see a woman, not much older than Romy, who has sat down beside her in a nearly empty sunroom. She wears a single silver clip in her curly hair. Her dark eyes and bemused expression convey interest and intelligence. Her pale brown skin reminds Romy of silk; her figure is nice; her legs sensational. But her most notable feature, aside from her legs, is a sort of radiance.

"I'm not really a guest," Romy tells her, drinking from a bottle of champagne.

"I know. You're with the photographer," says the woman, which causes Romy to snap, "I *am* the photographer," and the woman to say, in a still-friendly tone, "Hey, I stand corrected."

"I'm sorry," says Romy.

"My name is Apple Norris." She shakes Romy's hand.

"Are you friends with Miss Bisset?" asks Romy.

"Actually, I like her a lot, but I don't like the way she acts at times. She's very influential, you know."

"I know," says Romy.

Just then a man embraces Apple from behind, which causes her to laugh, as he kisses the top of her head. "Oh, Lee," she says happily, "where you been lately?"

Then to Romy he asks, indicating the champagne, "Are you going to share that?"

"I don't have a glass, so I've been—"

"Say no more," says Lee. "I decline. Nothing personal."

"Lee's a little fastidious," says Apple.

He still has his arms around Apple, and she has placed her hand on his. Soon they are discussing people Romy does not know. This gives her a chance to realize how strange it feels to be in the friendly presence of a white man; how much her life has changed.

"I have to go look for Lena," says Lee to Romy. "I'm

sorry, I didn't introduce myself, I'm Leland Grandin, and you are—"

"Romy March," she answers.

"Maybe we'll meet again," he says before bestowing a last kiss on Apple's cheek.

That night Romy goes up to bed well before Augustine. She lies on the bed sobbing, frustrated and angry. How she longs to be somebody! She wants people to accord her respect, not so she can bully or embarrass them, but rather so she can choose what she does and doesn't want and people will understand that she is making a choice. That she is not living a life dictated to her by others. Oh, hell, she thinks, it always comes down to the same thing: freedom.

She opens a book to read, and before she knows it, she falls deeply asleep. When Augustine comes in, she feels his hands in her hair, taking out the pins, and on her body, loosening and removing her clothing. And she can't be sure if she dreams it or not, but she thinks she hears him say, "I promise that will never happen to you again."

More and more, Romy is handling the business of their business. She schedules appointments, accepts payment, does the books. Perfect Fish Photography is thriving, and Augustine is very much in demand. The more work he does—calendars, a U.N.I.A. parade, Talented Tenth portraits and gatherings (those class-conscious members of Harlem's social elite), birthdays, anniversaries, and weddings—the more work he is offered.

And the less time there is for Romy's own photography. She's lucky to get behind the camera or into the darkroom once a week and often fails that.

Two more weekends are spent at Tea Bisset's villa,

where Romy is invisible to Miss Bisset, but her new friendship with Apple Norris makes it bearable.

Romy sees Lee Grandin two more times as well.

Every time Lee is around Apple, he is always very affectionate with her. Romy see them walking the gardens, arm in arm. He kisses her hello and good-bye. He strokes her back as they sit at the table following dinner. And, moreover, his wife, Lena, when she is around, doesn't appear to mind.

Romy wants to ask about Lee but doesn't wish to intrude. Besides, there is so much tension between Augustine and Romy during these working weekends that she can barely muster up enough interest in the romantic complications that surround her.

"I'm not going," says Romy after Tea sends over a driver with yet another invitation for the weekend.

"Fine," says Augustine, irritation in his voice. "Suit yourself."

Lee Grandin stops by to find Romy in the studio alone. "And where is your busy husband?" he asks pleasantly.

"Busy," she says.

"And how about you?" he asks.

She shuffles the papers that obscure the surface of her desk. "Me? I'm a different kind of busy." She turns her palms to the ceiling in a helpless gesture.

"I was wondering if you'd like to drop by our apartment on Friday. We're having some people over. Thought you might like them."

For a minute Romy fantasizes going alone. "I'd love to," she says.

"Augustine, too." Lee laughs, moves a little closer. "Or

were you thinking of abandoning your husband for the evening?"

"Oh, no. No. Of course, we'll be there," she says.

"My friends are fairly mixed, you know. It won't be completely white."

Romy looks at him and makes no response. Sometimes she forgets the details of her new life: that she is someone's *wife;* that her husband is gaining a reputation as a fine photographer while she is only known, when she is noticed at all, as his little lemon-colored wife; that she is black, which in Harlem is easy to forget until someone mentions some club she cannot enter, or some downtown restaurant where she will not be served, or, still downtown, the way white people look through her. Or the cramped balcony where, even in Harlem, she sits when in the theater. One night, the author of the play sat beside her, complaining to his companion that he was the goddamn writer of the goddamn play and look where they make him sit.

"That's fine," she says. "It doesn't matter to us."

"It doesn't matter to me either," says Lee quickly, smiling again.

"I'm supposed to go to Miss Bisset's house that weekend," says Augustine when Romy tells him about Lee's invitation.

"Why do you have to see that woman at all?" she asks.

"Look around you, Romy. Look how well we're doing." He picks up the appointment book from the desk in the anteroom of their studio and holds it up open.

"That's my point, honey, we don't need her anymore," says Romy, taking the book from Augustine and placing it gently on the desk. "We're doing all right."

"That's *my* point," he says. "All the more reason for me

to go." He puts his arms around her, says, "Life is capricious, baby. Who knows how long anything will last?"

Romy and Apple go to the Grandins' together.

Apple calls Lee and his white crowd of money and artists Negrotarians. It is not easy to read Apple when she says things like this; the way she tosses off some slangy, abbreviated description (for example, she will refer to a gathering involving the Talented Tenth as some "dicty bash," or refer to the boardinghouse where she resides in the company of other economically strapped artists as "Niggerati Manor") because her delivery is often wry and shining. Regardless of the topic, judgment might hide among her words; it is too hard to tell.

At the Grandins' Upper East Side apartment, everyone is talking about a Harlem Renaissance. Every time Romy hears the expression, her thoughts settle on Giulietta's box, and how fitting that it should survive one Renaissance to make an appearance in another.

"New Negro? What's a new Negro?" asks a man Romy recognizes as the playwright from the theater balcony. "Wait until they find out we're all just the same old Negroes they wanted nothing to do with."

"But don't you see?" says Lee as he pulls out his lighter to light the other man's cigarette, "what do you think the *Opportunity* dinner was all about?"

Augustine and Romy attended this event, Augustine more excited than Romy, and Romy more excited for Augustine than for herself. For here, in one room, were Negro writers, cultural leaders, and intellectuals, all being presented before a mixed audience. "Can you believe this?" asked Augustine enthusiastically. And, not long after that, "Can you believe this?" again.

For Romy, it was a fancy dinner and a job; she did not see what Augustine saw. Later she understood what he had so presciently identified.

"Whatever," says the playwright. "I need a drink." And he left Lee standing alone, the cigarette unlit, the lighter still held aloft.

By the bar, Romy overhears the playwright saying to the Negro bartender, "We do what we do, and then these Negrotarians involve themselves and *discover* us. Yeah," he says, downing his drink in one swallow, "they discover us like Columbus discovered America. They slap a name on this 'movement,' and we're the fashion." The bartender says nothing. The playwright glances around the room, his gaze falling on Romy, who answers his scowl with an even stare. He slams his glass down and mutters loudly, "I don't know what the hell I'm doing here!" and rushes out of the apartment, leaving the front door standing wide open.

"That's Able Williams," Apple says to Romy. "Brilliant, alcoholic, makes you want to kill him. He lives down the hall from me."

"Is he always this bitter?" asks Romy.

Apple stares at Romy, and for once Romy can see clearly what's on her mind: Apple's thinking, what don't you understand about bitterness? Then she shrugs. "He's Williams," she says.

Romy finds Lee and asks where he wants her to set up her camera. She thought he would mention it when she came in the door, but a number of guests descended at once and she was soon forgotten.

"Lee," she says, "it's getting late. What do you want me

to do here?" Of course, she has some ideas of her own. There is an American heiress, in town from Paris, where she divides her time. She has a wild reputation, and stunning, antique ivory bracelets up to the elbows on both arms. Romy desperately wants to capture her likeness.

"Oh, Romy, dear," says Lee, his arm across her shoulders, guiding her across the room as he speaks in intimate tones. "You don't need to sing for your supper. You are my guest. Next time. When you and Augustine come again."

But Romy doesn't feel like a guest; she feels like the dismissed half of Perfect Fish. And she thinks, what am I doing with my life? I pretend to be married, I pretend to be a Negro, and I pretend it doesn't bother me a bit when I am politely brushed aside. I do it, she knows, for love of Augustine.

Her clothing becomes more colorful and elaborate the longer she lives this new life. Part of the influence is the well-turned parade of Harlem itself. The hats and gloves and suits and fur and feathers and shoes and scarves and flowers of the citizens of Harlem are wonderful, a procession of finery that passes like a river of light down Seventh Avenue. The street itself invites elegance.

This environment, in conjunction with her inability to take her own pictures due to time and opportunity, expresses itself in her attire. She wears men's clothing, silks, velvets; her silver brooch holds light jackets closed, and soon she almost ceases using buttons altogether, preferring the ornamentation of jewelry. There are hats made from diaphanous, pale pink crinoline, adorned with cloth flowers, and a man's plain black bowler. Her sweaters are beaded, her blouses sometimes embroidered, her skirts unfashionably long. She borrows Augustine's plain white shirts. Bracelets climb one arm, a watch hangs from a long chain wrapped around her waist. The shoes she wears alternate between modest, everyday black boots and pearl-ized pumps.

In the evenings, she wears a slightly less theatrical version of the makeup worn by the movie stars at the studio.

Augustine's clothes are solemn and quiet. His appearance does not appear to be that of an artist, but rather of a solid, working man. There was nothing about him that announced his profession.

Other artists seldom view her as one of them (those who make art), instead deciding she is One of Them (those who don't make art).

So they make an interesting couple, a study in contrast, Augustine subtly attired, holding the hand of Romy, who resembles an actor without a play.

"Here's my wager," says Romy to Augustine, in the morning as they lie in bed and he mentions another invitation to Tea Bisset's. "I bet she wants you and is getting ready to let you know."

Augustine laughs and says, "Some imagination you got, baby."

Romy is laughing as well. She does an imitation of Tea, says in a parody of her voice, "'Don't mistake me for a patient woman.'"

"Please," says Augustine, then, "I feel I owe her, Romy, that's all."

Romy shakes her head. "That's fine," she says, "and maybe the introduction was from her, but the work is all yours. These people who find you forget that all they did was find you. What you do belongs to you."

"It's not that easy," Augustine says.

She knows exactly what he means. Look at her—people might hire Perfect Fish Photography Studio, but they are really hiring Augustine, and Romy working behind the camera sporadically, taking a graduation or anniversary picture. All the grand ladies that she wants to work with clamor for Augustine.

"Sometimes, Romy, I get so tired," says Augustine, curling up beside her, laying his head on her bare shoulder.

This is the reason for his exhilaration and his weariness:

*A Handful of Pictures* by Augustine Marks:

1. The salons of Tea Bisset, Lee and Lena Grandin, Miss Fauset (the most genteel, where French is frequently spoken).
2. James Reese Europe, a classically trained musician who backed the dancing team of the Castles. Irene Castle once said of his music that "it was the only music that completely made me forget the effort of the dance."
3. The Renaissance Basketball Team. And, another time, Jack Johnson.
4. Charles Gilpin, one of America's finest actors, who could be found, during the height of his career, manning the elevator at Macy's.
5. Harry O'Tanner, artist. Aaron Douglas, artist. Palmer Hayden, an artist who eventually painted a picture called *The Janitor Who Paints.*
6. Adam Clayton Powell, Sr., as well as exterior shots of the Abyssinian Baptist Church.
7. Marcus Garvey. W.E.B. Du Bois (Augustine's father's hero). Alain Locke.

8. The general population of Harlem, those who worked, and raised families, and fell in love, and battled sadness, and were young and grew up and grew old, and were happy, and tired, and angry, and pleased. All those people Augustine originally wanted to record on film because it seemed important. These were some of the pictures he liked best.
9. The writers: Claude McKay, Wallace Thurman, Zora Neale Hurston, Langston Hughes, Countee Cullen, Jessie Fauset, Jean Toomer, and Arna Bontemps, who said, years after it all ended, "Within a year or two we began to recognize ourselves as a 'group' and to become a little self-conscious about our 'significance.'. . . In Harlem we were seen in a beautiful light. . . . We were the first born of a dark renaissance."

For Augustine, taking pictures of the people of Harlem was what he wanted to do; the artistic atmosphere of Harlem inspired his art. And though none of the writers, with the exception of Countee Cullen, were natives of New York, he always knew that home is where your art is.

Augustine and Romy show up at Miss Fauset's, as well as Miss Bisset's, and Lee and Lena Grandin's, salons uptown and downtown. At night, 133rd Street (also called Jungle Alley) is studded with nice cars and cabs and white people with money. After the *Opportunity* dinner, the mainstream began publishing Harlem writers.

As usual, there are numerous debates about what it all means.

And Augustine (mostly) with Romy (occasionally) records it all.

* * *

Augustine longs for Romy when he goes to Tea Bisset's parties. Every time he looks up to see who has just come in the door, it is always a surprise and disappointment that with all the faces he sees, none belong to his beloved Romy. He misses everything about her: her increasingly fanciful wardrobe; the sly, funny comments about the other guests at the functions they went to; the midnight laughter when recounting the day's events. He misses her scent and her feel. He misses her companionship, and the way they talk and listen to each other. Sometimes it is as if they are the only two citizens of their own nation, speaking a complex language.

Augustine is in the darkroom, developing pictures of Easter Sunday on Seventh Avenue. The images of the crowd leisurely strolling down the street rise up through the chemicals. He has been so busy for so long, and grateful to be so, but something is bothering him. With all the activity of Perfect Fish, it is as though he hardly spends any time with Romy.

But I see her every day, he reminds himself. I am with her from the time we awaken in the morning, inside the studio, during work outside the studio, and socially. I see her all the time.

He can't remember the last time they went to the Garden of Joy or spent an extended period of time alone. The places they go are often well-appointed, sometimes luxurious, and the other guests lovers of wild conversation; yet he feels he is seldom with her.

There is a distance between them; they do not fight, they are not close enough to fight, he thinks. And she is unhappy not taking pictures. He can tell without being told, because, regardless, they know each other well. Or, maybe it's just that he imagines his own misery if he were denied what he likes to do best.

An unexpected tear falls and spreads on the photograph. He rushes from the darkroom to find Romy sitting at the desk, calculating rows of figures. She looks up, then says, "Are you all right?"

"I miss you," he says, his voice just slightly breaking.

Romy and Apple are walking down Lenox, enjoying the late spring day. They see each other often at various parties and such, or one will involve the other in such mundane tasks as marketing or taking in the laundry. Sometimes they just go for a walk together. Augustine calls them Roma Apple, as if they are a single woman.

"Do you ever think about having a child?" asks Romy.

Apple laughs. "Honey, I don't even want a dog."

"Oh," says Romy.

"Are you having a baby?" asks Apple, and as usual, nothing is revealed in her voice.

"Maybe. No, well, I'm just thinking, you know."

"Look," says Apple. "I've got no man. You know where I live. And I wouldn't have that if a child lived with me." She stops outside a store, saying, "I have to run in for a minute," and Romy nods.

When Apple emerges, she says, "Children just tie you down. A man wants all of you, but children want more, until they don't want you so much and you want them and what's the use in all that?"

"That's true," says Romy, "but I think about it—"

Apple turns to Romy, says, "You want to take pictures, right? What are you going to do with a baby when you get your chance? You going to look across the table at that child one day and think, because of you I had to give up what I loved?"

Apple is right: Romy does not want to blame her child for what she has not done with her life; she does not want to gaze at that child working arithmetic figures, or slowly eating dinner, or, maybe, drawing pictures of his own, and think, But for you I could've been someone. She has to settle something before she has a child because she cannot determine if children multiply or divide your love, and, without knowing the sum of the equation, she cannot do it.

It was true that most of the women she knew who wrote, or sang, or acted, or painted did not have families. Most of them, including Apple, lived nothing close to what her parents would call a "normal life." They appeared to live unencumbered, driven lives. Apple is right.

Romy gives a resigned little laugh. "I'm driven too," she says. "I want."

A week later, Apple says to Romy as they lounge around the empty studio, two ordinary women among the clutter of props, "You know I write a little. And, with the way I live, the things I do, there's no place for a family. It's not that I don't want a man and a child, but that I want it too much. And if you can't have the things you want, you begin to reject them until you convince yourself they were never good for you in the first place, and that you don't want them at all." Apple strokes the polar bear with the Japanese obi tied to its neck. "Where would I find the time?"

Augustine asks the residents of the rooming house where Apple lives among writers and painters, mostly men, if they would be willing to sit for a group portrait. What for? they ask, some suspicious, some pleased. For myself, he answers.

Romy's job is to assist him, gather everyone together and arrange them. It is not easy to get them to agree on a time, because they all keep step to their own private, unshared schedules. Some drink too much and have trouble in the morning; some are night owls, prowling the streets or working late on some project in their room; others are drawn to the music that spills out onto certain streets. Some have early morning rituals of walking, or going for coffee, or meeting friends. Some simply need to be alone a good deal of the day. And others will only participate in Augustine's picture if it requires no effort or planning on their part ("If I'm around, I'm around").

The place ("Niggerati Manor") is more like the home of careless, imaginative children than of adults. Augustine recognizes echoes of its style in the flat he shares with Romy. The furnishings, having once seen better days, have a residue of elegance that is enhanced by casual fabric coverings, or staining, or painting. There are knickknacks here and there that look inherited or found. The walls are hung with a variety of pictures, though some of the illustrations are painted directly on the wall surfaces. The images are often erotic, mostly male, once in a while political, and sometimes graphic. The colors of the place are bold and arresting, the effect unplanned but welcoming, as if all rules are relaxed within these rooms, an absence of judgment. It was a great house of mood and impulse.

As Romy sets up in the main parlor, she thinks of how much she rather likes this place, which feels familiar, and about the present-tense lives of children. In regard to artists, is there a part of you that can't grow up, or is it that you refuse?

Once the group comes together in the parlor, Augustine goes to work. The sitters look fatigued, or half-asleep, or exceptionally bright-eyed. Able Williams drinks liquor from a juice glass between pictures, grumbling but not leaving the room. Other people smoke tobacco or reefer.

Their manner of dress is as seemingly without thought as the decor of the house, their bohemian codes of manner and dress as strict as the black bourgeoisie of the Society of the Sons of New York. The paint-splattered pants, the woman wearing a necktie, the genteel poverty of a silk or velvet garment, the two-tone shoes, the inherited jewelry, all bespeak a life that defines them to (those they consider) outsiders. These odd modes of dress that serve as an erratic sort of uniform.

Able Williams is now joking with some of the other artists but treats Romy as if she were invisible. He is a man, she discovers from Apple's descriptions, who is so fragile and cruel that he almost dares people to befriend him. He is hard and critical about the work of other people but hard on himself as well.

There is the woman who minimizes her own stories by saying, "Oh, I just do 'em on the side. They're nothing really," when everyone in the house hears her typewriter long into the night.

And the poet who loves boys so much he can hardly concentrate on his work and the boys he loves became his form of poetry.

There is the painter who eschews canvas, choosing instead to decorate the walls and ceilings and bathtub and sink of the boarding house and, like the woman writer, acts as if he has no special love of painting.

There is the actor who used to drink and act but these days just drinks and talks about his wasted genius. He is not wrong, and has grown bitter and lost.

There is Apple, who mostly writes but also engages in other interests, and has, as of late, given in to Romy's request to take pictures of her.

There is Leland Grandin, not a resident, of whom Apple once said casually to Romy, "He spends some time at my place." Romy took Apple's statement to mean one thing, but in reconsidering the homoerotic wall paintings begins to think in another direction.

There are the singers and musicians who stay awake all night, often involving themselves with drink and drugs, saying, "It's because my life doesn't feel right, so I take a little something and I can tell myself that I don't feel right because I've taken a little something."

And there is Augustine, pulling this group together, wanting to set down their faces on film for all time. No flamboyance of appearance or personality, no destructive habits, nothing pegs him as kindred to the people in this house, yet he is just as serious about his art as they are. He is so different, so exactly like them. These people who live with feelings of being misplaced. Those who turned to drugs and drinking often connect better in a dream, until it becomes a habit. Nothing more dramatic than that.

Now Able Williams is saying to Romy, "What are you doing here, anyway? Shouldn't you be with your own people?" He is staring at her with contempt. Romy tightens with silent anxiety; for a second she thinks this unhappy man will tell everyone that she is white. How could he know that about her? Then he says, "You and your dicty girlfriends," a comment Augustine hears and, she can see, angers him.

It's true, Romy very much resembles one of the daughters or young wives of the black middle- and upper-middle class. The Talented Tenth. Where skin color was noticed, ranging from "high yaller to cocoa brown to blue," and most of them had lighter flesh.

Augustine and Romy were at one house for a Christmas party. The guests were unlike those at Tea Bisset's or Lee and Lena Grandin's in that there was almost no mix of classes, let alone race. It was very strange, for example, that the serving girls were white and European. Romy caught the eye of one of the girls as she served dinner, but the girl immediately looked away.

It was odd, too, to be in a place with people who could pass for white as easily as she passes for black; they are all virtually the same. Augustine was one of the darkest-skinned people there, and Romy noticed that, until it was revealed that he was photographing the event, no one approached him. Even as they spoke freely to her.

They were an aloof, privileged group until Augustine reminded her, as they packed up their camera, that these people, for all their education, money, debutante balls, elevated socials, and white servant girls still could not eat a steak at Delmonico's.

For much of the evening Romy found their world unappetizing and rigid. It reminded her of Pasadena, of the men who handed over their cash to her father; it brought out the natural antipathy she had toward middle-class values and the senseless rules and traditions that drove her from school and home.

But when Augustine reminded her that these people, regardless of their education, blood, and background, their snobbery and high society, were still black in America, Romy softened. She still did not warm to them but understood that they were nothing but prisoners, and all the worse for them because they could only hold together their illusions if they remained in their world. Better not to risk being turned away at a restaurant door.

Here is this playwright accusing her of being some rule-bound snob. Before she can answer, Augustine says evenly to Williams, "You don't know what you're talking about."

"I don't, huh?" he says.

"You don't want to do this," says Augustine, his voice calm.

Suddenly Williams seems agitated. He throws his glass across the room, where the remaining liquid runs down the torso of a naked man lusting after another naked man drawn on the wall. "What are you doing here?" he demands of Augustine. "You think something special is going on? This Negro craze, some sort of renaissance. You sit around like Hal over there—" pointing a finger at one of the other men in the room "—telling yourself that this is only the beginning of greatness? That the rest of the country will know what we've known all along?"

Augustine says, "Nobody knows anything."

"Go kid yourself," says Williams before storming from the room.

Everyone is quiet. The residents of the house sigh, indicating that this is usual behavior from Williams. They acknowledge that he is a difficult man, but they forgive him regularly. He isn't always like this, they say. Someone laughs and says, Actually, we're all like him, we just don't take it out in public.

Romy watches Augustine follow Williams; he doesn't get angry at the playwright. In fact, he is very patient with him. And when Augustine returns, it is with Williams in tow, who cooperates for the rest of the sitting.

"What did you say to Able Williams?" asks Romy as they walk home. The streets, as usual, are full of people; they bump into one another and apologize.

"I told him a story," says Augustine.

"What kind of story?"

"It's something I once heard, and I don't know if it's true or not, but as I listened to him going on in there, for some reason it just occurred to me." Augustine wants to put his arm around Romy, but they are carrying too many things. "You know, I think the pictures today might be great. When I was there, it felt like—" His voice trails off.

"Life as you know it?" asks Romy.

"Yes." Augustine smiles. "Anyway, it seemed to me that Williams was going to be trouble from the start, and that this all might go better if he were to leave. But once he was gone, I knew it was a mistake. That he was necessary to the picture. He belongs. As I went after him I was trying to figure out what I could say to calm him and persuade him to return. But the only thing that came to mind was this story."

"Tell me," says Romy.

"During the Renaissance, Raphael was painting a series of frescoes for a wealthy man. After preparing the walls, he left for a while. During Raphael's absence, Michelangelo, curious about Raphael, traveled to the place where he was working and came upon the prepared, untouched walls. When Michelangelo realized he was alone, he climbed the scaffolding and painted the head of an angel in black paint. When Raphael came back—Michelangelo was gone—he recognized, in the angel, the work of Michelangelo. Raphael decided to leave it alone. This angel is called the Visiting Card of Michelangelo.

"Then I said to Williams that nobody knows anything and maybe this time will fade, unremembered like a dream, but maybe it won't, and we're the visiting card of Michelangelo. He listened, then said, 'Black angels in the expanse of heaven.'

"'Something like that,' I said. 'I want a picture,' I said. And he followed me back."

perhaps the dream is only her face—
perhaps it's a fan of silver lace—

Romy takes picture after picture of Apple. The first time, she places an elaborate beaded headdress on her and wraps her body in an imported piano scarf. She ties one wrist with a thin rainbow of ribbons.

The next time, Apple is dressed in Chinese silk pajamas. The next time, an old opera gown of silk indigo and so much sparkling paste jewelry on the dress, at her throat, circling her arms, on her hands and in her hair, that she looks like the sky and stars. After that, naked under a fur throw.

Apple models with enthusiasm. She often appears to take pleasure in almost everything. It is her general willingness coupled with her natural privacy and lack of judgment that draw people to her. Later, they will speak of her beauty; she is not strictly beautiful, she is simply lit from within.

Each time, Romy paints the pictures with color. She tries using color film with glass plates and dyes, but she can't create the saturation of color she envisions. So she keeps begging Apple to model for her and experimenting.

Tea Bisset sends a white Egyptian cotton shirt for Augustine, along with a pair of platinum cuff links fashioned like tiny dragons with sapphire eyes. For Romy there is an evening dress of pale sage crushed-velvet. And, naturally, an invitation for dinner at her villa. Tea is, by nature, a generous woman, but Romy doesn't trust her.

"She's up to something," says Romy.

Augustine replies angrily, "You two women are making me crazy! Enough, Romy."

Romy says quietly, "If your life is so hard, Augustine, why don't you try being me for a while?"

"What the hell is that supposed to mean?"

"Try being the person who just happens to be with the person everyone really wants. Sometimes it's like I'm not even in the room."

Augustine's voice rises. "You think I don't know what that feels like? You think I have no idea what it's like to be invisible? Christ, Romy, how long have you been with me?" He takes a deep breath. "I like that I am respected for what I do. I like having people call me, and I like getting recognition for my work. But sometimes I still have to be a little nice to folks when I don't feel like being nice."

Romy is unmoved. "Yeah, but Augustine, when your work, or your patrons get to you, or you're tired, at least you have something to complain about. Something to worry about. You have something."

He is not in a conciliatory mood and stalks from the room.

The crushed-velvet dress fits Romy's body as if it were made for her. Decked out in Tea's splendid clothes, Augustine and Romy have to stop and stare at each other.

"You're so beautiful," says Augustine. For a moment he feels breathless.

"So are you," says Romy.

They have not really made up since their fight, and there remains a free floating tension. It is made worse by having to go to dinner at Tea Bisset's house. Romy so infrequently goes with Augustine anymore, and she is convinced that Tea has designs on Augustine. For a while she joked with Augustine about it, but with moments of trouble within their own previously happy home, it is less humorous to her now.

Tea has never liked Romy, and the only reason Romy can think of is because she is beloved by Augustine, who very much interests Tea. Tea has never had to work, and as with many people who inherit their wealth, she lives with a certain liveliness and self-indulgence. Entertainment comes easily to people like Tea because they seek to be entertained.

Almost everyone loves Tea, but Romy is not among their number. Augustine, as well, enjoys Tea's company, but he always sees her as more of a patron than a friend, and this engenders a certain distance on his part. Perhaps it is this friendly inaccessibility that so draws Tea.

*      *      *

When they come in the front door, Romy's eye is caught by a pair of shadows toward the back of the house. One shadow leans into the other, and a hand comes up, touching the other shadow's hair. The shadows merge into a deep kiss. Then part. Romy recognizes Apple's walk.

Romy hands her coat to the waiting butler, apologizing for having to be asked twice.

It's a small dinner this evening, a dozen people including Romy, Augustine, Leland and Lena Grandin, Apple Norris, and Tea. Tea's husband is not anywhere to be found, but no one seems to mind. Lee has told Tea to divorce him anyway on the grounds that he is "too common for her."

"Since we are still missing a couple of guests, why don't we have cocktails in the back," says Tea. All the guests happily follow their hostess to the glittering hall of mirrors. "Look," says Tea, turning around and around before the many mirrors, "we have become a gala." The guests are reflected and multiplied, every movement infinitely copied in the glass.

"That dress fits you very well, Romy," says Tea. A roomful of Romys in pale sage crushed-velvet dresses slightly preen.

"I want to thank you," says Romy. "It was so thoughtful."

"I can see why Augustine married you," continues Tea. Then Tea walks over and threads her arm through his. "I'll just have to catch you next time around."

"What makes you think there will be one?" asks Lee, smiling.

"Oh, honey, there's always a next time around," says

Tea, kissing Augustine's cheek with a lingering kiss that leaves a full imprint of her lips. Augustine smiles hesitantly, then politely disengages himself from Tea. He tells Romy, I'll be right back.

At the makeshift bar that has been set up in the hall, Tea pours herself some champagne. Romy crosses the hall to stand beside her. She says, "I don't know what I have ever done to you."

Tea looks at her. "Walk with me for a minute," and then to her guests, as she and Romy leave, "Enjoy yourselves. We'll be right back."

"What have I done?" asks Romy again as they break from the rest of the guests.

"It's not what you've done," says Tea, "it's what you have."

"But you can have whatever, even whoever, you want," says Romy.

"That's true. But you have Augustine. And you have your work. I've seen your pictures; Augustine has shown them to me." Romy tries to imagine Augustine showing her pictures to Tea. "It's not too deep, Romy. I'm jealous. I'm rich and I'm jealous. I have a good time, of course, but I don't have a passion. Even my mother, god bless her, had a passion. You have love and passion, and that makes me envious." She continues, "How can I say this? Because your bent is artistic—like so many people I gather around myself—you, good or bad, live inside yourself. Someone like me, I need to be entertained." She pauses. "I can see the ongoing need for company is foreign to you."

Romy starts to tell her that because she hasn't been able to do anything for so long, she might be more understanding than Tea can imagine. Instead she says,

"But the people around you are more successful than I am. Why me?"

Tea shrugs her shoulders. "I agree. Why you? I have no answer. And, you know, it's not even personal, as far as that goes. A reminder that jealousy is not a rational state."

Tea steers them back to the hall of mirrors. For one split second Romy is linked to Tea Bisset, and she to her. Theirs is not a joining of friends, but that equally rare attachment to someone it is a pleasure to dislike.

"Miss Bisset," says Romy before they come into the lights of the wonderful glass room, "you can't have him."

Tea says, "You're probably right. But it's possible you can't have him either." Tea is not looking at Romy, or at Augustine, rather; her gaze has settled on a newcomer. Romy gasps; standing at the other end of the room is a young woman, of unusual beauty, wearing a dress identical to Romy's; the same pale sage crushed-velvet. It is as if Romy's reflection has broken free of the confines of the mirrors to join the party.

At the same moment, Romy sees this woman in the twin velvet dress throw herself at Augustine, overwhelming him with her kisses.

"Two weeks ago I was at a party when I met Tea"—she smiles at Tea—"and we got to talking, and I had seen pictures by Augustine Marks, so I asked if she knew Augustine, since she seems to know everyone, and she said yes. We talked about Augustine, and she asked me to come tonight, gave me this pretty dress, so here I am." Polly tucks a wisp of hair behind her ear, her gaze connecting with Augustine's.

Lee is saying that Polly must come to one of his parties. His arm is resting on the back of Apple's chair; Lena sits on his other side.

"I had no idea that Augustine was married," says Polly, everyone hanging on her every word for the express reason of wanting to stare at her gorgeous face and figure. "Tea didn't mention it." Then flirtatiously to Augustine, "I can't believe I lost you." More smiles. More eye contact.

Romy can't think straight. Augustine mentioned Polly once, a very long time ago. What he said was, "I thought I loved her," then said it wasn't love after all because there was no generosity in it. There are times when she and Augustine are dangerously harmonized, when Romy knows what he feels and he knows what she feels; tonight he is embarrassingly (for him) happy to see Polly. The more he tries to act nonchalant, the more he gives himself away.

"Are you staying in Harlem for a while?" asks Lee.

"For a while," says Polly.

It occurs to Romy that she has experienced jealousy twice in relation to Augustine: once over Gill at the movie studio, and now, this evening. The first time it was over nothing; this time it's over something, and one feeling is indistinguishable from the other.

Of the range of emotions, jealousy is the one that Romy can least handle, because it makes her life desperately unbalanced, unstable, and closed. Everything is filtered through this horrible haze; she feels unfit to be with other people. It has been in her life infrequently and dispatched quickly.

As she lies there in bed at Tea's villa, beside sleeping Augustine, she realizes that Tea and she are alike when it comes to jealousy: Tea is correct when she identifies

Romy's life as internal, which is why Romy handles a situation like this as privately as possible. Unlike Tea, and her external life, who seeks to share everything with everyone.

The matching green dresses, worn by Polly and Romy, allowed a little informal comparison; but mostly they were just for entertainment.

Getting through the weekend is difficult, even though Polly feigns indifference. Which almost makes it worse. Even though Augustine is affectionate, Romy cannot shake the image of him as a man standing alone and far, far away.

More and more, Romy thinks Augustine is happy, cheerful but remote. He is kind to her, as always, and in some ways more attentive than he has been in a long time. He is with her, she thinks, without being completely *present.*

When she asks the reason for his preoccupied state, he merely says, "I didn't realize I was," then tries harder to mask it.

They run into Polly from time to time. Currently, she is in the chorus line at one of the glamorous Harlem clubs that allows Negroes inside only to work. Her dancing is not very good, but her beauty makes up for it. A little modeling comes her way; her name is linked with a boxing hero; she shows up at parties.

Romy always senses something passing between Augustine and Polly when she is with them. When she mentions this to Augustine, he counters by saying, "Don't you know I love you?" But he doesn't deny it.

She doesn't doubt that Augustine loves her; once she told Augustine that they were fated, as if they had no choice but to spend this life together. He said he didn't believe in fate and destiny, that it frightened him to think he was living a life without control, even if it was a good life. He added that he was sometimes afraid that one lifetime with her won't be enough.

"Enough for what?" she asked.

"Just to be with you," he said. Then buried his face in her neck as he held her.

Romy notices two kinds of artists: those who flaunt their outsider lives, showing the world, through their sexual situations, their choice of stimulants, their attire, their living arrangements, exactly who they are and who they never want to be. Then, there are the other artists, the quiet ones who don't appear all that different from their conventional neighbors but who, inside, are indistinguishable from the first group, their flamboyant brethren.

For example, Romy and Augustine do not announce the particulars of their living arrangement, which does not and will not include marriage. Nor does Romy make a big deal out of telling Augustine that if he wants to photograph Polly for an ad he has been asked to do, he should go ahead.

"This won't upset you?" he asks.

"It's fine," she says. "I'm not living my parents' life."

And she wasn't lying; it was fine.

The ad comes out great, and Polly is asked to do another. The more Romy sees Polly, the lovelier she thinks she is, and the less jealous she is of her. Augustine loves Romy, she knows that is unshakable, but Polly has nothing to do with love.

One day Romy comes home to find two used teacups in the sink. Her impulse is to smash them together; instead she rinses them carefully and puts them away.

the loss
of the dream
leaves nothing
the same.

A photograph sits on the table in the studio. It is a nude of Polly, her knees pulled up to her chin, her arms circling her knees. She poses before a painted backdrop of a fireplace, with a painted stairway in the back. Augustine has lit the picture giving the illusion of firelight falling on her face and body. The expression on Polly's face is neither inviting nor chaste; it is contemplative. Her thoughts seem random and consuming.

It is the look on Polly's face, not the fact of her nakedness, that gets to Romy.

Augustine comes into the studio, says, "What do you think?"

"It's a wonderful picture," she says. Tears threaten. "We started out as partners, you know. We weren't going to be like everyone else."

"I know," says Augustine, thinking, *somehow I have ended up with everything.*

Tears slowly slide down her face. "I'm sorry," she says. "I did say you could be friends with her."

Augustine looks away. "I'm not sure I want to be friends." This admission feels to Romy like a blow to the body. He says, "Oh God, what am I doing?" This is more to himself than to her, his expression as downhearted as Romy's.

They say nothing more, and when Romy packs her beautiful suitcase and tells him she is setting sail for France, he does not try to stop her.

# A Bridge of Biographies

### *James McNeill Whistler*

Though he was born in Lowell, Massachusetts, in 1834, he often identified his point of origin as the American South. He said, "I shall be born where I want and I do not choose to be born in Lowell."

He left the United States for Paris in 1855, eventually settling in England, where he developed an uneasy relationship with his new home. There was such a wild volley of rejection between the artist and the English that Whistler refused to allow his pictures to be hung in an English museum.

Yet he stayed on.

It was an American collector named Freer, in the country Whistler abandoned, who so loved Whistler's work that he purchased it with the offer to lend it to the artist on request. As if the owner of a picture is borrowing it and nothing more. And eventually it was Freer who shipped Whistler's phantasmagoric blue peacock room from England to America; not a single canvas but the entire dining room of the very wealthy, disappointed, angry patron who originally commissioned it. Freer's home, with works of art at every turn, was described as a "dream of beauty."

Freer said, "Many consider art a luxury, that is, they are blind to the fact that in its highest form it is really a necessity."

Back to England, where Whistler gave the world the *Nocturnes* ("like a breath on the surface of a pane of glass"). He painted "tone poems," symphonies of color, paintings with names like *Harmony in Brown; Mother of Pearl and Silver; Rose et Gris; A Red Note; Arrangement in Blue and Silver; Symphony in Green and Violet; Variations in Violet and Grey; Green and Pearl; Blue and Opal; Arrangement in Pink, Red and Purple; Harmony in Crimson and Brown; Arrangement in Black No. 5*; with subtitles like *A Felt Hat, The Andalusian, Genevieve Mallarmé, The Great Sea. Symphony in White No. 2* is a painting of the mother of his child.

Even the shimmering blue room that Freer had shipped across the Atlantic in all its wild extravagance (and its two peacocks fighting over pieces of gold) was called *The Story of the Room.*

*Harmony in Blue and Gold (The Little Blue Girl)* is a picture of Whistler's wife, Beatrice, as she stands naked, a scarf obscuring her hair. Her facial features are indistinct and blurred from the numerous applications of paint layered upon her bright face. The effect is strange, troubling, distracted. He loved her deeply, and his grief (for she died young) was so profound that he could not call upon his gifts to properly portray the shape of her eyes or the curve of her cheek.

On the other hand, the subject of *Symphony in White No. 2,* the mother of his child, his discarded mistress, is as recognizable as a photograph.

In England, Whistler himself was painted more than one hundred times.

In England, Whistler painted Mary Cassatt's sister-in-law, Lois. When Mary saw the result, the lack of animation in Lois's face, she wrote to her of Whistler, "He does not talk to his sitters."

***Mary Cassatt***

Mary did not paint her own sister-in-law because she harbored a quiet irritation, a dislike for Lois. The feeling was mutual. Mary and Lois were like upper-class bookends of their time: Lois the socialite and rather grand keeper of the rather grand house, Mary the funded bohemian with eyes for Europe.

Mary lived abroad as a child and returned as a young woman to live in France. Another warning to beware the desires we inadvertently pass on to our children.

It's possible, for all their trips to Europe and interest in art, that the Cassatts would have preferred Mary to be a little more like Lois, who was prominent in Philadelphia social circles, had power and money, a husband and four children. Maybe the willingness to paint pictures and say no thank you to wife and motherhood is as unsettling to the American population as a decision to enter a convent is to nonbelievers. And how else to explain the animosity of Lois, who had everything, toward Mary; or, in larger terms, America's near refusal to support art and artists at all? What do they do all day, anyway?

* * *

Mary once said of France: "Give me France—women do not have to fight for recognition here, if they do serious work." (Maybe it is not only artists in America who feel thwarted.)

Mary once said of Degas: "The only man I know whose judgment would be a help to me artistically."

Mary once said of Matisse, whose work she saw at the Steins' apartment (although later in life she would deny ever having visited the Steins' apartment): "He could not master Impressionism so he decided to achieve fame through notoriety."

Mary once made one or two anti-Semitic remarks regarding the Steins. This is a distressing thing to know about the rebellious woman who painted the relationship between mother and child (a relationship she herself was never to experience) with such an understanding and affecting love.

***Gertrude Stein***

Stein famously wrote *The Autobiography of Alice B. Toklas* about herself. (What writer does not write about herself?)

Gertrude Stein said that it bothered her that in America, the home—*I am an American and my hometown is Paris*—she abandoned many, many years before, and making the famous remark of the city of her childhood, *there is no there there*—that people were more interested in her than in her work, even though it was her work that made people aware of her, so shouldn't they be more interested in her work than in her? She said, "This is one of the things one has to worry about in America, and later I learned a lot more about that."

She lived with Miss Toklas, who was often relegated to

cooking and keeping company with the wives and consorts of the men who frequented their Saturday night salons. For example, Miss Toklas found Picasso's Fernande uninteresting with her talk of "hats & perfume" ("A hat should provoke some witticism from the man on the street or it is not a success"). Poor Alice.

When Miss Toklas saw Picasso's picture of Miss Stein she said that she liked it, and Picasso replied, "Everyone says she does not look like that but it doesn't make any difference, she will." Years later, when Gertrude had died, leaving Miss Toklas wrecked by sorrow, Picasso came by to say good-bye to the portrait, which was being shipped to the Metropolitan Museum. Miss Toklas said, "It was another parting and completely undid me."

***Paul Bowles***

Paul Bowles, young protégé of Aaron Copland, found himself, in the course of his travels, in Paris. There Bowles met Miss Stein, who said he was "delightful and sensible in the summer but neither delightful or sensible in the winter" and so should set sail for Morocco, which he eventually did, along with his wife, writer Jane Bowles ("Paul and I are so incompatible that we should be in a *museum*").

He is probably most famous for writing *The Sheltering Sky,* which in turn made Jane more famous as the model for the character of Kit Moresby than for her own work.

In 1950 Bowles wrote of "the sinuous Estelle, a half-Chinese, half-Negro prostitute who 'walked like a rope unwinding.'"

He made his home in the International Zone, a place best known for its unquestioning permissiveness. Who would want to return home after keeping house in a piece of the world called the International Zone? Seeming to be everywhere and nowhere all at once. With your taste for all pleasures tripping lightly toward the illicit and the exotic.

*Ernest Hemingway*

Perhaps the best-known American expatriate, he wrote one of the best lines ever written regarding the bottomless nature of the loss of love. It was an event that occurred during his years in Paris but had little to do with the expatriate experience and everything to do with the inner landscape of his own heart, where, it is said, home resides. Hemingway had begun an affair and was poised to leave his wife, and when he watched her as she stood on a train platform with their young son, he thought to himself, *I wish I had died before I loved anyone but you.*

He was a friend to Miss Stein and, she claimed, her student; she said she "taught him how to write." They eventually parted company, not in dispute over who found what writing style first (he insisted he did), but because he once overheard Miss Stein cajoling an angry or petulant Miss Toklas with the word *pussycat,* or some such thing, and the whole scene ran counter to his famous Code.

Here are three women known to Hemingway during his sojourn in Paris:

Sylvia Beach, another American, owned a bookstore and lending library in Paris called Shakespeare & Co. and was, in general, a good friend to writers. She published *Ulysses,* written by an Irish expatriate, when no one else would. Anaïs Nin said that Miss Beach was an artist because she had an artist's soul. The notion that being an artist is possessing a specific sensibility and not necessarily limited to the act of creation is a fine idea. Hemingway always spoke well of Sylvia Beach, never falling out with her, even though her choice of lovers was not that different from Miss Stein's.

Hemingway wrote the introduction to Kiki de Montparnasse's memoirs, saying, among other things, that Kiki was "wonderful to look at" and that she defined and ruled Montparnasse during the 1920s in the same way that Queen Victoria defined and ruled nineteenth-century England.

And one warm Paris night, he said, he danced at Le Jockey Club with Josephine Baker, who wore nothing but a fur coat and had "legs of paradise."

### *Josephine Baker*

American dancer with La Revue Nègre (1925). Janet Flanner described Miss Baker's entrance that first night: She was nude with the exception of a pink flamingo feather "between her limbs," and a "giant" carried her upside down upon his shoulders, and when he set her down "she stood, like his magnificent, discarded burden, in an instant of complete silence."

### *Isadora Duncan*

A dancer who, like Miss Stein, was from the Bay Area, Duncan said that her prenatal life consisted of her mother's "great agony of spirit and her tragic situation" and that her mother could only consume "iced oysters and iced champagne"; this, Isadora believed, was the genesis of her life as a dancer.

"Under the influence of books, [Isadora] planned to

leave San Francisco and go abroad." Isadora is buried in Père Lachaise cemetery in Paris.

*Richard Wright*

A writer. Buried in Père Lachaise as well.

He wrote in his journal, before any of his trips to Paris, that he felt the need to leave, to locate "some out of the way spot where one could claim one's own soul."

In the course of his first stay in France he was asked about the "black problem" in America, and he replied that there is no black problem in the United States, but a white problem. Then he returned, unwillingly, to America before turning around and leaving for good.

It was difficult getting out of America the first time, in 1946. The U.S. Government did not want to give this Negro Liberal Ex-Communist the papers to go. And it wasn't as if they wanted to celebrate him at home. With the help and friendship of Gertrude Stein, he received an invitation from the French Government, which the U.S. Government could not refuse. And Richard Wright and his wife and their daughter sailed for France.

It is said that when Gertrude Stein died in 1946, Richard Wright became the most well known expatriate writer in Paris.

He drove an American car, an Oldsmobile, through the streets of postwar Paris, turning the heads of the citizens, and he didn't know whether to feel "proud or ashamed. I'm ashamed most of the time."

Before he left America, he met James Baldwin, who wasn't James Baldwin yet, but Richard Wright was already Richard Wright, so the thrill of the meeting belonged to Baldwin.

There is a controversy surrounding Wright's death. He was not old; there were suspicious circumstances. However, the official report simply states that his heart gave out.

### *James Baldwin*

"I did not go to Paris, I left New York."

He quarreled in person and in print with Richard Wright, a writer he admired. No one knows the whole story; Baldwin said they remained in touch throughout Wright's life. They had strong disagreements regarding literature, though they seemed to be following a similar path, en route to a similar destination and arguing like a married couple about the best way to get there.

From *Notes of a Native Son: A Question of Identity:*

> Hidden, in the heart of the confusion he [the student] encounters here is that which he came so blindly seeking: The terms on which he is related to his country, and to the world. . . . The truth about [the American past] is not that it is too brief, or too superficial, but only that we, having turned our faces so resolutely away from it, having never demanded from it what it has to give. It is this demand which the American student in Paris is forced, at length, to make, for he has otherwise no identity, no reason for being here, nothing to sustain him here. From the vantage point of Europe he discovers his own country.

Within his work can be found America, and love, and jazz.

# Book Four: Paris

## 1927–1929

ROMY IS DRESSING FOR AN EVENT THAT WILL ONE DAY BE called the Last Ball of Paris, but for now is merely another costume dance at the Tiger Bar, located on the corner of Boulevard du Montparnasse and rue Campagne Premiere. It is a rather small, shabby establishment with a long wooden bar, tables and chairs, and a makeshift dance floor. Paintings of jungle animals cover the walls, courtesy of numerous penniless artists (though the Tiger Bar is quite affordable), of varied talent. Since space is so limited, parts of the animals have been worn away, rubbed off by patrons tilting their chairs, or leaning against the walls.

Her costume consists of green leggings and a tunic of deep blue velvet. The tunic laces up the front and sides, and the velvet is a little battered, worn down to nothing in some places. Romy purchased it at a flea market, along with the voluminous white shirt she wears beneath the tunic. The brocade jacket, trimmed with rabbit fur, is a castoff from a theater that specializes in Shakespeare. She wants to finish the outfit with a pair of delicate slippers she found but instead wears her sensible boots, which she needs to get through the February snow.

Romy has attended a handful of these dances during her two years in Paris. When she left America, she also left some of her own celebrations behind: her birthday (no one knew her here); Augustine's birthday; the anniversary of the day they came to Harlem. Christmas went unacknowledged because the first one without Augustine was the first one without Augustine. There was no Fourth of July. No Thanksgiving. And she was too new to France to participate in their holidays. So these artists' parties became the events that Romy used to mark the passing of the months. It is now 1929.

The Renaissance costume was a chance find at the open market, yet the moment Romy saw it, she understood its near perfection. It would have been entirely perfect had it been a Renaissance dress. Romy very much wants to look her best because tonight, at what will one day be called the Last Ball of Paris, she is anticipating the arrival of Augustine.

She is met at the corner by her friends Eve and Lionette, who are already complaining of the light snow and chill of the evening. Under their coats they are wearing practically nothing. Fortunately, the three women are not far from the club.

As they walk along the boulevard, Romy listens to Eve and Lionette's conversation, comprehending bits and pieces of it. Despite nearly two years in Paris, Romy's French is very poor. Lionette accuses her of being "too

American, expecting the world to conform to you. Even I know some English."

It is strange to be someplace where you cannot do something as ordinary as eavesdrop on a random conversation. She did not realize that these free floating comments, exclamations, opinions, and so forth were so intrinsic to her everyday life. Without knowing how long she planned to stay, she didn't make much of an effort.

Romy has always had a sense of misplacement. The conventional home of her youth was foreign to her, as was the university she attended with its airless classrooms. The first glimmer of life as she knew it, deep inside herself, was the weird, rushed world of the movie studio. When she lived in Harlem with Augustine, the day-to-day cultural life was not innate to her. In a large sense, she drifted away from being white yet did not completely understand what it was to be black.

Now she is living in Paris, lost in the complexities of language and navigating by landmarks because she has trouble remembering all but the most common street names. When someone asks her directions, she often ends up walking with them part or all the way to their destination because she cannot explain herself.

With each place—Pasadena to Harlem to Paris—she has felt more and more at ease. Not necessarily as if she belongs; that is something else altogether—but comfortable. She can trace it this way: Pasadena was externally familiar but internally foreign; Harlem was culturally foreign (she is not black) and culturally familiar (she is American); and France is overtly foreign (another country, another language). Yet, the more unfamiliar her surroundings become, the more herself she feels, because her outside is now in line with her inside. To put it another way, she has a clear, evident reason to feel outside.

In being so obviously a foreigner, she begins to relax.

Plus, she likes the artists of Montparnasse. As Kiki de Montparnasse once said, "Montparnasse is the land of liberty. . . . As for the middle-class citizens who happen to pass through, they do not know what it's about and are frightened out of their wits and do not stay any longer than they have to."

The middle class frightens Romy. It is how she grew up and what she left.

"What does *un violon d'Ingres* mean?" asks Romy of her friends.

Eve and Lionette say something to each other in French, disagreeing on the exact translation versus the meaning of the phrase. "It means women as a hobby," says Lionette.

"It means a passion," says Eve.

Romy lives on rue Delambre, near the boulevard Raspail. It is a narrow building, with a narrow, steep stairway that curls up five floors; Romy's flat is on the fifth floor. She doesn't mind the climb, and her rooms look out over the street, directly at other fifth floors. Every day she sees cats in windows or carefully walking out on the minuscule wrought-iron balconies.

She wishes they would come visit her; they make her nostalgic for her cats; which makes her ache for Augustine.

When she arrived she sent him a letter asking him not to contact her; what she said was, "I can't take it."

On the rue Delambre, Romy has one good-sized room and, through a wide arch, a second, extremely small room. The arch is hung with beautiful old silk curtains, which she keeps closed during the day but ties back at night, to reduce the claustrophobic quality of the little room that serves as a bedroom. The toilet, which she shares with the other inhabitants of her floor, is down the hall.

Eve and Lionette are immediately greeted by Masunaka, one of the hosts of tonight's ball. The other host is his wife, Suki, who is dressed in the sparkling costume of a circus bareback rider and standing across the room under a gathering of painted elephants.

Masunaka says a cursory, distracted hello to Lionette and Romy; all his attention is reserved for Eve. After she removes her coat, he grabs her hand, lovingly holding it behind her back so no one can see. Even though his affair with her is not really a secret, it is not yet, out of respect for Suki, openly discussed.

"I've missed you since Marseilles," he tells her.

Eve laughs and nuzzles his neck, the paste tiara on her head almost catching on one of his gold earrings.

Masunaka wears a flower-print dress, a scarf, stockings, and low-heeled satin slippers. He frequently dresses in women's clothing at these parties, though the gold earrings are not part of the costume. His usual attire is eccentric: wildly patterned overalls, gray velvet suits, gorgeous Japanese kimonos, so that he often appears to be in disguise.

Ten years ago, when Suki first laid eyes on Masunaka, she became utterly enamored of him. Two days after that, when Suki had persuaded a common acquaintance to introduce them, Masunaka likewise thought that Suki was the moon and stars. Her given name was Suzanne, but he shortened it to Suki.

"Most men settle for changing the last name," she said, flattered by his interest.

Masunaka was already a fairly successful painter, and once he rid himself of his mistress, he was all Suki's.

Their life was abundant in love and material goods; of all the artists around Montparnasse, Suki and Masunaka had a house and a car. They were generous and extravagant.

Now Masunaka is in love with Eve, so much so that when he and Suki took a trip to Saint-Tropez, he sent train tickets to Eve and Lionette, begging Eve to meet him in a hotel in Marseilles, where he had reserved two rooms. Though he was gone for five days, Suki knew nothing.

Lionette has left Masunaka and Eve to the shadowy corner of the club and made her way to the bar. All the guests greet her with a glance or a tossed kiss or the call of her name, and Romy knows it will not be long before Lionette clears out a section of the small dance floor and begins to sing and move. The songs are dirty but sung with such sweetness, Lionette could be a one-girl choir. She will show her breasts and raise her skirts and probably have nothing on underneath. And the crowd will respond with appreciation and respect. There is no one who charms strangers and friends as effortlessly as Lionette.

Romy spies Robert at a back table and pushes her way through the thickening crowd. She still has not developed a taste for wine and prefers reefer. Once she tried absinthe, and as she lay recovering the next day (or maybe it was two days) she thought of something Ernest Hemingway said about Pernod, which is that if you are going down, it'll get you there faster.

Of cocaine, morphine, and laudanum, all she would say is that she enjoyed it all a little too much and so stayed clear. She was close enough to certain people here to see what the excesses of drugs and drink can do to you. Smoking seemed to suit her.

The group seated at Robert's table smelled of perspiration, perfume, and smoke. The girl to the right of him is his latest conquest. She doesn't speak English and Robert doesn't speak Polish, and he exclaims, "Best affair I ever had! Love of my life!" Romy does not sit down; instead she leans in to Robert and asks if she can please borrow his pipe.

"No need," he says loudly. "I came prepared for this party." Reaching into his jacket pocket he pulls out three slightly bent marijuana cigarettes. "For you, my dear," he says, tucking them into her shirt.

Romy met Robert on one of the *terrasses* of Montparnasse, where she sat alone and wrecked over Augustine, and angry too, but mostly wrecked. Robert came along and asked if she would like some company. His French was not even close to being French; it was more like a parody of French.

"You're American," she said.

"Don't tell anyone," he said.

"I don't think I have to." The effort to be social was already exhausting her. "Besides," she said, "who would I tell?"

He was of medium height, good-looking and unaware of that fact, making him all the more attractive. Romy judged him to be a few years younger than she.

"How about a café crème?" he asked.

"Oh, so you think all Americans have money, do you?"

He smiled, and she smiled back, and they each had a coffee.

"I have to tell you," Robert said, "when I do talk to the American girls here, I never get the adventurous ones that you hear so much about. I always seem to end up with the ones who Come to Paris To Forget."

"You're saying my sadness is not unique?"

"Sorry. I thought you knew."

It was a perfect spring day, and all the tables were full. In many ways, before Robert sat down, Romy had been happy to be alone and watching the activity of the street.

"You should keep an eye on that fellow there," she said, pointing to a young man clowning around with the passersby. The man would find a couple, arm in arm, then, tapping one half of the couple on the arm (usually the woman) he would trade places with her so that her escort would be strolling the boulevard, talking and walking with the strange young man. He wandered into restaurants and cafés and down the street with a series of unaware men so sure of their girl they seldom needed to look over at her.

This, of course, entertained the *terrasse*-sitters no end. The reaction of the men, once they discovered they had been fooled, ranged from those who enjoyed the joke to those who threatened violence. The young man ended each performance with a hand extending to receive change.

"The problem is money," Robert says. "I have the most wonderful studio, on rue Campagne Premiere, where I live and work. Central heating, electricity, toilet, walls of windows." His voice trails off.

"What if someone shared it with you?" asks Romy.

"I don't want to live with anyone. Not all the time, anyway."

"What if I shared the studio but lived somewhere

else?" She has long admired the building he is describing. It's wonderful. It's also close to her place.

"What do you mean?"

"We'll divide the time. Put your things to one side before I arrive, and I'll move my things before I go."

Robert thinks about her offer.

"I do live there," he reminds her.

"When you are not working or sleeping, do you stay inside?"

"No," he says.

"Why let it stand empty? I need somewhere to work."

"Let me think about this," he says.

"Of course," she says, "but if you agree, you must never encroach on my time. Ever. My time is my time."

"This might work," he says.

...............................

"Sit with us, Madame Romy." The man catches her hand as she passes his table on her way to the bar and pulls her into the chair beside him. He takes the lit marijuana cigarette from her other hand and inhales deeply. "This is very nice."

His name is Ben, and he is an American writer with recent substantial success, here and at home. He calls her Madame Romy because at a dinner party in the atelier of two well-known women he drunkenly insisted Romy tell his fortune. At first she declined, but because Ben was drunk and rude and overbearing to everyone that evening, she eventually said, "You will get your heart's desire."

And when his novel was so popular even he couldn't quite believe it, he sought her out, choosing, she thought, to disregard the complexity of such a prediction. "I didn't forget you," is what he said.

None of this is making him happy, and though he doesn't acknowledge this discontent, it is evident to those around him. He has become arrogant and exacting; he allows no opposition; he is beginning to believe his own myth and forget his old friends. Part of the problem is the set of unrealistic expectations he has for his formerly acceptable friends; part of it is his new friends; part of it is his pursuit of women who are not his wife.

After Ben demands that Romy sit beside him, he promptly begins to ignore her. This is because his interest in women is either sexual or maternal (generally not at the same time, and not in the same woman), though his interest in Romy is neither. Men are those he seeks out as equals, as friends. The reputation of Ben's wife is that of a classically long suffering woman. Romy scarcely knows her, so it may or may not be true, but Romy knows Ben and his relations with women and draws her own conclusions.

It is a saving grace that Ben allows her to be a part of the group at the table without being expected to participate. As a matter of fact, one of the blessings of Ben is that he is the next best thing to being alone. She can sit and smoke quietly, pleasantly stoned, and let her mind wander, and observe the entrance to the Tiger Bar.

..............................

Some of the time spent in the studio Romy shared with Robert was useless time, that is, she could get nothing done. She decided upon her arrival in Paris that she would try painting again and give up photography. She is crazy for color (the gray of the Paris winter makes her hunger for more) and thinks if she cannot find it one way, then perhaps she should try another.

For many hours, many days, she stared at the prepared canvas tacked to the wall, trying to adjust to the awkwardness of the materials. It was as if she had a working knowledge of the language of art but was hopelessly unfamiliar with the variety of dialects.

In another studio in the building was another American, a photographer who had enough work to need an assistant. When she asked Robert about him he said, "I've heard that the women he works with are frequently the women he sleeps with. Model, assistant, mistress. That sort of thing."

Romy continued to freeze up when it came to painting. One day she simply threw everything into a wastebasket and walked determinedly upstairs to the photographer's studio.

A single sentence was lettered in small, perfect script on the door: I WOULD PHOTOGRAPH AN IDEA RATHER THAN AN OBJECT, AND A DREAM RATHER THAN AN IDEA. MAN RAY. Below that: TIN TYPE.

Before she could knock, the door flew open and a young woman, clearly in a rush and mumbling to herself in French, pushed past her. Romy hesitated in the doorway, the door still flung wide, and called out, "Hello?"

"One minute," came a voice from upstairs. "I will be down directly."

She remained stationary in the hallway, until the voice asked, "Are you standing outside? Come in, please, and close the door."

Obeying the commands of the disembodied voice was like an inversion of Beauty's visit to the castle of the Beast, the invisible servants satisfying all her wishes.

The photographer's studio was very different from Perfect Fish. It too contained a number of objects, but the overall effect was of a space more modern, sleek and spare. There were miniature wooden artist's figures arranged in various stages of copulation; mirrors; shards of glass and smooth metal shapes; metronomes with eyes affixed here and there; a plaster torso; sculptures of found objects reassembled inviting new interpretations; highly polished wooden spheres; lengths of twine; there were paintings and ribbons of movie film. And, of course, photographs.

Robert had told her that this man was a member of the surrealists, and when she asked Robert the meaning of *surrealist* he said that he wasn't quite sure but the artists either paint *from* their subconscious, as if in a trance state, or they tried to paint things to *resemble* their subconscious. He also understood that they could be quite austere in their personal habits.

Oh, was all Romy said.

The photographer came down the stairs, neatly dressed in a suit and tie; his shoes were black and white leather. "Can I help you?" he asked politely.

"Yes," said Romy. "I worked for eight years in a photography studio at home, and took pictures before that, and I want to work with you."

"I don't know if I can pay you, or pay you very much." He paused. "I do most of my work myself."

"I've worked with someone else before. That is, I do nice printing." She took a deep breath. "I need access to a darkroom. I want to work with a camera; I have my own ideas."

He sat down on the bottom step. The humor and intensity in his gaze were compelling. Romy stopped herself from laying her hand on her chest to quiet her heart. What she felt, she knew absolutely, had little to do with love.

"What is your name?" he asked.

"Romy March."

"Okay," he said. "Let's see how it goes."

She thanked him and asked what she should call him. "You can call me Tin," he said. His name (not his real name, apparently) was almost embarrassing for her to say aloud because she was afraid she would fall into a laughing fit. Romy told herself if she didn't have to use his entire name, she'd be all right.

As Romy's eyes remain fixed on the door, she sees Tin enter the bar dressed in women's clothing, like Masunaka (who looks at Eve as if he would like to consume her). Romy giggles from the pot and from the observation that Tin looks quite nice in his skirt and sweater. He is a very slender man but very masculine. Though his work explores, among other things, androgyny and homosexuality, there is nothing sexually ambiguous in his appearance or personality; something Romy thinks he sometimes regrets.

He catches Romy's eye, then looks away. She sighs and thinks how hard it is for everyone just to be happy for a while.

..............................

Romy continued to rent studio space from Robert, who is her friend. When Romy was especially lonely, it was often Robert who came to her rescue. Her life was made up of tiny routines; she liked this sense of the mundane counterbalancing all that she doesn't quite understand in this new home of hers. And sharing the space with Robert was one of her routines; one of the things that made her feel connected to another person.

In their good friend manner, they slept together once. It was uneventful, but they liked each other so much that they slept together a second time, just to be sure. Thankfully, they still liked each other.

In spite of all that, Romy was unyielding in her condition that Robert not cross over into her studio time.

"I don't see why you are so hard on that point," he complained.

"I have my reasons," she replied.

Then, one day, she went to the studio and heard noises from within. In one way, she was happy Robert was there because it released her from the drudgery of her work. This painting business was a struggle. In another way, she thought he was taking advantage of her by violating their arrangement.

A young woman with jet black hair and exotically set blue eyes (maybe Slavic? Asian? Siberian?), with a long, slim neck and small, short-fingered hands that rested in her lap. Her feet too were small, though not delicate. Though she was seated, her torso appeared a little long for her body. Her legs, however, were beautiful. All in all, the look of the woman was arresting, and Robert, in the throes of painting her portrait, seemed captivated by her.

Was she some new girl? The most commonplace relationship of all, Romy discovered in her brief sojourn in Paris, was that of the model/lover adored by the model lover.

Romy said nothing and left.

Shortly after that, Suki and Romy were going to Suki's house after a particularly good lunch, on a particularly sweltering summer day, when who should emerge from Masunaka's studio but the same beautiful Slavic/Asian/Siberian girl.

Not long after that, sitting on the *terrasse* at Rotonde was the girl. This time she was accompanied by Max Vien, one of the surrealist painters.

Similarly, the girl showed up with many of the known painters, sculptors, and even Tin, in Montparnasse. Picasso, Léger, Man Ray, Foujita, Derain, the list went on. Everyone was committing her image to canvas, wood, metal, marble, plaster, and film. Yet no one seemed to know anything substantial about her.

All of these events took place in a remarkably short time.

"Come with me to Martha's," said Robert.

Romy loved going to Martha and Cory's atelier; they had the most wonderful collection of pictures and an equally wonderful collection of people: painters and writers mostly, accompanied by their assorted mistresses and wives, sometimes both, though frankly that arrangement was frowned upon by Martha and Cory. It was at Martha and Cory's that Romy told Ben's future.

Martha and Cory were American but had been here before and gone through the war, so it was easy to forget that they had not lived in Paris all their lives. Martha talked endlessly with the men, while Cory was in charge of the food and the various women.

While Romy enjoyed listening to Martha hold forth, a privilege accorded Romy since she was an artist of sorts and often had no man of her own, she secretly preferred the brilliance of Cory. And the food was always very good.

When Martha and Cory extended the invitations for that night's dinner, they informed their guests that they had something special planned. They asked everyone to arrive at precisely the same time; not an easy task for the same reason it was not simple to gather everyone together that day Augustine took the group portrait at the rooming house.

The collective *aaahhh* when the guests walked into the atelier was audible. On every wall hung the portraits of Feodora (the Slavic/Asian/Siberian girl); in each corner, the few sculptures. The many interpretations of the radiant, mysterious Feodora turned the salon into the most marvelous prism. The artists looked at the paintings, drawings, and sculptures, then they looked at one another, then back to the paintings. One of the mistresses whispered, "Who *is* she?" And a torrent of answers followed: She is an heiress, she is a girl of the streets, she is an actress, she is the runaway wife of a tyrant, she is an ex-spy, she is an adventurer, she is the youngest Romanov Grand Duchess, miraculously spared, now grown and incognito. Regardless, her personal magnetism came through in all of the works.

Cory announced dinner, and everyone sat down in their assigned places. "How odd," thought Romy, because normally the placement of dinner guests wasn't quite so exact.

The food, as to be expected, was excellent. The wine ran out, and they had to send for more. No one seemed to want to leave the table; instead they sat and ate and drank, and when there was nothing more to eat, they drank some more.

As usual, Romy's single glass of wine lasted all evening, but she had smoked a bit of weed, and it was not long before she caught on to the arrangement of the myriad images of Feodora: Martha and Cory had seated each artist directly across from his own work.

She began laughing, and every time someone mentioned what a marvelous party this was, Romy would catch the eye of Martha or Cory (who knew she knew) and burst into fresh laughter.

Nobody wanted to leave such a fine dinner party, and in the end Martha and Cory practically had to shove everyone out the door. For months people spoke of the night. And Laroux ended up publishing a book of the portraits.

Six months after the dinner a man who claimed he was Feodora's manager showed up at the place where the portraits were stored and said he had been sent to pick them up. Neither he nor the art nor Feodora were ever seen or heard from again.

..............................

The smoke gets thicker, the voices louder, and Lionette, Romy knows, is gearing up to sing. Against the far wall, painted with faded, prowling jungle cats, Romy thinks she can see Sal and Adair Angell, though she is not certain for they are not known for appearing at public gatherings, preferring their own, close company.

They are inclined toward each other, Adair leaning her back against wild cats, ferns, and palm trees, talking, as Sal places his hand above her head, facing her, listening. They seem entranced by their own conversation. Their movements are slight, intimate, and sexual. Laughter passes between them. A touch. They act as if they are newly acquainted. The party only seems to interest them as a topic for commentary, not as something to join, but as something to observe before passing again into their own conversation.

The first time Romy saw Sal and Adair was on one of the *terrasses*. They were sitting at a table, drinking espresso and reading. Even when absorbed in their separate activities they gave the distinct impression of being tightly connected.

"You know," said Robert, when he saw Romy staring at them, "Sal is known for painting his wife. Just his wife."

"Don't most of the men here paint the women they love?" asked Romy.

"Of course," said Robert, "but only for as long as the love lasts. Sometimes it lasts as long as one picture. But with Sal, it is always Adair."

Romy thought about Sal, glanced at them again. "Do you think it's love, or something less savory?"

"It's love. If you get to know them, you'll know it's love."

Romy did get to know them, marveling at the way they could spend their daily lives apart and still give the impression of uninterrupted togetherness.

Sal painted, Adair socialized. There were days she visited friends, rode her bicycle, toured and complimented them on their gardens, played with their children. She read books and wandered the city's galleries and museums. Sal and Adair had no children of their own and now, in their early fifties, were past that time.

Sal referred to his pictures of Adair as hand-painted dream photographs.

Sometimes Adair sat for Sal, but mostly he painted her from memory.

Adair and Romy walked in the woods one brisk, autumn afternoon. The forest at Fontainebleau always reminded Romy of Robin Hood; she would not be surprised in the least to see him and his merry men flash by.

Romy said, "I always think of you and Sal together, even though you seem to spend a great part of each day alone."

"That's true," said Adair. "I even travel without him. But not for very long, and not very often."

"Then why do I always imagine you are inseparable?"

Adair shook her head. "Because even when I am not with him, I am with him. And he with me. That's just how we are."

It was easy to lose track of time when in the Angells' company because they were so entertained by each other that they entertained their guests by extension. They laughed and argued and bantered and touched. No matter how adamantly they disagreed, there was always a kindness toward each other.

Romy had to quit them finally because they reminded her daily that she was here and Augustine was there and on days like those she could not summon the energy it took to pretend she was whole.

..............................

Tin makes his way over to Romy, who still sits, ignored, next to Ben. He leans down, the garnet beads of the necklace he wears grazing her cheek, and kisses her deeply before again walking away, camouflaged by the crowd.

..............................

Tin, true to his word, loads his pictures with ideas and dreams and visions. The development itself is sometimes dream-evocative. Some of his works are more seductive or startling than others, but all of it commands your attention. It is difficult, Romy thinks, to stay uninvolved with Tin's pictures and sculptures. Even if they simply make you laugh, they get to you.

Romy no longer shared Robert's studio, since all her

time was spent with Tin. Besides, it was too difficult to pay for living and working space.

Romy left America with some money of her own. Augustine was willing to give it all to her, but she only wanted what was hers. He insisted. She said no. He made her promise that she would ask him if she found herself running short.

Since she knew she wouldn't ask, that left only her parents when her money ran low. Though she and Helen were never out of touch, it was not an easy decision to ask for funds. Particularly when Romy was unsure of her father's feelings, and knew that her parents would certainly disapprove of the life she was living.

She asked anyway. And envelopes addressed in Helen's handwriting began arriving with bank drafts inside.

Romy wondered who was actually sending her the money. She sent an impersonal note to her parents saying, *Thank you.* The reply read, *You're welcome. Lorenzo.*

She worked in the darkroom, learning a great deal from Tin, who had been a dadaist and then a surrealist, always avant-garde. While Romy admired much of his work, it was his photographs and experiments with film that she liked the best. He filmed a former mistress, nude, through fractured glass; a woman crying glass tears; he made a moving picture for the express purpose of projecting it on guests at a ball who had all dressed in white and danced upon a white floor; he made eyes out of closed eyelids, eyes out of car headlights, an arm out of a metronome.

One of Romy's favorites of Tin's pictures is a group portrait of the surrealists. In place of himself, Tin had another artist hold a mirror bearing Tin's reflection. Romy likes it for its perfection of depiction and because it reminds her of Augustine's group portrait of the artists of Harlem.

The most interesting was Tin's fashion photography. His many pictures of well-to-do women, not necessarily professional models, in designer gowns.

"Why do you like these so much?" Tin asked Romy.

"They mean something to me," she said.

"What?"

"Something beyond the pictures. They connect with my own work."

"Which is?"

"I'm still figuring that out," she said. One thing Romy did know was that her pictures would be drenched in color. She didn't mention anything more.

The culmination, it seemed to Romy, of all his lanky, rich women in their extravagant clothes was a series Tin took of mannequins clothed in identical gowns. The progression of a real woman modeling her wealth to an imitation woman modeling wealth fascinated Romy. In one picture, a mannequin who looked as if she were walking up a rather elegant staircase always made the viewer look twice because its posture made it appear so real.

At Select one night, Tin's enraged mistress, the one who had rushed past Romy the first time she went to Tin's studio, ran up to their table, throwing Tin's dinner of Welsh rarebit down the front of his clothes. She slapped him and cursed him in rapid French. Romy couldn't make out the words, but the gist was unmistakable. Then she flew out of the café, shoving other diners' meals off *their* tables. *Just because,* guessed Romy.

"What was that all about?" asked Romy.

"You," said Tin.

And that was how Romy became Tin's lover, in addition to being his assistant.

The spurned mistress wrote on Tin's studio door, in English: HERE LIVES AN AMERICAIN HORE. Romy wondered if the mistress meant Romy or Tin. Romy still kept her own apartment and only slept at Tin's on occasion.

One morning found the mistress curled like a kitten on the landing outside the vandalized studio door.

Romy was walking down the boulevard du Montparnasse when the mistress appeared suddenly and said, "He doesn't really love anyone, you know."

Romy answered, "It makes no difference. I'm not sure I do either," which caused the mistress to burst into tears. Romy was at a loss, the girl seemed so forlorn and defeated. Without thinking, Romy took her in her arms, and to her surprise, the woman allowed it.

And that is how Lionette and Romy became friends.

..............................

Five women have just come to join the increasingly crowded party in the Tiger Bar. Romy waves to the tallest, most striking of the group, an American heiress from Chicago, and squeezes through the throng to see them. Romy greets them with a combination of American and European-style kisses.

"Is there anywhere left to sit?" asks the tall woman in a very loud voice.

"I don't know," says Romy. "You're tall, you tell me."

The tall woman, who goes by her surname, Trent, motions to her companions to follow her. At an exceptionally little table, where they do not all fit but find enough chairs nonetheless, the women seat themselves. Their costumes range from Apache dancer to sailor, except for Martha, dressed as she is always dressed, who says, "I came as my public persona."

"What are you doing here?" asks Romy, unaccustomed to seeing these women at these sorts of masquerade dances.

"We were bored and wanted to see how the other half lives," says Trent.

"I just go along with Trent," says Louise, who is as hopelessly enamored with Trent as Trent is with the perpetual pursuit of new girls. They have been together ten rocky years already.

The other two women, who are without inheritance or trust funds, struggle with their bookstores and small presses and their own writing. One is an American with an American bookstore, the other French with a French bookstore. They have been together longer than Trent and her long-suffering companion Louise. The rumor is, the French woman, Marie, is leaving the American woman, Sarah, for a Spanish expatriate named Montserrat.

"It's so loud, you can hardly talk here," complains Martha, who loves to talk, while Cory looks around and smiles.

"Of course it is," says Romy, "that's the point, I think. Maybe this will help," says Romy, lighting one of the marijuana cigarettes given to her by Robert.

"Perfect," says Trent, taking a drag.

"I haven't seen Daisy around lately," says Romy to Trent. "Or Talia, for that matter."

Trent holds in the smoke as she hands off the joint to Louise, who inhales with about as much enthusiasm as she exhibits for being here tonight. As Trent exhales she says, "They are in the country, with Talia's brother and his family."

"What are they doing there?" asks Romy.

"Driving them all to drink, I believe," says Trent.

Talia and Daisy have recently found religion of the mystical, eastern sort based on the beliefs of a woman named Madame Blavatsky. At least, Romy thinks there is some eastern philosophy involved. She's a little unclear, despite being buttonholed by Daisy and Talia on separate occasions.

"They wear quite a lot of blue these days," adds Martha. "Something to do with blue being a higher consciousness."

All the women order more wine. "To a higher consciousness," Trent says, and everyone laughs.

Romy happened upon the "girls," as they are often called, through an invitation to Martha and Cory's home, which came by virtue of her knowing Robert. It was Trent who found Romy and insisted she attend one of Trent's Thursday Afternoons.

Because Trent was an American and Romy a recent arrival and knowing practically no one, she accepted.

At Trent's townhouse was a roomful of women: tall and short, stunning and plain, masculine and feminine and androgynous, friendly and shy, laughing and troubled and carefree and, primarily, English and American, with a French woman or two. All of them were artists of one sort or another: painters, poets, novelists, journalists, one photographer, and Sarah, the owner of the American bookstore, who was not technically an artist but who everyone agreed owned the soul of an artist.

It was Sarah who said to Romy, "Watch out for Trent."

"What do you mean?" asked Romy as she saw Trent move from woman to woman, laughing, flirting, touching.

"She's rather fickle," said Sarah.

Romy didn't know if this was a good time to bring it up or not, but she had no interest in Trent or any of the women here. Not in that regard.

Growing up, Romy had not known many men or women who preferred their own sex. Actually, she realized later, she might not have known them because they did not make themselves known. During her years with Augustine, starting with the movie studio, Romy understood that some people simply desired their own, or both, sexes. Romy didn't care why, instead accepting it as another of life's facts.

That the Garden of Joy, where Romy and Augustine went dancing in Harlem, was a "mixed club" suited them immediately; they liked the idea of being mixed. Augustine, with Romy assisting, took pictures of some of the drag balls of Harlem: the women in suits, the men dressed like tango dancers, society girls, and mannequins.

Almost all the male writers and artists in the rooming house where Apple lived were homosexual. ("Can you imagine me living in a house full of men otherwise?" Apple asked.)

Augustine and Romy never cared. Romy still doesn't care. Her "tolerance" has always sprung from the same impulse: her own desire to be left alone.

"That is not to say that Trent is a bad person," continued Sarah. "She is always the first to help out."

Louise joined Sarah and Romy. "Are you new to Paris?" asked Louise.

"A couple of months," said Romy.

"How do you like it?"

How could Romy explain that she was too brokenhearted, too numb to know if she liked anything or not? "It's fine," she said.

Louise turned to Sarah. "I thought Juno was supposed to be here today," she said.

"She can't. I mean, you know she's divorcing, and he has to say that she deserted him, even though he's getting paid very well, but she has to keep out of town for a while."

"Oh," said Louise. "Too bad. She always makes me laugh."

As Romy listened to them discuss their friend, she found herself wishing Apple were there. They had each written once, but Romy could already tell there wasn't going to be much of a correspondence. Ironic, considering that Apple is a writer. Romy knew the friendship would last, regardless; when they again met, it would be as if no time had passed. Still, at that moment, she missed Apple's good humor.

"Romy's a photographer," offered Sarah.

"Then you must meet Martha," Louise said, and Romy started to say she already had, but Louise continued speaking without listening, turning to Sarah. "I hear that Martha and Tin Type—I'm sorry, I laugh every time I say that man's name: Tin Type, Tin Type," laughs Louise. "It's well that he is so good at what he does—anyway, Martha and Tin Type are working on the French government to bring some American photographer over."

"Why can't he come over on his own?" asked Sarah.

Louise turned up her palms. "I think he's a Communist with a passport problem or some such thing. Ask Martha."

By the time Romy got around to seeing Martha, she forgot to ask. Likewise by the time she met Tin.

* * *

And so Romy went to Thursday Afternoons at Trent's about every other month or so. The primary difference she could see between the male expatriate artists and the female expatriate artists was this: The men seemed to want to sleep around and drink, and the women wanted to be free of the expectations of marriage and children. They also liked sleeping around and drinking, but that seemed a by-product of their new lives. The men could just as easily stay home and drink and fool around and get away with it. The women left lives so much more proscribed and contained.

Of course, everyone wanted to make art. And love. And art. And love. And art.

..............................

"Nice costume," says Trent to Romy, rubbing some of the fur of the worn Renaissance tunic between her fingers, "who are you, Michelangelo's lover?"

"Nice getup yourself. Czar?" asks Romy.

"Cossack," says Trent.

Just then, Lionette sings the final notes of one of her most requested songs, and everyone looks up to see her stripped to her slip, now fallen to her waist.

"Goodness," says Trent, "I'm more familiar with that girl's breasts than my own."

Tin comes to Trent's table, intercepting the joint, inhaling, and passing it back into the circle.

"Dance with me, Romy," he says.

She smiles, excuses herself to be pressed against the other dancers on the unbearably tiny dance floor. No one is really dancing because there is no room to move.

Romy and Tin are not dancing so much as they are pushed close together and swaying a bit.

"I miss you," he begins.

"You see me all the time," says Romy, reminding him that she still works with him.

"But I don't have your attention," he says.

"I know, I know," says Romy, thinking, *Look, you knew what we would be from the start. It's not my fault that you've convinced yourself you're in love.* Despite Lionette's statement when Tin and Romy first started up, Tin does love Romy. Whereas Lionette modeled for Tin, Romy has spent more darkroom time with him, as well as doing a little modeling. "You're trying to change everything," says Romy.

"I don't like to think of you with other men," says Tin.

"Then don't think of it," says Romy.

"Believe me, it's not deliberate."

That's the problem of the colony of artists; they are a small group who seldom go outside their tribe. The life of a secret under these circumstances is brief. Love and loss seem equally distributed in general, though this does not hold true on a personal level, where some people appear always to get more than their share of one or the other.

Big love, as Romy calls it, is for her now so threaded with melancholy that she cannot feel one without the other and so chooses to feel nothing at all.

"Look over at Lucie and Piet," says Tin. "They are leaving each other and they don't even know it."

Lucie and Piet have been together for three years and have a daughter. Like so many of the couples here, they have a rather relaxed marriage, each allowed to find anything but love on the side. Lately, Piet is said to be recklessly courting a girl of seventeen whom he can't forget, and Lucie is seeking comfort with an ex-lover who never got over her, and all this causes Romy to wonder, if you explode the rules and smash the boundaries, how do you know when you have gone too far?

Is there such a thing as too far? How do you know when a thing is beyond repair? How do you know who you love? What is the meaning of loyalty? Is your life together enhanced by the outside affair, or finally brought to ruin? How do you build your life when everything is permitted? Are the things you engage in action or reaction?

Romy, once she began sleeping with Tin, did not say no to the other offers she received. Not that there were that many, or that it occurred that often, but she allowed herself to say yes to whatever she felt like, whenever she felt like it.

"Do you have to see Augustine?" asks Tin.

"You brought him to Paris," says Romy.

"Don't remind me," says Tin.

It was only a few months ago that, traveling the short distance between Tin's studio and her apartment, Romy saw Augustine. The late autumn day was clear and mild. She stepped quickly along the boulevard Raspail, noticing and not noticing her surroundings, having taken this route too many times to count, when she noticed a figure coming toward her. He was looking around in the same way she used to look around when she first came to Paris, that is to say, in his preoccupation, he didn't notice her.

But the sight of him made Romy walk faster. Seeing him thrilled her, rendering her excited and anxious; his face brought on a rush of recent memories: She remembers herself restless and sleepless; sobbing wildly in an empty room; awakening in the morning, feeling normal for the few seconds it took to come fully awake, when her loss threatened to level her. She thinks of her inattention toward Tin. Augustine's face filled her with excitement and love and a sense of arrival and home. She quickened her pace.

Romy was almost running when Augustine finally saw her. And when they come together and she stood before him, he spoke her name over and over, as she slid her hands into his jacket, holding him tightly, thinking, *I'll never let you go.*

When they pulled apart, Romy had said nothing except his name. They said each other's names because they were the only words for the past eighteen months that they had no reason to use. Within this peculiar conversation that consisted solely of their repeated names, Romy slipped her hand into his and turned Augustine around, leading him in the opposite direction of his destination (What is his destination? She doesn't know. She doesn't care), and took him to her apartment.

On the way, Augustine interrupted their progress to kiss her. It was the sort of private kiss that often evoked joy, judgment, discomfort, or envy in observing strangers. It wasn't until much later, after everything, that Romy realized she had received her wish to wander down a street, together, a black man and a white woman, in full view of an indifferent world.

In her bed, Augustine reached out for the Renaissance box that sat on the table. He picked it up, set it on his bare chest, then opened it to see if it still contained the bit of marble. When he closed it and returned it to its former position by the bed, all Augustine said was, *You.*

* * *

"What are you doing here?" asked Romy, as they sat on the *terrasse* of Coupole, drinking a café and wine, respectively. They are lazy and rumpled from the last few hours in Romy's room.

"A couple of American expatriates each wrote to me, complimenting me on my pictures. They said they would be 'interested in my point of view' on the artist community in Montparnasse. I wrote back and told them I would love nothing more than to come and see Paris, that as a black American I had heard stories that life in Paris was nothing like home. And, of course, the life-of-the-artist business.

"I looked into leaving, but I was having difficulty." He touches her hair. "Some problem due to photographs I had taken of 'known Communists.' It was decided that I was 'sympathetic,' politically speaking."

"But we didn't join anything," said Romy, puzzled, even though they had come close more than once. Then, with some hesitation, she said, "After I left—"

"No," he said emphatically, "but I guess we are judged by the company we keep," Augustine said. "When I wrote again, they—the Americans here—contacted the French government, urging them to bring me over. Citing my work"—he corrected himself—"our work in Harlem. All those pictures of everybody and everything. They said we need a similar record, please come."

"What are their names?" asked Romy. "The Americans."

"One is Martha—"

And before he can finish his sentence, Romy remembered that first Thursday Afternoon at Trent's ("I hear Martha and Tin Type are working on the French Government to bring some American photographer over here," said Louise), said Romy, finishing his sentence, "—Tin Type."

"Why, yes," said Augustine, surprised. "As a matter of fact, I was on my way to his studio when I found you. How do you know him?" He holds the end of her cashmere scarf between his fingers with absentminded affection. His joy is palpable. She senses his thought: *What made me think that a life without you was a life?*

Romy hesitates. She doesn't want to reveal the nature of her relationship with Tin. She doesn't want to say, You know, I work with him, and pose for him, and, oh, yes, I sleep with him. She certainly doesn't want to talk about how Tin loves her and his unexpected possessiveness.

Does Tin know that she was once Augustine's "wife"? Impossible; she has never said anything about Augustine.

"It's good that you're here." She almost starts laughing at their situation; the one man who wants her with no man, save himself, working for months to bring over the love of her life. And the love of her life, eagerly anticipating meeting the man who is giving him a chance for an international artistic reputation (at most) and a great experience (at least), never dreaming that this agent of dreams is the love of *his* life's lover.

"Well," said Romy as she stood on a corner with Augustine. He held Romy's face in his hands. His touch was so familiar that Romy felt no distinction between her face and his hands; they felt of a piece. "What, Augustine?" She smiled. "What's on your mind?"

He looked as if he was about to speak, then, "Nothing, baby."

She thought about Tin, and how she was to meet him tonight and work with him tomorrow, and how it was all over for her. Even so, she did not mention Tin to him and was relieved when Augustine didn't ask to stay. So relieved that she didn't think it through until much, much later.

"Must be fate," she said, finally.

"Must be, baby."

"How can I reach you?" she asked, not really wanting to know too much. Augustine thought for a moment. "Well," he said, "my situation is temporary—"

"I know," said Romy, "the Tiger Bar. I'll leave you a note." And she explained where it is located.

"Okay," he said. Then, in a rush, "I want to see you."

"Then see me tomorrow," she said. "So, good-bye."

"Tomorrow," he said. And kissed her as if there were no tomorrow.

Augustine left her a message that read: *Have you ever been to Nice?*

She left one back: *When do we leave?*

He wrote: *Meet me at the train station Tuesday.*

And when she told Tin she was going away for a while, he was silent, then said, "Everyone is going to the South of France these days. Well, have fun. I'll see you when you return. I'll think of you."

It was as if Augustine and Romy had never been apart. They ended up near Cap d'Antibes, in a modest hotel, up a flight of concrete steps from the street. They walked through a beautiful, lush courtyard before entering the lobby. They took a room in the back of the hotel, at ground level, with its own bathroom.

Each day they walked the two blocks to the beach, where they sunbathed, read, napped, and almost always touched each other. Never in their lives could they recall being so purely happy. "So this is bliss," Augustine said to her one evening as they strolled along the sand.

"I never want to go back," Romy said. "I never want to be anywhere you are not." At night, she would half awaken, wondering who was beside her and where Augustine was, then wake fully to the realization that this person was Augustine, and his presence would overwhelm her.

Perhaps the most surprising, pleasing aspect of their time together was the immediate fall into routine. The days on the sand, the walks at night, the swapping of books and stories, their old betting habits. They laughed a great deal together, Augustine endlessly kidding her about the quality and breadth of her French. He pretended to be teaching her the language. It cracked her up. Everything about them seemed the same and not the same.

*Your face,* he would think when he glanced at Romy, *God, how I missed your face. And your voice.* "Talk to me," he would sometimes say suddenly, in the middle of a long silence. If he was playing with her, "Oh, *sing* to me," a reminder of the Christmas concert. It was seeing her again that made him fully understand the profundity of her absence.

Two weeks went by, and neither made a move to leave. "Who would miss us?" they asked each other, both knowing the answer but not wanting to tell the other.

After another week, Romy said, carefully, reluctantly, "Augustine, I have something in Paris I promised to do. I'm going to have to think about going back." She explained about Trent and her Thursday Afternoons and the "girls" and how one of them was writing a book based on the group, with easily decipherable pseudonyms. Romy promised to take a series of photographs. Still, no mention of Tin.

Augustine laughed. "Just out of curiosity, why would the author change the names of the women who will appear in *photographs*? Won't they be recognized?"

Romy laughed too. "Of course. It isn't exactly surrealism, but a nod; the real women in the pictures, combined with the fake names that everyone can figure out; as if we are ourselves and characters based on ourselves all at once."

"This idea, these photographs, the way you describe them, sound like you," said Augustine.

"It is my group portrait of the artists in their time and place. Like you with the artists of the rooming house at home. Like Tin with the surrealists. This one is mine."

"Do you know that this is the first time in our lives that you have been you and I have been me in a public place? We are living public lives," said Augustine with amazement in his voice. "So this is what it feels like." He held Romy aloft, above the advance and recession of the waves on the beach. "Should we write and tell them the world didn't go to hell over it?"

"I think they want the world to go to hell," said Romy.

He lost his footing, and they both fell into the blue of the beautiful blue sea.

When Romy came back to Paris, Tin said, "I should have mentioned it sooner, but I am not an exclusive sort." Romy nodded. He continued, "For example, I have someone else," but he said it with a shadow of doubt, as if he were testing his own words.

"I understand," said Romy.

"It doesn't mean we're over," he said.

"I understand," said Romy again.

Romy touched him between the shoulder blades. His body was so fragile, so strong. "Thank you," she said softly, grateful for being offered an exit.

Romy didn't see Augustine for a few days. She was busy with the women at Trent's house. There was some argument regarding the content of the book. The women wanted to know what the author, Claire, was saying about them.

Claire said, "I'm part of this group. On the inside. What do you think I'm saying? I need to write what I need to write; either you agree to that condition or that's it."

So the women, torn between ego and caution, finally favored ego. They wanted to see what Claire would make of them; those who had been Claire's lovers wanted to see how she thought of them; those who hoped to get close to Claire wanted to see if they stood a chance. And the rest liked the idea that their artist group would be set down for posterity.

"What about our families?" asked one woman.

Claire laughed. "Since most of us don't live around our families, and since this book may never make it out of the country, I don't think we really have to worry. But more than that, our families will believe what they want to believe. I really wouldn't give it a thought."

Romy loved working on the project. These women who had come so far, who made their art, who loved whom they chose, who were honorable, who were sometimes difficult, who ran from family and societal expectation, who were better than saints for all their flaws, were well worth committing to paper.

What had begun with Romy's mother, Helen, in her evening gown in the kitchen and garden progressed through Apple in Harlem, and the techniques she learned from Tin and his high society ladies was now being partially realized with this book. It still wasn't the thing Romy was dreaming of, but she knew she was closing in on whatever it was she was trying to do.

When Romy told Tin about the project he said, "I'm jealous," but congratulated her just the same.

They grew cautious and careful around each other. There was kindness in their polite distance. They were suddenly shy about sleeping together, and neither made a move. Regardless of this shift, Tin didn't break up with Romy. More mystifying, Romy didn't leave Tin.

He also said, "We've been invited to dinner at Martha and Cory's."

"I love seeing Martha and Cory," said Romy.

A few days before the dinner, Romy went to buy a new dress. She was extraordinarily happy these days: She had Augustine (though he was busy) and this book (though she was busy), and Paris turned lovemagical. For a moment, Romy thought, astonished, *why, I have everything!*

Then, turning a corner on an unfamiliar street, Romy's hand went to her throat. A woman and a man, far ahead of her, walked arm in arm. The woman threw her head back, laughing, and when she did so, Romy could've sworn it was Polly.

*Of course, it's not Polly,* she scolded herself. *Polly's at home.* Then, asked herself, *How the hell do I know where Polly is?* The man definitely wasn't Augustine, but that meant nothing. In an attempt to calm herself, Romy believed that the woman at the end of the street wasn't Polly, that Romy only imagined Polly because she was preoccupied with thoughts of Augustine. That was the connection. *She can't be here.* Romy started pulling distractedly at her collar, as her heart skipped and raced. *She can't be here.* She had the sensation of free falling without any hope of salvation.

There was no way to reach Augustine, to ask him all the questions she had avoided asking. And to answer similar questions that he had not asked as well.

To Augustine:
Where are you staying in Paris?
How long will you be here?
What ever became of you and Polly?

To Romy:
Are you in love?

They sent messages to each other by way of the Tiger Bar. Even with the common association of Tin, they seldom ran into each other. Romy didn't know how much Tin knew of her private life. Augustine's name did not come up.

Empty-handed, anxious from what she thought she had seen, Romy sat and smoked a cigarette in the Luxembourg Gardens. The day was cool and brisk and threatening snow. When she finished, she made her way to Tin's, pulled him onto the bed, and there they stayed until the winter moon rose.

* * *

It was when Cory opened the door, before Romy saw who the other guests were, that she knew. It was unpleasant but not a surprise to see Augustine in the same room with Polly. Polly was so involved in flirting with the husband of another guest that she took no notice of Romy. But Augustine caught Romy's eye the moment she entered the room.

Tin registered the look that passed between Augustine and Romy in turn, causing Augustine to take in Tin's reaction. A slow understanding of Romy and Tin crossed Augustine's face, and by this time, Polly glanced up to see Romy. Polly then looked at Augustine, as if something had finally dawned on her.

"And I thought I might not have any fun tonight," said Polly, smiling her expansive smile.

One dining arrangement at Martha and Cory's home was inflexible: artists, writers, and Martha at one end of the table; wives, mistresses, and Cory at the other. Romy usually sat in the Martha circle, since she was neither wife nor mistress. Her status as a photographer and friend "promoted" her, though Romy loved listening to Cory more than Martha.

"I'm wondering," said Polly, who sat among the women, "why Romy isn't sitting with the rest of the wives."

"Not all of us are married," said one of the women, ignored by all.

"Martha actually wants to set up a children's table," said Tin. "But that might cause confusion."

Martha gave a slight smile, the look in her eyes cold.

Romy gripped her napkin in both fists as it lay on her lap. *Augustine is married to Polly. She is one of the wives.* It had not crossed her mind until that moment that Polly might be married to Augustine. Even if they weren't married, Romy now knew, unequivocally, that Polly came to Paris with Augustine. Romy's stomach turned over; she fought the desire to bolt.

Augustine, Tin, Martha, the painter with whom Polly had been flirting, as well as two other painters were clustered together, Martha at the head, Augustine on the dividing line of men and women, and Romy across from him, beside Tin.

"How long have you lived in Paris?" Polly asked Romy.

"Two years," she answered.

"Are you going to stay?" asked Polly.

"Maybe," said Romy, and Martha interrupted, "*I* don't want her to go."

Romy smiled. Her shoot with Martha and Cory, separately and together, had gone very well. "You captured how deeply we care for each other," said Martha, "without making too much of it."

Tin fed Romy a piece of bread. "Romy would be someone to miss."

Augustine watched the bread as it traveled from Tin's fingers to Romy's mouth. Romy chewed the bread but could not swallow it without a long drink of water. Tin replenished the water in her glass from the pitcher. "Relax," he said.

The husband-painter that Polly had been flirting with asked what time Polly could come to his studio tomorrow.

"Anytime," said Polly.

"Maybe you should check with your husband," said the painter.

"She's not my wife," said Augustine quietly. He looked directly at Romy. "Polly is not my wife."

The table fell quiet.

"I was only joking," said the painter, quickly, but Polly was already out of her chair. She slowly, and with a great deal of grinding noise, dragged it over to the men's side, wedging herself between the painter who wanted to paint her and one of the other artists.

"Well," she said brightly, "I guess I'm all yours."

The wife of the painter knocked her silverware to the floor, catching the attention of no one except Romy, who then saw the embarrassed wife retrieve her fork, knife, and spoon.

"Polly and I travel together," said Augustine, his voice dull.

Polly laughed. "Is that what we do? I thought we lived together. My mistake."

"You know, Romy and I *work* together," said Tin, laughing. "I like this game. What other euphemisms can we find?"

"Roommates," said one of the wives.

"Friends," said a mistress.

Again, the comments from the women went by without remark. The food on the table grew cold from lack of interest.

"You are really quite extraordinary," said the husband-painter to Polly.

"Aren't you sweet," said Polly, draping an arm over his shoulder.

Polly was as breathtaking as ever.

Cheese and sweets scattered the table before the guests.

Romy pulled a piece of paper from her pocket and with a pen wrote: *Who are you being unfaithful to, her or me?* She folded it and handed it to Augustine.

Everyone, including Polly, quietly watched this transaction with curiosity, until Polly interrupted the silence. "Have you ever been to the South of France?" she asked Romy.

"Yes," said Romy.

"Augustine tells me it's spectacular." A hardness came into Polly's face before vanishing again into beauty. "I am so surprised that you didn't see each other. In the South of France."

Before Romy could respond, Augustine said, seemingly to no one, "I don't know. I just don't know." Then he rose, opened the door, and disappeared into the street, without a word.

As Augustine worked in Tin's studio on rue Campagne Premiere, Robert knocked on the door.

Robert and Tin greeted each other. "Come in, come in," said Tin, "disturb us, please."

"I need to talk to Augustine," he said.

Augustine glanced over at Robert. "You look familiar," he said.

He began, "Romy asked me to tell you—"

"Oh, *Robert,*" said Augustine, placing him.

"—that she will be at the masquerade at the Tiger Bar," said Robert.

"You've just made me sorry I let you in," said Tin.

"That's it?" asked Augustine. "That's all she said?"

Robert shrugged.

"Christ, what more is there?" said Tin, walking into the darkroom and slamming the door behind him.

Polly followed Romy to Tin's later that week. "You might as well know, I'm staying in Paris."

"Fine," said Romy.

"I'm not like you. I won't run away."

"Then don't," said Romy.

..............................

Romy frees herself from Tin's embrace, pushing her way off the dance floor. In their disguises, Tin's woman is lost in unrequited love for Romy's man.

Romy needs to be left alone. The emotional course of her evening went from small anticipation to excitement to anxiety and now defeat. Tin, she knows, is not a comfort; he is too overcome by angry love for her. She is not expansive enough to excuse him this evening, for she can barely stand her own disappointed heart, let alone his.

It is almost two o'clock in the morning. The party grows wilder. Romy leans against a wall, almost lost among the gorillas, lemurs, and monkeys. Her eyes move from the door to her watch and back to the door. She is exhausted from waiting. If only she didn't experience such a deep sense of belonging with Augustine. Has she so miscalculated his attachment to her?

And just when she starts thinking about the February snow that awaits her, she looks up once more, a breaking tide of love.

For there he is.

# Book Five: Florence Revisited

1929–1930

ROMY EXPERIENCED DIFFICULTY WITH FORGIVENESS. AUGUStine understood that she could be in love with him and have a hard time forgiving and forgetting; the same way that Romy knew Augustine could adore her and still take up with Polly and work with Tin. In this way, their love was unaltered and unshakable, but it wasn't their love for each other that was in question.

Love, in its pure state, divorced from our lives, might escape and remain inviolate, even as our lives might be tainted. Ideally speaking.

Following Augustine's entrance into the Tiger Bar, Romy and Augustine held an extended, exhilarated reunion. Polly and Augustine parted simultaneously, with Augustine moving into Romy's place.

Then began their good days and bad days: a picnic in the country that made them feel as if there had been no separation; the tearful fights and defeats that lasted long into the nights. It was as if they built up their love by day only to demolish it by morning.

"Why is all the effort on my part?" Romy would demand, then sob, "It's too much for me, Augustine. I thought I was strong, but I'm not. I'm not."

"I love you so much," he said softly, wanting to persuade her to forgive, to stay, to love him back. Knowing the impossibility of persuading anyone about love.

"Well," she said, "well, I don't know if I love you anymore. I might. I can't tell." Romy lifted her face to his. "I don't know if I feel anything." The numbness of her heart terrified her. She didn't want to say that seeing him again brought rapture and misery, and in order to steel herself against the unhappiness of their past, she had to forfeit the sweetness of the present as well. "You must understand," she said, "I want to love you, but for now there is nothing."

Montparnasse is small and interconnected, and Polly was everywhere: in cafés and clubs, on canvas, at parties, everywhere. Polly was not so much a rival as a reminder of disconsolate times, and Romy was more vulnerable to her presence than she had anticipated. Polly reduced the scope of Romy's Paris to nothing.

Having Polly in Paris was intolerable. One of Polly's admirable qualities, thought Augustine, was her manner of moving on without a backward glance. Since Augustine was over her almost before it began, he could manage the proximity of Polly. Such was his indifference toward her. What he could not manage were Romy's fluctuating moods in regard to Polly. For that reason alone, he sometimes wished her gone.

* * *

More than half a year had passed when Augustine came home one day to see Romy's beautiful suitcase by the door and the bedside table bare of the Renaissance box. As his heart crashed, he thought, I will plead, if that's what it takes, I will cajole, promise, if that's what it takes, walk her through the best of our years, if that's what it takes.

Romy spoke before he could engage in any of these strategies, and said, "Please let me go." Her request ran counter to every impulse he had, and she held and kissed him in a way that made him momentarily trick himself into believing that she would stay. But in the end again he let her go, even as he began the involuntary vigil of awaiting her return.

Romy travels aimlessly, to sort herself out, until she reaches Florence.

*What shall she do about Augustine?*

(Her beautiful suitcase bumps against her leg as she walks to her *pensione,* located off a street whose name she does not know. She navigates the city purely by landmark and memory. It does not make her uncomfortable to do so.)

Romy and Augustine have known each other eleven years. He is the only man who will ever know both her young girl self and the woman she has become. From this point on, any man she spends time with will miss the girl but see the woman.

*What shall she do about Augustine?*

(She wanders into the Piazza della Signoria, by the Palazzo Vecchio, and unexpectedly sees Michelangelo's

*David.* It quite takes her breath away. Though he is in the company of numerous other statues, Romy sees only *David.* She walks closer, confused that he has been left outside at the mercy of vandals, pigeons, and the vagaries of weather. She stands before him, amazed that the citizens of Florence casually pass him by without a second glance.)

I love him without end.

*What shall she do about Augustine?*

(She sips espresso alone and observes the passing parade of people.)

For the first time in eleven years, Romy is not living among a community of artists. Her days are not full of incessant talk of art and work. There are no jealousies to contend with: Why one artist receives the acclaim and rewards, while other, equally deserving artists scrounge for every crumb. There were those artists who lived in squalor and thought that those who did not gave nothing to their art. The issue of poverty made Romy uncomfortable, since most of the French were reeling from the war.

Some artists she has known were so bitter that all she could think was, please, God, give them something, anything, so I don't have to hear it anymore! They would drone on, why? why? why? until she wanted to say, "The universe is random! The universe is indifferent!"

There was an elderly, revered artist Romy used to see from time to time in Paris. When she sat at a café, some painter would always note her presence, followed by the comment that "she is not the best painter around." It was not uncommon for the speaker's voice to carry traces of gladness when making this pronouncement.

One day, the elderly artist heard these words, turned

to the speaker, and said, "I never said I was the best. Maybe I could have been better. But the public likes what I do, what I have done. Somehow I was in touch with my time."

Romy reminds herself of that exchange in the café when she falls prey to jealousy, those days when she feels slighted. *I can control what is on film,* she would say to herself, *that is all.* Then scold herself, *there is work to be done.*

It is envy, Romy is sure, that fuels the perpetual exchange of partners among the artists, spouses, models, writers, and such. Such criminals, trading in thefts of affection. Combined with those whose passion is for those with passion. They are such an incestuous, high-spirited, covetous crowd. Unusual for them to desire each other's work directly, so common to want what someone else might have: love, money, time.

Romy misses them terribly.

*What shall she do about Augustine?*

(She lies in her bed, with the window open. The insensible sounds of the street fill her room. She is so accustomed to not speaking the language, the mystery of their words no longer makes her lonely.)

Robert told Romy that his French mistress is pregnant. If his child is French, will that make France Robert's home as well?

As Romy walked back to her apartment, she thought about children; no one will expect that Robert give his life over to his child.

It was odd that a child was not something she and Augustine had much discussed. He came from a happy home full of children; even Romy's upbringing had been warm and loving. They liked children, and Augustine, in particular, was beloved by the children they knew. Their lives seemed to allow no space for children. And still she sometimes wanted them.

They could see, from the movie studio to Harlem to Montparnasse, there was so little left over from the parents for their offspring. Unless one parent, always the woman, Romy noticed, was not an artist. In which case, being a parent divided her from the rest of the crowd, who often behaved selfishly and impulsively except where their art was concerned. Romy thinks they lavish all their big emotions and patience on the things they write, or paint, or make, or sing, with nothing left for their family. It is not much of a life for children.

This is the problem, as Romy sees it: You need to be connected with other people, and these connections often lead to love. In contradiction, you need to be alone. If you are alone, then you are leaving your loved ones alone. If they are alone too much, they might find someone new who won't leave them alone so much.

If you are always alone, what life do you have to put into your work? And with an excess of company, when do you work?

*What shall she do about Augustine?*

(She crosses the Ponte Vecchio, this marketplace of gold with almost no glimpse of the river below.)

Can she live a life without missing him daily?

*What shall she do about Augustine?*

(There is a light rain as she wanders the Boboli Gardens. She is crying.)

This is something she once read.

## A SHORT POEM BY MICHELANGELO
c. 1545–1546

Dear to me is sleep, and even
more to be like stone,
in these days while prejudice
and shame persist;
not to see, not to feel, that is
my fervent wish—
on this account, wake me not,
oh, pray, speak softly!

Would that be life without Augustine? Wishing to sleep, to be made of stone, beyond sensation? What is the length of heartbreak?

*What shall she do about Augustine?*

(Romy heads toward the Galleria dell'Accademia.)

Briefly, this is what became of Giulietta: She continued to learn at her father's knee until she was nineteen years old, after her tenure as a spy and model, respectively, had ended. She grew to be quite beautiful and eventually caught the eye of a wealthy man who offered to keep her.

Instead, she traveled to England, where she dressed in extravagant and bohemian styles and spoke Italian-accented English, which soon (along with her beauty) attracted one or two important men. She told everyone that she was a painter, with emphases in *cassoni* and portraits.

She had two casual lovers and many commissions. Then one very profound love and a daughter. Many times she had asked Sandro to live with her, but he refused, until she told him that her man had died. More commissions, more lovers, and serious royal connections; a son came along, and by this time she had changed her name from Marcel to March. Her life was long, her work sought after and admired. Giulietta was respected and well off, privately grateful for her good fortune but publicly confident.

Sandro died around the time Giulietta met the man she would love forever. They grew very old together.

She gave her daughter the box with the curl. Never mentioning the curl.

And when she was very old, with the man she would love forever, she often thought back to her Florentine youth, her father's flying cathedral ceiling, her children when they were small, her work and how she once thought such a life would be denied her, the two quick encounters with Leonardo, her life at court, and, rarely, M.'s kiss.

*What shall she do about Augustine?*

(She enters the room at the Galleria dell'Accademia where *David* is kept.)

Here the tourists stare reverentially at *David,* the genuine *David,* not the copy in the piazza that Romy mistook for this statue before her. Something inside her connects with the beautiful, frightening, wonderful, and terrible statue, reducing her to tears. The effect of *David* is inexplicable to Romy; it is not the way she felt in the piazza, which she would classify as the usual emotional transport one feels when finally face-to-face with an admired work of art. No, this is almost breaking her heart with its mixture of longing and loss so great she is mystified.

She feels that she desperately wants something she cannot have.

It must be about Augustine.

# Book Six: America and England

1930–1945

*1.*

One month turned into two, two into three, three into four. Nothing from Romy. Then Augustine got a letter from his mother saying that Orlando had an accident, could Augustine please come home?

Prior to receiving the letter, Augustine believed he was almost indifferent on the subject of leaving or staying. With Romy gone and the request to return, he realized that his stay in Paris, as wonderful as it had been, now hinged on the reappearance of Romy.

Augustine had no idea what Romy was thinking, or intending; in fact, he had no way to reach her. Was she coming back to Paris? He did not know. Since he did not know, he could not write or leave her a note. He despaired of losing her in the world. He remembered what Romy always said about fate and translated that idea into one of faith, which led to hope.

## 2.

Romy's travels lead her here and there. She goes from Rome to Greece, where she basks in the sun and loses herself in reading about the mythic lives of the gods and goddesses. Their behavior was so perpetually vain and vengeful, the mortals constantly, unknowingly provoking them to misuse their power. Someone was always bragging about an abundance of beauty, love, or wealth, only to be punished in the end. Romy concludes that it's a good idea to treasure privately whatever you hold dear.

As Romy drifts from city to city, images of home assail her. When she first went to Paris, there was no question of visiting home. Staying abroad is like taking a stand; a lover's rejection and a way of coming into your own; who you really are. She sees this defiance, this victory, among the other expatriates, who had to leave home to find home.

And these new places feel like home. The expatriates fall in love, build lives, forge friendships, experiment with all manner of sensual experiences. They come into their elemental selves. Then, at some point, they find the unexpected: They begin to miss the other home. They turned awkward in their adopted home, unable to return to their previous home because the home they miss is not real at all, but a dream of home. Similar to the way their adopted home once existed in a dream. Hard to stay, hard to return, because of the reality and illusion of each place.

The dream home generates novels, paintings, poetry, and plays.

The place where you don't live is transformed into the dream; the place with which you cannot make peace until you have a new home. Real homes can be mundane and oppressive and make you want to run; dream homes allow you to indulge in the luxury of nostalgia. They make you wistful.

The pursuit of a dream is always the point. Some wanderers fashion lives and become true citizens of their new home, accepting that everyplace is flawed. Others explore each new location as a matter of curiosity, and still others are made restless by their dreams and, in a reverie of ideal homes and better lives, move from city to country, leaving little pieces of themselves behind.

In the aftermath of the stock market crash, Romy sends a cable to her parents. They cable back that they are fine and what is she doing in Amsterdam? Just looking, she writes, then moves on before they can write back.

She travels to Venice, Budapest, Vienna, Berlin, Barcelona, without rhyme or reason. Each place seems more heartbreaking than the last, because she misses Augustine. Things cannot be the way they once were, she decides, and that was the problem in Paris; she wanted an impossible return to the past, classically yearning for what she could not have.

## *3.*

It is in Florence that Romy realizes, in a manner mysterious to her, that she could spend her life with Augustine. In something akin to an epiphany, Romy understands she has gone about their reunion all wrong. In Paris, she desperately wanted the past altered (wanted the things that had happened to never have happened), only to understand that if that were to occur, the good part of their past might be erased as well. It would have been like the gods giving you a little too much of what you think you desire most.

And her random travels have made her long for a home. Augustine is home.

*4.*

It is a pleasure seeing his own family. Since his brothers and sister are busy with their chosen professions (pharmacist, teacher, journalist, and proprietor of *Orlando's Gift*) and children, Augustine spends a great deal of time with Suzanne and Orlando, thinking how much he likes his parents. And how wonderful it is to sit in their home of roses and palm trees that rustle with the warm breeze.

He tells his parents about Harlem and Paris. About Perfect Fish Photography and the famous people he has met, but he doesn't mention Romy. Until Orlando says, "What about your girl, Augustine?"

"Yes, where is Romy?" asks Suzanne.

He tells them everything. He tells them about Romy, confessing the lie of her race. He explains how Polly showed up, rekindling his old obsession with her ("not love," he said, and they said they understood); the need to be with her was something akin to needing the last word. No time for Romy's photography. Again stating that for all the love he bore Romy, he could not resist Polly's attention. Something about how busy he was and the natural ebb and flow of human relations.

The minute Romy was gone, he says, my life was out of my hands. Everything began to crumble into dust. And rising from the ashes, like his own personal phoenix, was Polly. Like a man momentarily lost, he accepted the earned consequences of his haste.

*   *   *

"What will you do now?" asks Suzanne.

"I'll go back to New York. Maybe open up another studio." Augustine pauses. "You know."

Suzanne leans over and adjusts the pillow under Orlando's broken leg.

"She doesn't know where I am," says Augustine. "Maybe she's been trying to find me since I left."

Suzanne says, carefully, "Honey, it's you who doesn't know where she is."

Orlando says, "Don't throw your life away, Augustine."

"It's not that easy," says Augustine, looking down.

*5.*

Romy hurries back to Paris, moving more purposefully than she has in months, only to find Augustine has gone. She cries with disbelief; she searches for a message left behind (the Tiger Bar, a mutual friend, their old apartment on rue Delambre); her thoughts scatter in disarray. Martha and Cory say he went home, then fell to the task of comforting her. ("Stay with us," they say.) For a while she thinks about sending a letter to his parents, asking them to forward it, but she cannot bring herself to do it.

Martha and Cory are having a party to celebrate the private publication of Claire's book, *Hats & Gloves.* "I imagine only women would pick up a book with such a title."

Everybody loves Romy's photographs, but there is some complaint about Claire's text. It is a satire, but even so, Claire showed clear preferences, settled old scores.

As Romy holds a copy of *Hats & Gloves,* she, for the first time, has a clear sense of her own work. In her excitement, she can hardly speak. It is so close to miraculous that one minute her pictures were abstractions in her head and the next they were realized on the page. The photographs of the women please her. In actuality, her portraits are more subtle, complex, and true than Claire's words. Romy feels a closeness to what she wants to do with her pictures. "I can do this," she says, unheard.

As she sits in Martha and Cory's atelier, looking at the pictures on the walls, listening to the women discuss their own novels, poems, and pictures, holding a book with her own photographs within its pages, Romy thinks about art and work.

This sets her to thinking about love and art and things that last. She thinks about Augustine, understanding that she does not wish to return to their old life, the life where he worked and she didn't. They live by the dual compulsions of their love and their work, unable to determine which is more important, their love and their work equally important. Her adoration continues uninterrupted, yet somehow, for them, love suffers under such an uneven arrangement.

Maybe she is wrong about fate, and love lasting.

Her response is to continue to travel. Though she always feels like a tourist and not a traveler, she can lose herself anyway. But this unquiet life cannot go on indefinitely, so when she reaches London, with its shades of steel, pewter, dove gray, and green, she decides to stay.

*6.*

The first thing Augustine does when he arrives home is to reopen Perfect Fish Photography Studio. Even though the location remains the same, he changes the name to M & M Photography Studio. It could not be Perfect Fish (nothing was perfect without Romy), and M & M stood for Marks and March, including Romy's name as wish and prayer and preparation for her return.

He airs out the flat upstairs, cleans it from top to bottom.

He goes to retrieve their two very old cats from a neighbor good enough to take them in. The slightly younger cat has died, but the other is so happy to see him she reverts into excited, kittenish behavior. When he holds her in his arms, she purrs ferociously and grazes his face and neck so many times that he is covered with hair and saliva.

It is peculiar to be home after his Paris sojourn; everything is, at once, familiar and foreign. He thinks his feeling is the result of trying to readjust to life in America. When he was in France it seemed to him that he was almost untouched by his extended visit. This disappointed him; he wanted to believe the experience of being in another place would slightly alter him. It was when he arrived in America that he felt the effects of his time in France.

He thinks this difficult transition has to do with life without Romy. Yet, he had been in Harlem without Romy before.

Then he thinks it's having gone to California to see his parents between his return from Europe and his resettling in New York. He blames this feeling of slight dislocation on the aging of his parents, that sense of constancy and flux.

It wasn't Pasadena, he decides. The town had changed somewhat in his absence, but it was still provincial and fundamentally the same. He had spent many, many more years away from Pasadena than he had from Harlem, yet Pasadena seemed the less altered of the two.

Then he realizes that what he feels is not restricted to his internal life; huge changes surrounded him. When the stock market crashed the previous year, he had been in Paris. Though he knew it was false, he initially considered this event something that happened at home, away from him. Additionally, he felt that whatever happened to the Parisians did not necessarily happen to him.

In America, Augustine was accustomed to people who worked hard to get by. It was true in Pasadena, in Harlem, and, for a time, in his own life. So a difficult economy was not something he would readily notice. Besides, it did not seem possible that America could go under. Money woes for certain citizens did not strike him as a change; hardship for the majority of Americans was something new.

Augustine has less business, was spending more and more time idle in the studio. Money that people used to spend on portraits now went for more pressing items. As for those who could afford pictures, many had their own cameras now. Never mind that they took snapshots of a lesser quality and different style, it still cut into Augustine's revenue.

The "celebrity Harlem" was shifting as well. He had some work, but not like before.

Walking the streets in the evening, past the clubs and joints and restaurants, he sees that there aren't quite as many patrons as there once were; maybe it's the tenor of the crowd that's changed. It seems these white people are caught up in a more pressing, less pleasant distraction of worry.

* * *

Apple Norris occasionally stops by, her presence a sad contrast to Romy's absence. Augustine and Apple converse in the slow workday hours or take walks around the city, sometimes marketing or cooking together. She is fine company; she's fun to talk to because she knows something about everyone, or most subjects. She has a generous laugh.

They take a train upstate for the day. It is spring, and Apple says, "I've just got to see flowers and grass and sky." The air is mild but pleasant, with all of the plants coming back to themselves. They talk about their recent dinner at Lee and Lena's, Apple making Augustine laugh with her rehashing of the evening's guests and events. Augustine thinks, is this what life was like for Romy when I was busy with my own work? Am I living Romy's previous life? He can see the attraction of these lazy days spent with Apple, the relaxed entertainment of it all. Simultaneously, he understands that to be unable to do the work you love can leave you wasted and blue.

Augustine and Apple fall into a system of work exchange: She models for him; he reads her stories and essays. They grudgingly admit to wishing for an audience for their pictures and words.

"Are you publishing anything?" he asks.

"Here and there," she says. "Not much. You know. There isn't the same kind of interest in us. Those Negrotarians must be busy elsewhere. Been a kind of falling off."

"The economy," says Augustine.

"Sure," says Apple.

Neither one wants to talk about abandonment, the withdrawal of money and support, or the withdrawal of love and companionship. Love and work. They don't want to talk about it.

It is in Harlem, with his ever-slowing business and his visits with Apple, that he realizes Romy isn't coming back, but he still cannot quite stop himself from expecting her any minute. Her absence/presence is constant; his longing for her constant. He wears himself out with wanting.

He tells Apple about the daily exhaustion of missing Romy and how he is at a point where all he desires is a release from this useless love. He quotes Rilke: *I would like to step out of my heart and go walking beneath the enormous sky.*

**7.**

With a loan from her parents, Romy opens up her own studio, in Knightsbridge, on Trelawny Road. As in New York, Romy lives upstairs. To enter the studio, one walks to the side of the house, through a door, and down five steps. Though it is set slightly below street level, it has windows and light—not too many windows, not too much light. High ceilings. She doesn't know what to call her new studio.

Not long after arriving in London, she hears about a book party for her old friend from Paris, Ben. In the interim, Ben has divorced the wife who had his child, stood by him when he was unknown, and loved him, more or less completely. Many, many years later, he will write one of the most beautiful memoirs ever written of Paris during the twenties and make one of the most beautiful confessions of love within its pages. But that is a long way off.

Ben is now even more famous than when Romy knew him and in the possession of a new wife. He will make her suffer as he did the previous wife, but in a different way. In the meantime, there is a party celebrating his newest novel and Romy is going.

"Madame Romy," calls Ben, joyfully, when he sees Romy across the room. Everyone who has been hanging on his every word turns their heads at once, in Romy's direction, making her horribly self-conscious. For the first time in her life, she wishes to be famous to justify this entrance and the crowd's attention. The guests part to let him pass, and when he gets to Romy, he hugs her tightly and for a long while. She is so moved by the hug and the memories of another time, that she finds herself responding in kind; she is genuinely glad to see him. There is a faint alcohol smell about him.

Ben looks like Ben, handsome in that robust sort of way, but a little tired. For the second time that evening, Romy feels self-conscious in regard to her own appearance. Not too much time has passed, except that she is no longer in her late twenties; she is in her early thirties. Her hands go to her hair, which is now threaded with a little gray, and as wild and wiry as ever. Even the hat she has so recently removed cannot calm it. She is still slim and small, wearing a thin, floor length, red skirt and a tweed jacket. Though she does not see it, she looks younger than her years, but more beautiful than in her youth. As if her looks are being deepened and refined.

"How are you, Ben?" asks Romy, when they pull apart, though he still grips one of her hands.

"I'm great," he says. "Look at you." There is appreciation in his eyes. Gesturing toward a wall of windows where four women stand, talking, says, "I'm writing. I'm remarried."

"Really," says Romy, not asking what happened; she has a pretty good idea of what happened.

"I left Paris. I never saw anyone anymore, just tourists. You know," he says.

"I read you were in Africa," says Romy.

"Beautiful country," he says, then launches into a vivid description of hunting lions, which Romy can hardly listen to. Same old Ben, she thinks, going on and on, regardless of her interest. His admirers surround him, person by person, and soon he, same old Ben, is holding court in that way of his; that way where he acts as if he doesn't know *why* the crowd clings to his very words, but would turn subtly cruel if they refused.

As she eases herself out of his conversational sphere, Romy laughs a little to herself that she is still happy to see him, his self-involvement unchanging and rather comforting.

She is sipping the same glass of gin with which she began the evening when she recognizes Paul Robeson. He is standing, smiling, speaking with a group of people, less in number than Ben's audience. Romy wants to say hello; Augustine photographed him more than once, but she is not sure he will remember her.

As she contemplates approaching him, he spies her, hesitates as if he believes he knows her but cannot quite place her, then waves. Romy smiles and waves back. Paul excuses himself from the people around him, and makes his way over to Romy.

"Hello, Mrs. Marks," says Paul. "I believe I know your husband, Augustine Marks? The photographer."

"I wasn't sure you'd remember me," says Romy, pleased.

"Why would you think that?" says Paul.

"Because I haven't proved to be very memorable," says Romy. She laughs. "And what are you doing here, Mr. Robeson?"

"I'm talking with some people about a play. And what about you?"

"Traveling. Well, actually, I'm somewhat settled—I opened up my own photography studio. Here." She stops. "I'm alone," is all she can say, and Paul is too polite to press her.

"Weren't you in Paris?" he asks.

"For a time," she says.

"I found Paris quite congenial."

"I loved it."

"Hmm," says Paul and Romy finally grasps what he is saying which is, *why* London and *not* Paris?

"I know," she says, "I have my reasons." No place is home, she wants to tell him. "Hey," she says, "would you mind very much if I took your picture?"

"I would be honored," he says.

They arrange a time, and she writes down directions to her studio. "It's a little tricky," she says, "not being on a main street. Wait," and proceeds to draw a crude map on the back of the paper she is giving him. That done, they find a comfortable place to sit and reminisce and benignly argue and laugh for a good part of the evening.

Romy is in her studio, sorting through the numerous props she has already acquired: rows of glass fish, and plaster busts of Caesar, Nefertiti, and Venus, and butterflies, and a clear double glass floor screen with wild flowers pressed between the panes, and a stuffed owl, and a wide array of stars: gold and silver metals, glittering stars, paper stars, painted stars on backdrops. She has all manner of costume jewelry and silk flowers and a queen's crown. Two pairs of wings: one feather, the other water silk. Tons of hats, and yards of beautiful fabrics. Strings of fanciful lights and lanterns.

Upstairs, where she lives, her rooms are spare, lacking the color and texture and *objets* of her work area. One of the reasons for choosing London was her belief that she could work with color more clearly in this gray city. Her sofa, her chairs, her desk, her lamps, her Renaissance box beside her bed, her beautiful suitcase.

There is a knock on the door and before she can open it she sees Ben, his hands cupped on either side of his face, peering in the large window by the door.

"Madame Romy," he says when she lets him in, "I've come to ask if you would take my picture."

"For any particular reason?" she asks, smiling.

"I just think it would be wonderful to have my picture taken by you," he says. "I will pay you, of course."

She says nothing, thinking that she could use the cash and it occurs to her that he must have found that out.

"When can you do it?" he asks.

"I'm very booked," she says, laughing, "so how about right now?"

The first pictures are conventional. Rich black and whites with plush shadows. Ben is pleased. The photographs have a fine elegance about them. Then she asks if he would be interested in letting her take some color pictures. "I'm working with this lab. They would be for me. No charge."

He agrees and in the pictures, wild with color, he reclines in a gold velvet armchair, wearing ultramarine trousers, and a pressed, apple green wool shirt. A red fox stole thrown, unnoticed, at his feet, as Ben sits absorbed in the book he is reading.

She poses him with a few of her props: a metal floor lamp with a purple shade, and a footstool of sky blue silk nearby, as he gazes out a window covered with a hundred butterflies. "Well, Madame," he says, "this is a bit too whimsical for me." She puts it away; agreeing that her idea did not work. She sticks to resplendent clothing and furniture and lamps and drapes.

Not long after that, Paul comes to her and she again begins with black and white. Again she takes a conventional, gorgeous picture. Again she asks if he would allow her to take a few color photos.

But when she sets up, she is hesitant. Some of her ideas, as with Ben, cannot work properly with a man. The juxtaposition of the fanciful with each man's particular masculinity falls apart. Again, she decides to give color to the picture through clothing, though she has more freedom with Paul, since he is an actor and accustomed to being in costume.

She positions him in front of a pale blue backdrop of white paper stars, in a midnight blue tuxedo.

Clothed in a robe of sharkskin silk that collects the light and changes color, he sits in the gold velvet armchair, focusing his gaze past the huge globe that is almost out of the picture; behind him are scattered tiny, sparkling musical notes.

Her favorite picture is of Paul in a suit of lights that she borrows from an opera company for the day, his red cape held casually in his hand, pooling at his feet.

* * *

The set of pictures of Ben are printed in the United States in a small magazine devoted to art, and in *Life.* There is an offer to have three of them included in a show of photographs of celebrities (Ben, a writer, has made such a crossing). The curator also asks if she has pictures of anyone else (famous, naturally) that could be included. The letter is addressed to, and the credits for the photos noted as, *Madame Romy.*

Romy is amused—she knows it is Ben's doing—and considers correcting her name, except she actually prefers it. It fits.

She writes that, yes, she does have another picture, and sends the image of Paul in the suit of lights with the red cape.

*8.*

"I have to close M & M," Augustine says to Apple. "I can't afford it and my home. I'll have to hope that people will still call me to come to them to take their pictures." It hurt him to give up his fanciful painted flats, his weird and beautiful props. He could store many things in the apartment but not everything.

It does not seem that long ago when Augustine looked at Romy's tear-stained face, thinking, *she's right, I have everything.* Now that is reduced to nothing, though it has been several years. "I'll still be able to take pictures," he says, "but without my studio and props, they won't feel like my pictures."

"I have a friend who knows a woman," says Apple, "who is old, rich, and white and has some crazy ideas and money to spend on them. My friend, Dr. Arnett, says she is looking for Negro artists for hire."

"I'm not sure I understand," says Augustine.

Apple smiles. "She thinks the Negro can unlock some primitive path to enlightenment."

"Through art?" Augustine says.

"Through art," Apple says.

"And she's wealthy?"

"Drowning in it."

Augustine says nothing.

"Look, Augustine, all I'm saying is that I'm broke. The country's in a mess, and it isn't like I've never taken cash for my labor. Do you want to go with me or not? Just to see what she's about?"

"Why not?" says Augustine, "what would I be giving up?"

Lorraine Hume Ross is old, rich, and white. When Augustine and Apple visit her palatial home on the Upper East Side, they are as highly sensitive to the impressive surroundings as she is indifferent. When they have been in the homes of people with money in the past, there was always a self-consciousness, no matter how slight, on the part of the host: a nod, a look, a comment on this painting, or that carpet; discussion of antiques or exotic travels where something precious was purchased like an ordinary souvenir. Not so with Mrs. Ross. Her family's fortune has a history so deep she acts as if she believes her life to be, well, normal.

For example, she always buys the best (clothes, furnishings, vehicle) because she doesn't fully realize that there is anything else.

Mrs. Ross sits in a massive silk upholstered chair ("Like a throne," Apple says, laughing, later). Apple and Augustine wander toward the sofa when Mrs. Ross says, "No, please, here," pointing to the two zebraskin footstools near her chair.

Apple and Augustine surreptitiously exchange a look before seating themselves. "I'm sorry," Apple apologizes as she tries to keep her short dress from riding too far up her legs.

"Dr. Arnett recommends you both for my endeavors. I trust Dr. Arnett, so I will simply tell you the conditions. I will pay you each a monthly stipend of two hundred and fifty dollars. You will have one car between you to share. I provide clothes, meals, other incidentals. I have been known to give gifts. You shall call me Godmother." She smiles. "All your projects under me will belong to me. You may not show or publish your work without my approval and permission. This is not negotiable.

"I believe in the pure, undiluted spirit of the Indian and Negro people. I am estranged from Judeo-Christian philosophy. My desire is to become the child of a more primitive god. If you are wondering how I know the innate goodness of the Indian and the Negro to be true, I shall tell you, it came to me in a vision—the first of many—upon the death of my honorable husband, Dr. Aaron H. Ross. Through your art, you will connect to your homeland of Africa and, in that connection, you will save me."

She smiles a smile of such genuine sweetness, then reaches out, taking Augustine and Apple's hands in her own. She holds them for close to a minute, her touch unexpectedly warm and sympathetic.

Augustine and Apple need the work.

*9.*

A wealthy American woman who has seen Romy's photographs of Ben calls Romy and asks to come by.

"I wanted to meet you," says the woman and introduces herself, though she needs no introduction, she and her husband are that rich. Accompanying her is a titled Englishwoman named Cornelia. Romy is struck by Cornelia's natural beauty, suddenly imagining her dressed up as Medusa. Both women are in their early thirties. "The color photos of Ben are extraordinary," says the American woman, as Romy muses on their closeness to her age and the enormous differences of their circumstances.

Romy uses a Vivex camera and a special lab that, under her direction, produces highly saturated colors. It is unlike anything Romy has seen before, and for months now there has been a low-grade excitement infusing her waking hours. For years she has been drawn to color in photographs; she has experimented and looked without understanding exactly what she was looking for. "I'll know it when I see it," she told herself in frustrated moments; she couldn't even tell Augustine what she wanted; how can one explain something that is nothing more than a vague idea?

How could she have known, for all that time, that once she had the tools, her ideas would follow? Instead, she thought it was the subject that was lacking. But when these two very well dressed, well-cared-for women wandered in, Romy's vision takes hold.

The American woman, Anne Chase, asks for a portrait.

Romy quotes a price, then asks, as she had Ben and Paul, "Would you be willing to sit for me, no charge, for something else I am working on?"

Anne smiles, flattered to be asked to have her picture taken. "Well—"

"And you, too," Romy says to Cornelia, "I could use you as well."

Cornelia looks at Anne, who looks at Cornelia, until they laugh and say, "Why not?" That's the thing about the rich, Romy thinks: Nothing stands in the way of impulse.

***The Goddess Series by Madame Romy***

*Arethusa* (Anne Chase, American, heiress): A water spirit. Green cellophane over the lens. She wears glass-green lingerie and imitation tiger lilies. Her hair alive with shiny metal bulrushes that look as if they are caught in the current of a stream. She looks down, a greenish cast to her flesh, at a passing parade of glass fish.

*Medusa* (Lady Cornelia): Green light. Her skin deathly pale, her lips painted deep purple and the lines around her unusual blue eyes smudged. On her head and circling her throat is a mass of rubber diamondback snakes. Close cropped. You cannot look away from her beautiful face.

*Europa* (Lady Anne): Amber velvet toga, her hair held up by pins. She embraces the stuffed head of a bull, adorned with flowers and grapes. The distant blue ocean in the background, barely noticeable.

*Venus* (Mrs. Marquand): Her gaze is dreamy, downcast, a giant scallop in her hair, and pearls strung from her clothing and wrists. Her gown is off-the-shoulder and pleated, and veils fall from the shell in her hair and her wrist, catching the light in their spangles.

*Helen of Troy; Hecate; Dido* (all three are duchesses): All are bathed in a light so blue it makes their white flesh appear as stone.

*Circe* (Lady Theodora): Against a cloth of teal, scarlet, gold, and white, seductive Circe, golden scallop shells and pearls hanging from her ears, bears a large, ornate cup. It looks baroque with its painted faces and swirls of green and gold. On her head is a wig of blond ringlets, fashioned to appear fake; her dress yellow and falling from her shapely form. Her attention is not on the camera.

*Andromeda* (Mrs. Bennett-Dean): Green filter, for she too is associated with water. Her green Fortuny gown draped upon her slim, captive form. It is hung with slick seaweed and seashells, her wrists imprisoned in the ropes of chains that hold her to the rock. The white light behind her gives the impression of a particularly unforgiving sun.

*Ariadne* (Lady Rowan): Silvered blue cloth is draped like a towel across her chest. A background of midnight, with four white stars. A band of blue green and pearls holds back her hair, and in her hands is a sword tangled with golden thread.

*Minerva* (Mrs. Davies): Minerva, born fully grown from the head of Zeus; keeper of the thunderbolt; goddess of war and wisdom. She stands, gun in her hands, soldier's helmet obscuring her hair, a stuffed owl stands on a pile of leather-bound books, its bright eyes staring directly into the lens. She is covered, neck, to wrist, to feet in cloth of shimmering, fragile gold.

These were some, but not all, of the goddesses. The more titled and society women sat for Romy, the more titled and society women wanted to sit for Romy.

And those she couldn't use wanted their portraits done anyway. Sometimes they brought along husbands who stood stiffly in the grand, almost comical uniforms of their stations; or their children.

Romy also took pictures of the classical plaster busts that sat in her studio, with sunglasses and exotic hats, beads and necklaces, and her butterflies and stars. They were echoes of Tin Type, but the humor had less of an edge, a little more self-deprecating. She sometimes wondered what he would say of her work.

And her collection of clocks and globes; Romy caught up in the notion of world enough and time.

### *10.*

Godmother sends Augustine and Apple into the South, "to merge with your past," she tells them. The ride down is glorious; the world in bloom and fragrant. They revel in the freedom of having their own car and their own income. They laugh and gossip and tell their life stories. They don't miss the city because the open space and lush green landscape soothes them.

Sometimes they forget the rest of the country is suffering, until they pass families living in fields or walking the roads with one or two bundles. And they travel quietly; they understand they are no longer in Harlem.

Here and there they stop in at juke joints, listen to music and dance. Apple gets them invited to a voodoo ceremony; another time they witness people handling snakes and talking in tongues. They listen to stories, true and folk, and keep to the back roads. They meet a famous blues singer, have supper with a famous writer, visit towns and homes they previously read about in books. Apple spends the night with a reclusive painter, while Augustine stays back at the hotel.

If anyone asks, they say they are married, or siblings, or cousins.

Augustine does a picture series on churches, from grand to storefront, and another series on cemeteries.

Apple collects love stories.

Mrs. Ross sent them through the South to gather oral histories of ex-slaves; their lives during slavery and after. Apple interviews and Augustine photographs. And that is all she wants them to do. If she knew the side trips they took, the people they met, or their interests in the lives they found that included but went beyond the people Mrs. Ross wanted them to see, she would be furious.

Mrs. Ross would scold them, insist they not waste her time ("That's rich," says Apple) and money. "If you wallow in the dirt, you become as the dirt," she told Augustine later, when he tried to describe some of the wondrous things they saw and people they came across.

They meet Naive painters and take pictures of their pictures. They examine quilts and carvings. There isn't anything even remotely a part of Negro life that does not enthrall them. Unfortunately, Mrs. Ross doesn't share that feeling.

"Stick to the task at hand," Godmother demanded. Whenever Apple and Augustine have to get in touch with her, it leaves them both sullen and moody. "It's from the effort of having to kiss up and pretend," Apple says when Augustine complains that Mrs. Ross wears him out. And they refuse to call her Godmother unless they are in the same room with her; it's never used with any sincerity in any case.

There is a five-generation family they want to talk to, and they decide to drive into the night instead of stopping somewhere to sleep. As the sun sets, Augustine says to Apple, who is driving, "Turn on your lights."

She pulls the knob. "They are on," she says.

"That can't be," says Augustine, and Apple agrees they don't seem to be very effective. "Pull over."

Apple gets off the highway on the first road she comes to. It is a narrow, nowhere road that ends at a set of railroad tracks. They are in the middle of nowhere. Augustine gets out and stands in front of the car, saying, "I think we have a problem."

"Are you sure?" Apple says, fiddling with the knob. "How about now? And now?" Augustine shakes his head, until she gets out of the car to join him at the front bumper.

She pops the hood. They peer inside. They look at each other and Augustine says, "I feel so much better, knowing we've exhausted every possibility," and they burst out laughing.

They scrutinize their location; they are somewhere in Virginia.

"Are you warm enough?" asks Augustine. He is bundled in the backseat, while Apple lies across the front.

"Fine, I'm just-so-damn-uncomfortable," and she can already anticipate the soreness of her body in the morning.

"You know," he says, "we are supposed to call Mrs. Ross tonight." He smiles. "Something good out of this, anyway."

"She's not going to like this at all," says Apple. "Not at all."

"So what," Augustine says, turning over on his side, "so goddamn what. She's not hungry and aching in some car with busted headlamps, facing railroad tracks in the middle of who knows where."

"I'm sick of her too," Apple says quietly.

They are thinking the same things. They are thinking of the wealth of material each has—Augustine pictures, Apple tales—and how Mrs. Ross "owns" these materials and how unless she gives her permission, they can never do anything with them. Mrs. Ross has made that abundantly clear. She keeps harping on the subject of salvation, and all they can think about is art.

Augustine remembers reading about an artist named Jawlensky who painted his lover's face over and over until the configuration of eyes, nose, and mouth resembled Eastern Orthodox crosses; this marriage of agape and erotica: *My work is my prayer, an impassioned prayer spoken in colors.* Augustine considers his own twin passions of art and Romy. He practically never speaks her name.

"Spirituality," he says bitterly. "What the hell does Mrs. Ross know of spirituality? Do you know what Jawlensky says? That the artist should express that in him which is divine. And that a work of art is a visible god, and art a longing for God." He is silent before muttering, "Isn't this a fitting end to our distinguished renaissance. When someone else owns our work and inspiration."

"I was thinking about that," Apple says. She starts laughing, with Augustine joining her but unsure what is so funny. It just feels good to laugh. "And I thought marriage was a tight box," Apple says, laughing.

They grow quiet.

"Augustine?" says Apple. "Does this make you nervous?"

"This?" Augustine asks, indicating Apple and he alone for the night when usually they are in separate rooms.

"Or this?" meaning being black and spending the night on a southern road. "I'm not scared," he finally says. And he means it, wondering if all people who are denied the things and the one they love feel so reckless.

"You know, Augustine, there are days I think this trip with you is the closest I'll ever get to marriage," Apple says as they sit on the banks of the Mississippi, eating a picnic lunch. They have been traveling for two and a half years, investigating, collecting, photographing, cataloguing, crisscrossing the southern states as if it were impossible to find the road home except by some random process.

The times he refers to Apple as "my wife" he almost believes it. They tease and disagree and are ultimately loyal to each other. When threatened or criticized in any way, Apple and Augustine become protective of each other. Now Mrs. Ross is talking about renting a house for them, in the South, of course, "your true home in this land," she says, so they can work on a series of books together.

Mrs. Ross never asks what they want; they give up what they want every time they cash her checks. Apple and Augustine increasingly resentful and secretive about the things they will take with them when the inevitable end comes with Godmother. ("It's all our hard work," Apple says. "It isn't stealing if she's not going to use it.") They know the ties will be quickly, irrevocably severed once Mrs. Ross understands that Apple and Augustine are not children.

For now, they need the money.

The government has begun a variety of programs to put people to work, even artists. Around the time Apple and Augustine wind up their work with ex-slaves, they find themselves running into writers sent down for the same purpose by a cultural arm of the Works Progress Administration. It is with some curiosity that Apple and Augustine muse about the sort of story these earnest white writers will get as opposed to the ones given Apple. Will one version carry more truth than the other? More likely, they will support the adage of many sides to a story.

***11.***

In 1938, when Romy is thirty-nine, she has her first solo show. She helps to hang the pictures and asks to be the last to leave the night before the show opens. She wishes Augustine were here; his is the praise she wants to hear. She misses Apple, she wrote her two letters quite some time ago but doesn't know if she ever received them.

But as she stands in the gallery, surrounded by her eccentric, peculiar goddesses, and a handful of black-and-white portraits, and her Paris pictures, as she refers to the ones that recall Tin and his surrealist ideas, she buries her face in her hands and cries tears of gratitude. *At last,* she thinks. *At last.*

She could barely attend opening night of the show, it made her so uncomfortable to be in the gallery. It was a success, and the good reviews (most of them were good) called her brilliant. They loved her use of color. They said, *This is new.*

The not so good reviews found her extreme colors garish, faddish. They said her goddess series was an "interesting gimmick." They said her goddesses were really just fashion work grasping for art; they talked about her subject, women, and were slightly dismissive, calling it "light weight." Sure, her tricks were new, they said, but they were, finally, tricks.

The majority loved her pictures, and their enthusiasm generates talk about taking the show to New York, which is how Romy discovers that, back home, she is thought to be a Communist. This makes her laugh; Romy has never been a political sort. She thinks the government can't be serious; she is nobody.

It seems that between Augustine's previous passport problems during the twenties, her "marriage" to Augustine, and her time out of the country, it was decided that she had socialist leanings.

Back home Romy is also thought to be a Negro. People who knew them in Harlem think she is Augustine's wife. Lorenzo sends Romy money, but her family does not seek her out. A consequence of Romy and Augustine's affection. Romy passed as black in Harlem. A consequence of Romy and Augustine's affection. But in Paris, the city of light and love, they knew what it felt like to be together, and no one cared. America has proved itself intolerant on issues of race (in some states it is illegal for Romy and Augustine to love each other) and is now exhibiting a political intolerance as well.

In any case, they will not allow her work to be shown; particularly suspect are the goddesses, with their mixture of farce and commentary, beauty and sex. So she is forced to choose between staying behind with her work or returning home to Augustine.

When Romy came back to Paris to find Augustine gone, she felt maybe it was for the best. Maybe things only last as long as they last. Now she has a handhold on what she wants to do (and a show) and she is ready to see him. To see if he still wants her as well. But the possibility that the government might confiscate her pictures kept her away. Again, the choice is between Augustine and work. Again, she reluctantly chooses work.

Romy has more work than she has time. She does the work that she loves, combined with more traditional portraiture, which doesn't much interest her but provides her with a comfortable living. She has spent so many years not doing, not fully knowing, what she wants to do, that her life feels fairly normal. Still, there are those moments of wonder when she hits all the right notes.

She takes self-portraits, standing with her cameras, one massive, the other, smaller one still heavy at twelve pounds. She works so closely with the film lab that they have stopped correcting what they think are mistakes. "No, no," she used to patiently say, "you've altered my effect." They like her so well that they get her developed pictures back to her quickly, often within a day.

Romy sometimes spends an evening with the writers and painters who congregate in other, more modest sections of London. Middle-class, not poor. They are fine. As with Los Angeles, New York, and Paris, it is all variations on a theme: They reject many of society's values; they champion rights for women (since everyone is voting, they are on to the finer points), children in and out of wedlock (the ones within are not always the husband's offspring); all forms of sexuality and love (the intricate change of partners); a variety of living situations, and art. And a great deal of talking. One of the things she likes best about the group here in London is the ongoing conversations; one of the things that wears her out about this group in London is the ongoing conversations.

She is a good listener, which is why she thinks she is often included; somebody needs to listen. They refer to her as Madame Romy.

Her favorite place to visit is the country cottage of a woman painter, her children, husband, and lover. It is itself a work of art, with the painted walls and furniture—all available surfaces ornamented, detailed, decorated. For Romy (who asked to take pictures of the interior and garden) it is like stepping into a painting.

As for the complications of the artists who inhabit the place, they don't interest Romy half as much.

## *12.*

Godmother installs Apple and Augustine in a house in Charlottesville, Virginia. They initially love the fields of green that encompass them, almost like a series of calm seas. They love the dogwoods that bloom pink and white. Then, with an overnight suddenness, they cannot tolerate the natural extravagance of their surroundings. "It makes me feel as though I've eaten too much candy," Apple complains.

Augustine craves the muted colors of the city. He calls it "the curse of my photographer's eye." Basically, he can't stand the overgrown beauty of the place.

"Why should we like it here?" Augustine says. "We're not from here."

When he explains this to Mrs. Ross, she insists they stay.

Apple tries to talk sense to her, only to be informed that she, Mrs. Ross, "knows what is best."

So they pack up their notes and negatives and typewriter and camera and clothes, lock the door, and head back home.

When they get home, Apple moves in with Augustine. She doesn't have the heart to move back into Niggerati Manor; her old friends are gone, some dead. "What was once sort of a life," she says, "is no life."

Augustine likes the company and is used to having her around. It is as if he is again living with family. There is enough sexual chemistry between them to keep the friendship lively.

"Thanks for letting me live here," says Apple, to which Augustine replies, "Don't mention it."

This is a better arrangement: Apple sees whom she likes, and Augustine involves himself where he chooses. Sometimes they converse on these matters, but not often, which also seems to suit them.

Predictably, things ended on a harsh note with Godmother, who called repeatedly in Charlottesville, until she was told the phone had been disconnected. Augustine patiently tried to explain about Jawlensky and his feeling of religion in art and the human face, but Godmother cut him off, saying, "Godless white European painters. What do they know of the true, primitive spirit?"

That ended that. Augustine before Apple, but Apple following in his footsteps just the same.

Apple works on compiling her research (the love stories she collected) into a manuscript. Augustine finds himself putting in for work from the Federal Art Project of the WPA. He now takes pictures of whatever he is asked: buildings under construction; murals; people in bread lines or lining the streets; Harlem scenes of children, lovers, politicians, performers, artists, workers, homelessness and charity, shops, and places of worship.

Augustine's longing for Romy has worked itself into the fabric of his being. So much so that it no longer feels separate from who he is; that is, he cannot *not* miss her. In a way, this has made living without her a little easier, but then there are the days when he is restive and anxious, when sadness threatens to do him in and he is reminded that he loves someone who is not here. He mistakenly thought that if he gave up hope she would come back, the love he had for her would fade or relax its grip on his heart.

He saw other women, made possible by the fact of Romy being just another part of him. His love for her made mundane and extraordinary all at once. He found himself liking the women he saw and having a good time, only to realize that one thing did not affect the other.

When Apple sees him like this for the hundredth time, she says, "I don't know how you can live this divided life."

"Neither do I," he says.

## *13.*

On a rainy fall afternoon, Augustine and Apple sit together in the kitchen; he is polishing his shoes, she reads the newspaper. The kitchen is pleasant and light. Augustine and Romy's elderly cat stretches across the table, with Augustine periodically scratching it under the chin.

Apple and Augustine are spending the day like truant students; Augustine not working for the WPA today, and Apple joining him.

The WPA/FAP is closing down. Within a few years, the government will rid itself of thousands of paintings by selling the canvas at four cents a pound. The entire lot, including many by Jackson Pollock, among others, is bought by a plumber, who intends to use it to insulate pipes.

Apple looks up from her paper and says, "If you could, would you go back to Paris?"

"Tomorrow," he says, "I'd go tomorrow."

She nods, then asks, "Do you think there was a Harlem Renaissance, or was it like Du Bois said, just a 'transplanted and exotic' thing that had more to do with white desires than anything else?"

Augustine is thoughtful. What he wants to say is, For me, Harlem was a dream made real. He thinks about his group portrait of the artists of the rooming house with a nostalgia so powerful his heart feels on the verge of collapse. His adoration of Romy, inseparable from those times, comes to mind, threatening to do his heart in entirely. "The artists came first," he says without hesitation.

Apple considers this, then says, "Romy's white, isn't she?"

But since Apple isn't really asking, there is no real reason for Augustine to answer.

## *14.*

"Oh my God, what are you doing here?" Romy exclaims as she rushes across the room to open the door to Apple.

Romy heard the bell but was in the darkroom, and by the time she emerged the bell stopped. It is then she sees Apple's figure, through the large window, turning to go.

Romy is euphoric. Of course she knew she missed Apple, but until she embraces her, she has no idea how much she missed her.

"How are you, Romy?" Apple smiles. Their joy mirrors each other's.

"I'm fine. Come in, come in." Romy takes Apple's suitcase and brings her inside. "What are you doing here?"

"I'm going to Paris," says Apple. "I just want to see for myself what it's all about."

"I want to hear everything," Romy says, "I do, but for now, I'm just so glad to see you."

"These are very good," says Apple as she examines each print Romy hands her. They are sitting in Romy's studio, the windows open to the sounds and smells of the street. A summer breeze makes a brief appearance. Apple is curled up in the gold velvet armchair; Romy reclines on a sofa losing its stuffing, feather by feather, miniature escaping clouds. "I love this," says Apple of a portrait of a young woman with vibrant red hair, dressed in red against a red background. There is another, similar shot of a blonde against yellow and amber. "This is great, too," says Apple of another picture of a titled woman, sitting in a simple, flowered afternoon dress, one hand cupping her elbow, the other supporting her chin as she looks off into the distance, contemplating, a globe nearby. She sits before a gradient blue background of good-sized cut-out white stars.

"Oh, hey, this could be me," says Apple of a solarized head of a woman with a live dove resting on her hair.

Romy is shy and pleased that Apple likes her work. Apple says, "You seem to know who you are now," and Romy agrees. They joke and trade stories. It is as if no time has passed.

Apple tells her about Mrs. Ross.

"She really made you call her Godmother?" says Romy, not quite knowing if Apple is kidding or not.

"Oh, yes," says Apple, "and sitting on one of those cramped little footstools at her feet was no picnic either."

Romy shakes her head. "I find this unbelievable," she says.

"She paid very well. I had a few nice years and an extended trip down south."

"But you couldn't publish without her permission?"

"I kept two sets of notes." Apple smiles a sly smile. "I wrote a book." She takes a deep breath. "Are you ready? Someone's publishing it. Unbelievable, I know."

Romy jumps off the sofa to hug and kiss her friend.

*15.*

"You want to hear about Augustine?" asks Apple.

*16.*

Augustine's work is starting to pick up. When the artists of the WPA are let go, Augustine worries that he'll end up in the restrictive employ of someone like Mrs. Ross. Not Mrs. Ross herself; there is no way to recross that burned bridge. He misses Apple's easy companionship. Even the cat is gone. He has never hit the bottom of his own loneliness, and finds himself wondering if such an experience is imminent.

It is jazz that happens to save him, in general, and

Coleman Hawkins, Duke Ellington, Gene Krupa, and Lena Horne in particular. Augustine takes photographs of them all. Which sets off a chain reaction, leading to more pictures of jazz musicians.

This is a different sort of work for him—somewhere between portraiture and snapshots—since most of the pictures are taken during performances. Or backstage, as if Augustine has briefly interrupted a conversation. Even when Augustine goes into people's homes to record their anniversary parties and weddings and coming-out dances, there is always something planned and posed about each picture.

Of course, there are the photos of the Harlemites hurrying around Lenox Avenue or the occasional parade, but these are relatively few.

The rush of the crowd and the physical movement of playing jazz have a similarity for him in photographic terms. Paradoxically, all this club work provides him with enough money to reopen his studio, where once again, he can retrieve his painted flats and props, creating a romantic, still place.

## *17.*

Romy and Apple walk along the Serpentine. "You must have gotten my letters." Romy throws an arm around Apple's shoulders, quickly embraces her. "You're here. I mean, you found me. I didn't hear from you for such a long time, I wasn't sure."

Apple rummages around in her pocketbook, withdraws one of the letters. It was addressed to the old rooming house, then someone else's handwriting obscured Romy's with a couple of p.o. boxes. Then the rented house in Virginia. Then Romy's and Augustine's old address.

Romy stares at the envelope, without moving, without speaking.

"Romy," Apple begins. "I only meant to show you—I moved around so." She touches Romy's arm. "Do you want to hear about Augustine?"

Romy's body reacts to his name with a constriction in her chest, and a fear of losing, and the sheer dizzy happiness of getting what you want. She has never had calm reactions to him; even when they were still together, his entrance into a room or the sight of him strolling down the street thrilled her. Romy thinks she is going to answer Apple's question with a shake of her head, no, but instead hears herself saying, "I always want to hear about Augustine."

Apple tells her about M & M Photography Studio.

"Marks & March," says Romy, moved by the gesture.

Then about the studio's failure, and Augustine's association with Mrs. Ross. "We left on rough terms. Augustine left first. His fall from grace harder," says Apple, the word *grace* sarcastic. Romy imagines how rough it must have been for Augustine, as he is not a temperamental or argumentative man. That old woman must have pushed him over the edge. Romy is laid low by the image of Augustine trying to please such a difficult person.

Finally, there are Apple and Augustine's travels together, and their living situation. "I had nowhere else to go, and he was kind enough to take me in," she said.

Romy is jealous of Apple's life with Augustine. She finds herself eyeing her friend with suspicion, dying to ask, biting her tongue. The question looms so large within her that there is space for nothing else: *Was there anything between you and Augustine?* There almost isn't enough room inside her to remember the love and trust she feels for Apple. Or her own willful absence. Her focus on this thought is intense; she has lost all track of Apple's current conversation.

"Apple," Romy begins.

"Yes?"

Romy hesitates, cannot bring herself to ask such a thing. The women watch each other. "Apple," says Romy, suddenly knowing the answer lies in an entirely different question, "do you think Augustine still waits for me?"

"Yes," she says. "Does that settle it?"

"It does," says Romy, with relief and an awakening of love that washes over her.

Apple stays with Romy through the summer. Before she can leave, however, Germany invades Poland, war is declared, and Apple rethinks her travel plans.

"Can you stand having me around a little longer?" she asks Romy, who says forever, if you like. As Americans they are advised to go home, but neither is ready. Romy often mentions that she hadn't intended to live in London, but she made a life and a name for herself, and "it became a habit." Who knows how long it will last and, it must be said, as Americans, inexperienced with war in their own land, they expect nothing to happen to them. They expect to be safe.

They seldom discuss Augustine because Romy is too unsteady, too unsure of how he still affects her. For example, Apple might innocently reveal some detail of Augustine's life that Romy wouldn't want to know. Or, worse, some small thing that might make her fall in love madly with him all over again. Who really knows if they could be together again? Romy knows they can be apart.

But, once he is reintroduced into her world, Romy can't trust herself to accept whatever might happen. She's unhappily certain that she won't be able to let him go, no matter how lightly he holds her.

Apple is writing essays and articles and sending them home to be printed in newspapers and magazines. Romy does a great deal of work for hire. Advertisements, mostly. She takes pictures of soldiers and sweethearts, which make her think of Augustine and his photograph tattoos; it seems so long ago. She sometimes thinks to write him but stops herself. For now, her color work is over: The color lab has closed, because of the war.

Besides, Romy's eyes have begun to bother her. They are sensitive to the ultraviolet rays from the lights she uses, "chronic edema," the doctor said. Sometimes the area around her eyes swells slightly, as if she were trying to recover from a bender.

She tries changing the lighting system and reducing the wattage; she has to wear dark glasses all the time, inside the studio and out on the street, for months. They are small, oval shapes of light metal, and though she is eventually able to take them off for short periods, her eyes never fully recover.

The bombings unnerve Apple and Romy. Romy closes the studio, packs her beautiful suitcase, her Renaissance box, her cameras, and as many negatives and prints as she can carry and moves, with Apple, to Dorset, where the roll of greenery relaxes her eyes and the threat of bombs seems remote. Not that it is; Apple and Romy finally understand that no place is out of reach.

They take walks, alone and in tandem, in almost all

types of weather. Greet their neighbors; feed the occasional stray cat.

One evening Apple says, "You know, living with you is almost exactly like living with Augustine," and Romy has to leave the room without comment. If Apple were to follow, Romy would be unable to say which upsets her more: that Apple lived with Augustine or that Augustine and Romy are so mated they are seamless.

"I'm sorry," says Apple, when Romy returns. "Forgive me."

"Don't mention it," she says.

Shopping on the high street, Romy overhears three women talking in a shop to the grocer, who says some painter moved into a tiny stone house at the end of town. Then Romy hears the painter's name, Carlos Rio.

Rio was one of Tin's surrealist friends, and hers by association, in Paris. Romy walks out the door thinking to herself that all the surrealists had made their way to America. What was Rio doing here, and was his wife with him? He was from Barcelona, and when she went to Spain during her hegira from Augustine, she often thought of him. Ben had purchased one of his paintings, she recalled.

Apple said, "You sent me two letters, right?"

"I think so," says Romy, trying to remember, "yes. I did."

"I've lost one."

"Maybe you left it in London," Romy suggests.

Apple shakes her head. "I think I left it home."

For one month past a year, Apple and Romy lived in their cottage. Each longing for a million different things and contemplating home. They thought the country was romantic in an epic sense: the endless green fields, the wooden turnstiles, the roses and sheep, the constant changing of grays, blues, and whites of the sky. The estates said to be haunted, with their equally haunted gardens, orangeries, and occasional topiary. The trips to the sea.

Ever since the day Apple mentioned the lost letter, Romy has been anticipating Augustine into her life. No matter that he may have had Apple's letter a month or a year; he knows where she is. He can find her. Of this she is sure.

Off and on, Romy runs into Carlos Rio. He wears the same outfit daily: some sort of tweed trousers, impeccable white shirt, sleeves rolled above the elbows, even under his jacket, necktie, dark suspenders. His neatly combed hair; his magnificent eyes. They stop and chat on the street, in the most ordinary manner, except that Carlos speaks in combined sentences of English, Spanish, French, with a smattering of Italian. Romy saying, "Carlos, in English, please," then apologizing for being so embarrassingly provincial.

They talk about his wife ("Bella stayed behind with our family. She had no choice, you know"), and the war, and the occupation of Paris, and Bella some more ("I am too sick with worry"). Their conversations move toward gossip, and the mass migration of Carlos's surrealist colleagues to America.

"I was supposed to go as well," he said, "but I got so far as England and could bear to be no farther."

They talk about Tin and Augustine. Romy invites him to join her and Apple for their pathetic dinners. This becomes a regular engagement. They discuss Romy's involuntary hiatus from her color photography and Carlos's isolation from the surrealists and any sort of gallery contact. ("What do you think about Miró saying 'one must be ready to work amidst total indifference and in the most profound obscurity'?" Carlos throws his hands in the air. "That's the reality of it, isn't it. What is there to say?") But mostly he talks about Bella. The *bella* Bella, as Romy and Apple refer to her.

He asks Romy and Apple to come to dinner one night, and Apple declines in order to work on a story. It is on this night that the intimacy of the dinner for two, their place and time in history, their life dictated by war, their fears and old-fashioned loneliness and longing for the human embrace, results in their sleeping together.

This turns out to be not an isolated incident, but their assignations are infrequent. Mostly, Carlos and Romy's affair consists of conversation and a great deal of affection.

As soon as she can, and with as much delicacy as possible, Romy asks about Bella.

"Not to worry," he says, kissing Romy, "we have always been with other people. We just don't fall in love with them." He smiles. "I don't think this is a new idea." Romy smiles back.

Years into the war, Romy receives a letter postmarked New York. It is from Augustine. *Where are you?* Oh, Augustine, she says softly, her sense of him correct, and places the paper in her pocket.

For a handful of years Romy and Carlos see each other. They hear the war is coming to an end. It is around this time, one morning, before Romy leaves, that Carlos brings her upstairs to the other room of his two-room house.

"This is my studio," he says as they ascend the staircase.

From the moment Romy walks into the room, removing her small, dark glasses, she is lost in the absolute bliss and wonderment of his paintings. She is almost speechless with joy, whispering *oh, look!* under her breath, to herself; or, *I love this,* in the same breathy voice, moving from picture to picture.

They are ecstatic with stars, dots, amoebic forms, in blue, red, green, black, gray, and yellow; they appear in constant, musical motion. The background fields composed of numerous colors and textures. The pictures are remarkable, comical and moving. "They are like miracles," she says to him. Then, "I don't know if I should laugh or cry."

"*The Constellations,*" he says. "All of them, I mean. That is what I call them."

"What about this one?" asks Romy, pointing to a picture with a galaxy of small, black forms. A piano score gone feral.

"It is *The Beautiful Bird Revealing the Unknown to a Pair of Lovers,*" he tells her.

She stands before it a long while.

"You are going home, aren't you?" he says.

"Yes," she says.

"If you see anyone I know, give them my regards."

"No," she says, "I'm going to say that Carlos Rio spent a world war turning a small room in a country town in England into a paradise of stars."

# Immortality

ART IS THE THING THAT LASTS. THE POPES, THE DUKES, THE princes and kings wanted a small piece of immortality.

But art is a dream. Someone somewhere—artist or subject—becomes enthralled of a vision: how something might be seen, how someone is seen. How it will all be recorded and, perhaps, remembered. Suddenly, out of almost nothing, comes something. Where once lay paints, or canvas, or wood, or marble, or paper, there is now an image. There is now the realization of a dream.

Take love. The body is the giver and receiver of love but not exactly love itself. Love, like the vision of a picture before it is made, is an abstraction without weight or smell or color. It, like the finished painting (statue, structure), is animated by someone's passion. Someone feels passionately about a certain bit of art; someone feels passionately about a certain someone.

Can you touch love itself? Can you hold the idea or emotion of a work of art as it is coming into being?

The canvas carries the idea the way the body carries love. What do we care for more: the idea of the picture, or the picture? The love expressed by the body, or the body? And which is immortal: the idea or the picture, the body or the love?

Maybe more to the point, are the two things (idea/picture, love/body) separate? Are they rendered almost meaningless if separated? Why get upset if an artwork crumbles after a number of years; why scream with hurt and jealousy if a lover has been faithless?

It is said that the problem with art made in the twentieth century is that it is art that cannot last. The materials, execution, and process almost insure its alteration (destruction, decay) within an artist's lifetime. There is a work by de Kooning that still wasn't completely dry thirty years after he finished it. At what point is it finished, can it be finished, as it slides down the canvas?

What of stretching and cracking and fading and chipping and pieces falling to the ground and slipping and fingerprints and dust and light?

Some claim that artists are commenting on the nature of time by the deliberate yellowing of once white canvas, which discolors from not having been properly prepared; others say it is a way of reminding the buyer that nothing can really be bought. Can someone truly devote his life, maybe sacrifice something quite dear, to remind the consumer that not everything can be consumed?

Or is the notion of a work that began as an idea, then became a picture, then falls to ruin until all that is left is the original idea, satisfying?

During World War II, when the art previously held by the Hermitage in Leningrad had been removed and hidden away, the city under terrible siege, a former guide gave a tour of the empty picture frames to the workers replacing broken windows. He explained, pointing to the vacancy within each frame, where each picture hung, who painted it, and what it depicted, though there was no picture to see, only the guide's description of its memory.

Giulietta was not surprised when Leonardo's work showed signs of decay before his death, because she considered art ephemeral, and Leonardo an "extraordinary dreamer." But in the twentieth century are more people compelled by the ideas in his notebooks or by the *Mona Lisa*? At the time, Giulietta could not decide if Leonardo meant for his *Last Supper* to mildew: if it was an oversight, deliberate, or indifference.

Then she thought about M.'s preference to sculpt in carefully chosen blocks of marble and his statement that he was primarily a sculptor and not a painter and that sculpting is closer to being like God. Marble more durable than canvas.

Romy March, descendant of Giulietta Marcel, keeps in her possession a box, with a boy and a girl gazing at each other across a mirror, made by Giulietta. Inside is a marble curl from M.'s *David.* Romy is unaware of the significance of this bit of marble; for her it *is* a "bit of marble," and it does not occur to her that it is a part of something as grand as *David.*

Does it matter? Romy owns a box that she knows nothing about except that it is dated from about 1502, or so, and that an ancestor made it. Should she love it any less? Without understanding its meaning and importance to Giulietta, does it mean less, become less important to Romy? Is there ever a single meaning?

Or, perhaps more to the point, Romy was breathless at the sight of *David* in the Piazza della Signoria, until she learned that it was not the original. Her initial response was the same as if it were the original *David,* her reverence altered once she knew the truth. Is this, the object without the idea, immortality? Do artists consciously think about immortality when they work?

# Book Seven: San Francisco

1946–1956

ROMY HAS LIVED ABROAD FOR SUCH A LONG TIME THAT SHE has sometimes lost track of the exact duration. There were the final years of Paris in the twenties; artists beginning to drift away, return to their native homes, settle into quieter lives, find new loves, or leave for parts unknown. The Depression and the war finished those years off for good. It was as Ben said to her when they ran into each other at the book party in London: No one was around anymore.

Well, some of the crowd stayed in France, though not necessarily in Paris. That wasn't what Ben meant in any case; the transformation was indisputable. Apple wants Romy to accompany her to Paris, but Romy, in her forties, is already fighting nostalgia. She thanks Apple for the invitation but explains that her experience of Paris is over. Even London can get to her if she dwells too much on the past. But not as much as Paris. Not with Augustine having been in Paris.

She lived through a war that is pretty much over. The

American soldiers who seem to be everywhere remind her of what she likes and dislikes about home, what she craves and rejects. She realized her art. She made a living off her photography; the work was fairly tedious, but she learned from Augustine that every picture you take isn't going to be the one you *want* to take. She shared a home with Apple, who she loves calling "my friend." She had assorted lovers. And she and Augustine eventually struck up a correspondence. She calls him My Pen Pal; he refers to her as My Foreign Correspondent.

It is difficult to leave as quickly as Romy wants to because of the politics and logistics of the war and its wake, but there has always been an emotional component to Romy's travels. It is something she wrestles with each time she packs her beautiful suitcase.

*This is the problem,* thinks Romy to herself as she looks at her beautiful suitcase sitting in the corner of her bedroom, *with all this coming and going, there is always someone, or something, to miss.* It is possible to make a list of her desires, divided into categories and columns, like a bookkeeper's ledger: for every credit, a debit.

The categories could cover such items as weather conditions (a specific rainy afternoon in London; a shining spring day in Paris); flora and fauna (the palm trees and oaks of Pasadena; the golden roll of the hills outside San Francisco); architecture (the curved script of the Metro sign in France, and Tin's old studio; the extravagant bungalow in which Romy grew up; the high ceilings and tall windows of the apartment she shared with Augustine); crowds (the elegant parade of Seventh Avenue in Harlem).

Then there are the people she loves, with whom there is never enough time.

"Do you ever think about going home?" Romy asks Apple. Romy already knows how hard it will be to say good-bye.

"Sometimes, but, you know, I *still* haven't been to Paris," she reminds Romy.

"After," say Romy.

Apple turns up her palms. "Who knows what I'll find in Paris?"

There are the things Romy does not miss; she does not give them too much thought.

She sits at the kitchen table in the house she shares with Apple, thinks about leaving, sets her tinted glasses down, rubs her tired eyes.

Romy receives a letter from a prominent movie studio in Los Angeles. It seems someone had seen her *Goddess* series in London and wants her to come and take pictures of their "screen goddesses." They wrote, You seem to have an eye for the theatrical. She smiles. They wrote, as a selling point she supposes, We have more stars than there are in heaven.

"Well," Romy says when she tells Apple about it, "it's almost as if they knew I was ready to go home."

"It's in the air," Apple says, ladling potato soup into bowls for dinner. "Maybe if I send out a telepathic resume, they'll hire me to write screenplays. For thousands of dollars, and I'll develop a wide and winning range of affectations. What do you think? Are you going to do it?"

"I hadn't considered California," Romy says.

Apple slides a bowl over to her. "How much will they pay you?"

"Enough," says Romy.

"Do you want to do this kind of work?" asks Apple.

"Oh, yes. If I can do it the way I want to do it, it's almost perfect for me. The sort of shimmering, exaggerated fantasy of it. Unless they want something more standard, which, as you know, bores me to distraction. It won't be the first time," Romy says. "It'll be strange to be back at a movie studio and not running around getting things for people who didn't even know my name." She laughs. "I can almost imagine me colliding with some sort of ghost of my young self there. Like a wrinkle in time. What I mean is, I'll probably feel like that young girl all over again." She is about to say, *I just don't know how I'll stop myself from looking everywhere for Augustine,* then thinks better of it. "I could see my family."

"Your family," Apple says.

"I think it might be time."

"Well, then," Apple says.

"I was thinking about New York," Romy says.

Apple puts down her spoon and looks Romy in the eye. "Tell him where you are."

"I think I just get scared," Romy says.

Romy hates the Atlantic crossing. She hated it the first time and hates it now. The endless expanse of water that surrounds her leaves her unnerved, feeling vulnerable and claustrophobic. Being prone to seasickness does not help. All she does is read sporadically, walk perpetually, and count the hours and days.

In New York, before she takes the train home, she calls Augustine.

Hey, she says when he answers the phone, It's me.

Oh my God, he exclaims. Where are you, baby?

Here. In New York. She tells him where she is staying, and he answers, No, stay here with me.

I can't, she says, Please understand.

Which, when he stops to think about it, he does. It's been a long time; Polly once lived in their flat; they are not the same people; they are exactly the same people.

You, she says, you come to me.

Romy has borrowed an apartment in Greenwich Village. It belongs to a friend of a friend of Leland and Lena Grandin.

When Romy hears the buzzer sound, she bolts from the sofa, checks herself in the mirror yet again, and instead of ringing Augustine up, runs down the stairs to the front door of the building.

They see each other through the glass: Augustine still slender, still wonderfully, quietly attired. His hair is going a little gray; he looks the same but older. In some ways, better.

Romy, too, is a bit gray. A few lines around her eyes and mouth; her cheekbones a little more noticeable from the aging of her face. He notices her clothing is not as elaborate as it once was, though she still doesn't dress like everybody else; she wears a man's undershirt, trousers, and pearls.

When she opens the door, he mentions the change in clothing style.

"Oh, it's funny," she says, "as I got more work, and became more busy, I didn't have the same kind of time or inclination, I guess. Maybe it all just got in the way. Well, I really don't know what happened. Maybe it's age." She laughs a little.

"Are you traveling incognito?" he asks, pointing to her dark glasses.

"I have some trouble with my eyes," she says. "Oh, dear, you don't like them."

"No, no," he says. "I think you look beautiful."

They have not reached out for each other, or touched, or kissed, or moved from the open doorway.

Though it is the middle of the afternoon, Augustine and Romy are sitting in a local bar; he is drinking wine, she is smoking a cigarette.

"You can't be forty-six," Augustine is saying. "Look at you. It's just not possible."

They have not seen each other in sixteen years, but it is truly as if it were yesterday. As if there had been no loss of contact, no war, no changes. As much as they try, they almost cannot see the sixteen interim years in each other's physical appearance. If asked, each would say, he looks like Augustine; she looks like Romy. Adding that each has the face they cannot love enough.

"Are you seeing that woman you wrote me about?" asks Romy.

"Not really. And you, what about you? Whose heart did you break in England? Or should I say hearts?"

Romy starts laughing. "Oh, listen to us. Aren't we adult?"

Augustine is laughing with her. It is so good to be together. "Do you hate talking like this as much as I do?"

"God, yes. It makes me feel as though I'm watching myself. And you know, there are those moments when one wants to keep body and soul apart, but not with you, Augustine, not with you."

He reaches out for her hand, casually holding it in his own, which rests on his knee. "I don't care about who you see."

It is like old times, when Romy and Augustine inhabit each other; it is not out of jealousy that neither one wants to hear about the other's love life—it is genuine lack of interest. That is, it doesn't seem to involve them.

They converse with great ease and enthusiasm. No awkwardness of time passed. They talk about Augustine's jazz musicians, Romy's goddesses, their work and art in general. She says, "So, I'm going to work in Hollywood, for the movies."

"You already have the dark glasses," he says. "May I?" he asks as he picks her glasses up off the table, in the shadows of the bar, and tries them on. "Ah, so this is what the world looks like to you."

"Okay, then, if you're me and I'm you, how do I appear in your eyes?" she teases.

"Like a sanctuary."

Romy reaches across to him, gently removing her glasses from his face.

They sit in the living room of the borrowed apartment.

"I'm here for three days, then I take the train to California," Romy says.

Augustine's expression flexes from contentment to poorly masked disappointment. "I don't suppose between now and then you'll reconsider."

"Augustine, I can't. I mean, I have a job. Who knows, maybe artists with artists are genetically indisposed toward one another. It has taken us, what, a million years to be friends?"

"I get out to California on occasion," he says.

"I'd look forward to it," she says.

She offers to walk him to the subway station. He says not to bother, and she insists it is no bother. On the way they talk about Paris and the changes and how it isn't like it was, and Augustine tells her that Harlem is not the same either. He tells her who has died (Able Williams, Countee Cullen, A'lelia Walker, among others) and who has moved and how new things have come up; the jazz musicians he photographs are inspiring, for example, but it's not the place they moved to after the Great War.

They are at the station, still talking, and Augustine says, "I can take a later train. Let me walk you back to the house."

In all their discussions of people and places, they never say, *It was so much better then, the people were more talented then,* because that really isn't the point. As Romy discovered when she thought about seeing Paris again, what she longed for was the past. And until she could travel to Paris and see it as it is *today,* it would just be an exercise in heartbreak.

They stand at the door of the apartment building, talking, and she says, "Look, why don't I just walk you to the station."

It was different for Augustine, since his absence from Harlem wasn't as long as hers from home; he moved along with his neighborhood. Still, he could not risk meditating on certain memories. But they do not want to talk about all that.

At the station, they still have so much to say, and it is getting so late that Augustine says, "I can't let you walk home alone. Let me take you back."

By 2:30 A.M. it is clear Augustine is going to stay the rest of the night. And that if he stayed this night, he would be with her every minute until her train pulled away from the station. Neither one could honestly say which would hurt more: to say good night right now or to say good-bye in three days.

*   *   *

Augustine brings his pictures to Romy. She was unsure about going to their old apartment, mistrustful of what memory can do to a person. In turn, she describes hers to him. "I shipped everything to my parents' house," she says.

They talk about technique and effects and ideas and color and black and white; about books they've read; people they knew and know; places they've been. Their conversations are so fluid that one subject effortlessly melts into the next, lofty topic next to bouts of laughter. They are never at a loss for things to say. Although they have always been just as comfortable not talking as talking, they have few moments of quiet. Partly because it has been so long, partly because they were starved for the sound of each other's voice (all that letter writing can create this sort of hunger), but mainly because there were all those empty years without any contact at all.

Inevitably, the time passes quickly. Augustine and Romy don't bring up being together. Curiously, it is their friendship that is keeping them apart this time. They cannot risk another misunderstanding, followed by the long, almost interminable silence that followed the last misunderstanding. Older now, they cannot take the chance that their friendship might dissolve into nothing. It is just so hard to risk what was so recently found.

None of this makes them feel any better once her train starts down the track.

The studio work is lucrative. Most of it is as prosaic as the society portraits she took in London. They prefer she work in black and white, though many movies are in color. Every once in a while she gets some great costume shots, or pictures taken on some exotic, elaborate set, but not as often as she'd like. What it comes down to is that she wants to do what she wants to do. Working for someone, even a job like this, is still working for someone. It is still their wishes, their money for her art.

She lives in her parents' house on the third floor, which is one huge room. Lorenzo even had a small bathroom put in up there for her. It is a house that gives the illusion of weightlessness and light, and each year seems to make it more so. The large central hallways on the first and second floors and the way the breeze passes through. All the screens and windows and the much-loved sleeping porches. The brilliant ambers, browns, gold, and greens of the stained-glass oak tree that spans the front door and two side windows. The sounds from the arroyo all but gone now with Pasadena having spread and grown.

Edward, his wife, Marisol, and their four children visit regularly from Atherton, where Marisol was raised. Lorenzo is gentle with the children, indulgent in a way he never was with Romy and Edward. Romy and Edward are close and easy with each other. They call each other simpatico siblings. Of her nieces and nephews, she is drawn to the middle boy, small with dark, curly hair, above the rest.

She and Augustine talk on the phone and write letters, but it has been three years and he has not come west. He is very busy, she understands, but deep down she is surprised. If someone had told her that, after she'd gone, Augustine died for love of her, she would've believed him. He seems fine, and busy. Since the laughing fit in the bar, they don't ask about each other's affairs anymore. She figures that if he wants to, he'll tell her.

Lately, she misses dancing with him, the whisper of his touch at her waist. Even doing fast dances with Augustine, she felt held by a string. She sits in the overstuffed, faded chair in her bedroom, her feet up on the ottoman, remembering all the dancing she did in college, and how she and Augustine used to go to the Garden of Joy in Harlem. They were so beautifully partnered.

Sometimes, when she sits in her chair, she picks up the Renaissance box that she keeps on the table beside it. More and more she wonders about the piece of marble inside it. She traces her finger along Giulietta Marcel's signature and examines the image on the lid of the boy and girl, face-to-face through the mirror; how they seem meant to be each other's reflection and wholly separate simultaneously. She wishes she knew something, anything about this object that has always meant so much to her, but a little mystery in life doesn't nag at her. That is, she accepts the inexplicable.

It all leads to thoughts of Augustine. And how, if he had pursued her after she left New York, she would have taken the risk and said yes.

But he didn't, so instead she works at a studio, with that unwelcome hint of nostalgia, doing well-paid work that she likes but doesn't love, living on the third floor of her parents' elegant bungalow, spending her evenings curious about a box she'll never really know about and dreaming, again, about Augustine.

Augustine and Romy write quite a bit about their work. In addition to photographing musicians, Augustine has also taken pictures of some of the downtown artists (the names Rothko and Pollock come up). Some of the photos are still and posed, while others show them at work. "I don't completely understand what they're doing," Augustine writes, "though I like some of what I see. Do you remember the automatic painting, I think it was called, in Paris, that tapping into the unconscious, or subconscious, or whatever it was called? These new painters" (de Kooning is mentioned) "want to show off their dreams, or nightmares, or paint pure feeling and sensation.

"I feel it in much of the jazz I listen to. It is as if things are losing their recognizable shapes and turning wholly rhythmic. Everything turning abstract, while I remain so hopelessly literal. The thing that strikes me, with this painting and music, is the artists' need to be elsewhere."

On the phone they laugh and talk about nothing. They relate their days: Augustine still taking pictures for himself of the commonplace in Harlem and the general population, getting beneath the ordinary, exposing what is extraordinary. While Romy takes pictures of the extraordinary (actors, people with money), in an attempt to push into the surreal.

She experiences little bouts of envy when Augustine talks or writes about his work. He is sought after, his name becoming as known as those whose pictures he takes. It is her love for him that saves her from being completely undermined by jealousy. But in those difficult moments, it is hard to feel charitable toward someone who is in a second wave of popularity when she has barely had a first.

Augustine is more in love with Romy than ever. The day he left her at the train station in New York, he took a cab home and began packing everything. That kind of crazy, rushed packing because you care so much more about where you are going than what you are bringing. You care very little about what you are bringing because the thing you want is in the place you are headed.

He grabbed his calendar to reschedule various jobs.

Then he saw that he had a reporter from *Life* magazine coming to write a piece on him. During the next month, a newspaper and another magazine wanted to photograph and interview him.

*I can't go,* he thought. He felt desperate and breathless. When Romy was in New York, they talked at length about her work. He did not miss the brightness in her face when she told him about her show in London. She has not stopped wanting something more. He is doing very well; he remembers the lazy days with Apple. Reluctantly, he put everything away. As hard as it was not to go to her, he could not bear to lose her again.

In the early 1950s, Romy's work is hung and shown in a small show in New York at the Museum of Modern Art. She has her own section but shares the show with three other photographers. Thematically, it is about California; some Imogen Cunningham, very early Ansel Adams. Her contribution is almost all actresses, so they consider her "a California photographer."

Romy calls this series *Goddess 2* but does not feel that it matches her first, "classical" goddess series. Despite the costumes and movie magic atmosphere, it lacks the "wondrous strange" quality in her earlier work. Even so, there is often a sly, quirky humor somewhere in each image.

She was allowed to add a few pictures of movie sets. These pictures stylistically echo her London pictures of plaster statues of Nefertiti and Venus, bedecked in jewels, carrying their pocketbooks like ladies who lunch; or Caesar wearing a fedora and sunglasses, situated in a cloud of butterflies pressed in glass.

The movie set pictures have similar, funny juxtapositions of objects and backgrounds, involving statues and stuffed animals and fish and the most glittering costumes Romy can coax from wardrobe.

Her part of the show gets attention because she has recorded the faces that no one seems tired of seeing. And it is for that exact same reason (the "inconsequential subject matter of movie queens") that Romy's efforts are subtly dismissed. Her shockingly bright colors are not as appreciated as they once were since Technicolor jaded the eye. No one knows how closely and patiently she has to work with the lab technicians to even come close to what she is attempting. As with her earlier show, audiences like her work very much, until someone decides that it is just so much smoke and mirrors.

"I'm moving to San Francisco," Romy writes to Augustine. "I've saved up what they call 'a tidy sum' and I'm going to open a studio up there. See what I can really do. I'm not going to live forever, you know. In that same vein, you know where to find me."

Lorenzo doesn't want her to go. He doesn't come right out and say it, for aspects of her father have changed as he has aged: He is no longer interested in running her life; in fact, he seems to enjoy leaving her alone to see what she does completely unguided.

The first time Romy didn't come home at night, showing up the next morning at breakfast, she was nervous to see Lorenzo. *My God,* she thinks, *I'm forty-six years old.* She decided simply to walk into the kitchen as if nothing were amiss.

"Dad, aren't you going to say anything?" she asked after a while.

He set aside his newspaper. "No, I'm not, actually."

"Well," she said, surprised.

Thinking about it later, she realizes it isn't so much that her father seems changed as it is that parts of his personality that she has known her entire life are becoming more prominent, while other aspects are fading back.

When Romy was growing up, her father could be playful and funny with her and Edward. He could be encouraging in their interests, unless they conflicted with *his* interests for them, in which case the matter would be decided without discussion. These days, he no longer exerts his will in opposition to Romy's.

"It's as if we are friends," she writes Augustine.

Lorenzo seems as taken by Helen as ever.

And Lorenzo and Romy never talk about what happened that day and night, so long ago, that sent her from the house. *What happened,* Romy explained to Augustine, is that between Lorenzo sending her money as she needed it and his laissez-faire attitude about her living her life, his genuine enjoyment of her company, and the dampening of his parental stance in all things, *we worked out everything between us through action, and not with words. We live our forgiveness,* she writes.

Now he doesn't want her to leave but will never again try to keep her back.

The gray and fog of San Francisco call to mind a milder London weather scheme. Romy has a spectacular apartment in North Beach. The entrance is through the kitchen, easily big enough for a table and chairs, leading into a hallway with two bedrooms and a bathroom. Upstairs is an enormous room, fitted with so many windows it turns two entire walls to glass. Since the apartment is situated up high, the view of the water looking toward the east bay is stunning. The place is spacious and saturated with light; the ceilings contribute to its airy quality. When she writes to Augustine she says, "I live like a bird."

She buys a massive loft space south of Market and begins the process of setting up her studio. Often she stands in the middle of the main room of the loft thinking, this is crazy, I have enough room for a couple of studios. She writes to Augustine, "I have enough space for two separate studios and room to spare." There are upstairs rooms as well. The thing she most wants to do when she is there is to roller-skate from one end to the other.

Which is what she does when Edward and Marisol's middle boy comes to visit her. For whatever reason, Romy has always adored this child. She has not regretted not having a child: During those ten years with Augustine it seemed they were too unsettled, then too busy to have children; they would think about it later, they said. Polly showed up, and suddenly there was no later. In Paris there was a possibility, but they had to repair their own love damage first, and Romy went off on her wandering before that was accomplished.

As Romy aged, she missed having a child less and less. Maybe she was getting more set in her ways, or maybe it was as Apple had said—if she didn't do what she needed to do, it would be very tough having a baby. Romy's artist timetable was, in the end, too long.

And she saw how the children of artists lived; sometimes there wasn't enough love and time and energy for them. No matter, the work of an artist is emotional work, and Romy felt, for her, between loving Augustine and trying to get her work done, it was enough emotion for a lifetime.

Once in a while she had a second or two of regret. She threw it in with her other regrets.

But Max, her nephew, was a new experience for Romy. The other three children of Edward and Marisol were fine: smart, fairly well behaved, playful, but they did not affect her heart. Once when Edward and his family visited her in Pasadena, Max, who was about three, came up to her room and was immediately drawn to one of her smaller, snapshot cameras.

"What is this?" he asked.

"A camera," she said.

"Can I hold it?" His little hand was already reaching for it.

"Let me help you," Romy said, walking over to hand him the camera. "Look through here," she said as he awkwardly held it, a little heavy for him, bringing his eye down to the viewfinder instead of lifting the camera up. "Can you close one eye?" she asked.

Max immediately closed both eyes. Romy laughed. "You know, I think it's better if you keep them open." And when he opened his eyes, she reached over and placed her hand over one eye. "Is that better?"

Max nodded. "But how does it work?"

She took the camera from him and directed him over to another part of the room, then took his picture.

He responded by saying, "I want to take your picture."

She hesitated. "Okay," she said. "Just let me focus." She judged the focus as best as she could, then seated herself in the armchair.

Max lowered the camera. "No," he said, "you go on the floor. On your knees, like this." He demonstrated the position he wanted from her. Romy kneeled on the floor. "Look at me," he said in imitation of what she had said to him when she took his picture moments before. It was hard not to laugh. He took three more pictures, directing her to different areas of the room, in various poses, before reluctantly returning the camera.

When she developed the pictures, they weren't too bad, nicely framed and she looked good. This made her chuckle and think about all those critics of photography as art who insist anyone can take a decent picture.

The next time she saw Max she showed him the pictures he took, as well as the one she took of him. He was most interested in the picture of himself but also somewhat fascinated by the ones he had taken. He asked to take some more.

"We went down to the arroyo," Romy told Augustine on the phone. "The thing about him is that he doesn't just take the camera and indiscriminately shoot whatever he sees. I mean, he looks around for what catches his eye. Or, if he's taking my picture, he thinks about the background of the picture as well as the pose."

"Really," Augustine said.

"And, if I take his picture, he'll come up with different ideas for me. He stood behind a tree, wrapping his arms around the trunk, so all I could see were his wrists and hands, and he said, 'Take a picture of my hands.' 'Now the back of my head.' 'Take a picture of my feet.'" She fell silent.

"Must be genetic," Augustine said.

They were quiet as they recalled that day in La Luna Park. They were also thinking, what if we had had a little boy like Max?

"I have to go," said Romy. And before they hung up, Augustine promised to come for a visit.

With Atherton so close to San Francisco, Romy sees Max regularly. He is ten. His parents drop him off, or she picks him up. They spend weekends together. He's a perfect companion, which always amazes Romy, who previously thought she would like to have a little girl around but never a boy.

They go to Golden Gate Park and walk across the Golden Gate Bridge; they wander around North Beach and go to movies. Every weekend Max is with her, Romy teaches him about photography. About silver halide, and parallax, and color filters, the importance of proper agitation in developing, and the camera obscura, which they visit near the Cliff House, and the reciprocity law, and so on. She explains about various cameras, what they can do, what they are best for.

Romy tells him what she can about how to get the picture you want out of your subject. But the psychology of this is still a little sophisticated for him; they will come back to it later.

They talk about many things: kid things, adult things. They pore over books; they look at Romy's own work; he likes the garish goddesses; they go to the one gallery in the city that shows photographs. These gallery jaunts are brief, he is still a little young.

They go to her studio, and she explains about light and shadows and color. They spend time in the darkroom, developing and enlarging prints. Romy fully expects that the next time she sees him he will no longer want anything to do with a camera, but it has not happened yet.

So, when she feels wistful about not having a child of her own, she asks herself the question: Which is your child? The one you give birth to, who has no love of the thing you most love, or the child who is not yours but who is absorbing and keeping inside himself all that matters to you? Is it the first child, born of your body, who will ignore his inheritance, or the second child, not yours, who accepts your legacy? Which is your child?

* * *

Around this time, Romy's goddesses have been rediscovered. She is to have a show of her own in New York called *The Goddess According to Madame Romy.* Everyone is calling her, and in San Francisco they want to show her movie goddesses. Another show in New York, of surrealist pictures, including her old friend, Tin Type, wants her surrealist photographs, as well as the ads she did. For that show, she takes a self-portrait, where she sets up her largest camera, placing it in front of her glass butterfly screen, and then a tiny image of herself amid the butterflies, painted wings on her back.

In New York, she is feted and celebrated. Newspapers and magazines want to interview her. Critics are writing pieces on her place in the "language of the camera." Almost anyone she could imagine photographing is asking to be photographed, "in your own style."

So this is what it feels like, she thinks to herself.

She had called Augustine to tell him that she was coming to New York.

"Goddamn it," he muttered.

"Well, what does that mean?" she said.

"Oh, Romy—this is unbelievable. I won't be here."

"But I'll be there for a week," she said.

"I still won't be there. Damn it."

"Where are you going?" she asked, her spirits, previously so high, now sinking fast.

"I don't even want to tell you."

"Tell me."

"I'll be in Los Angeles. Visiting my parents and doing a job."

"Can't you stay until I get back?"

"Are you coming to Los Angeles?" he asked, his voice hopeful.

"No," she told him, No, she has commitments in San Francisco, but she's so desperate to be near him she'll settle for knowing he is only just down the coast.

Augustine, as always, enjoys seeing his family. "When are you going to get a real job?" is the running joke.

He takes gorgeous pictures of a young horn player named Chet Baker, who plays romantic ballad after romantic ballad until Augustine can't stand it. He thinks, what am I doing? What have I been doing? He convinced himself, when Romy had come back from Europe, that if they were together things would be as they were when they turned bad. By the time she came back, his career was on the rise and hers seemed stalled. It wasn't his love that he feared would fail; it was her work and the state it was in. They would be back to the same place: he, busy and courted; she helping him, mired in the doldrums of her own work.

Augustine drove home, told his parents he was leaving the next day for San Francisco. "I'm moving there," he says.

"What about New York?" they ask. "You love New York."

"That's true, but I can't live like this. I tried and I tried. I want to be where she is. In the same time zone, in the same city. I miss her company."

He is packed that night and sleeps so badly that by morning he is already exhausted from the day.

When Romy comes home, there is a message for her in her mailbox: Pick you up for dinner at eight-thirty. Augustine.

She foolishly glances around to see if he is anywhere near.

* * *

When Augustine shows up at her door, Romy almost swoons at the sight of him. She feels such big love for him.

"I think you should get an apartment with a few more stairs," he says. "If I lived here, I don't think I'd ever go out."

Romy laughs, takes his hand, pulls him inside, and says, "Come with me," and leads him up to the enormous room with the stunning view.

In the moonlight that comes in the window, Augustine looks at her and says, "How is it you are still that same girl?"

"It's dark," she says, "my most flattering light."

They cannot stop kissing each other. They never make it to dinner.

"Have you heard about these beat people?" asks Augustine. They are sitting on opposite ends of the sofa in Romy's upstairs room, the one with the walls of glass. They hold each other's feet in their laps.

"You mean the Beats?" says Romy. "As a matter of fact, we're in the heart of it. There are poetry readings. I think they like jazz. I'm not sure about it, except that quite a few of these Beat artists are congregating here, and—don't laugh—I've even heard the word *renaissance.*"

"Again," Augustine says.

"Again," Romy says.

"What is it about artists that they need to migrate and colonize?" Augustine says. "What is this desire to leave?"

Romy shakes her head, says, "I'm done moving around."

"So am I. You are my home."

Romy would never say aloud what she is thinking, which is that love really is peculiar and miraculous and feverish and a dual source of misery and joy. It can be a constant inconstant state. She is thinking that, for all the time apart and together, Augustine and she remained known to each other. But, most of all, she considers how Augustine's face can mean so little to the world and still be an embodiment of love for her.

As these musings make her quiet and shy, Augustine says, "Marry me, baby."

Romy laughs. "I'm a fifty-seven-year-old woman. Too old to be a blushing bride. Besides, I think these Beat artists don't believe in marriage. No, that was the crowd in Paris, no, Bloomsbury, or was it Harlem in the twenties—"

"I get your point," says Augustine, laughing with her. "Marry me anyway. We'll be truly subversive bohemians."

"It seems, I don't know, a little ridiculous."

Augustine says, "I read somewhere that a Swedish marriage is one where the couple spend their lives together, raising children, caring for each other and sometime, near the end of their lives, they throw a huge party and get married. Marriage is for those who have spent their lives living their devotion."

"Is that true?" Romy asks.

"I really don't know."

They watch the moon as it reflects on the bay.

Augustine, who is absentmindedly caressing Romy's feet, says softly, "Your feet." Something occurs to him. He recites:

> "But I love your feet
> only because they walked
> upon the earth and upon
> the wind and upon the waters,
> until they found me."

"Marry me."

# Book List

Anderson, Jervais. *This Was Harlem.* Noonday Press, Farrar, Straus & Giroux.

Baldwin, James. *Notes of a Native Son.* Beacon Press.

Campbell, James. *Exiled in Paris.* Scribner's.

Cole, Alison. *Eyewitness Art: The Renaissance and Color.* Dorling Kindersley.

De St. Jorre, John. "The Unmasking of O." *The New Yorker,* August 1, 1994.

Driskell, David; Levering Lewis, David; and Willis Ryan, Deborah. *Harlem Renaissance: Art of Black America.* Studio Museum of Harlem, Abradale Press, Harry Abrams, Inc.

Gibson, Robin, and Roberts, Pam. *Madame Yevonde: Colour, Fantasy and Myth.* National Portrait Gallery Publications and the Madame Yevonde Exhibition held at The National Portrait Gallery, London, Fall 1990.

Green, Michelle. *The Dream at the End of the World.* HarperCollins.

Grizzuti Harrison, Barbara. *Italian Days.* Ticknor & Fields.

Hughes, Langston. *Selected Poems.* Vintage.

Jay, Bill. *Cyanide & Spirits: An Inside-Out View of Early Photography.* Nazraeli Press.

*Joan Miró's Constellation Series: A Retrospective.* Museum of Modern Art, Fall 1993.

Kluver, Billy, and Martin, Julie. *Kiki's Paris: Artists and Lovers 1900–1930.* Abrams.

Lawton, Thomas, and Freer, Linda Merrill. *Freer: A Legacy of Art.* Abrams. Also, the Freer Gallery in Washington, D.C.

Leeming, David. *James Baldwin.* Knopf.

Mathers, Nancy Mowell. *Mary Cassatt.* Villard Books.

Neruda, Pablo. *The Captain's Verses.* New Directions.

Photographs of James Van Der Zee.

Plumb, J. H. *The Italian Renaissance.* Houghton Mifflin.

Vasari, Giorgio. *The Lives of the Artists.* Penguin Classics.

Watson, Steven. *The Harlem Renaissance: Hub of African-American Culture, 1920–1930.* Pantheon.

Weiss, Andrea. *Paris Was a Woman.* HarperCollins.

Thank you.